THE PRYCE OF CONCEIT

An Historical Ghost Cozy Mystery

THE PRYCE OF MURDER
BOOK I

KARI BOVÉE

BOSQUE
PUBLISHING

PROLOGUE

MAY 27, 1885
LA PLATA SPRINGS, COLORADO

Narcissa Platte sat at her vanity, admiring her reflection.

Her eyes, large, soulful and jadestone green, stared back at her with a heaviness that made her appear older than her twenty-two years. Was that a wrinkle between her brows? A jolt of anxiety shot through her at such a notion, sending tingles into her hands. She was far too young to have a wrinkle.

She lifted her forehead and then smoothed it with her fingers. No trace of the crease remained, and she breathed a sigh of relief. She supposed the malformation was due to the stress she'd been under lately. She'd have to try harder to keep her emotions at bay. Her mother had always told Narcissa that to habitually frown or press her eyebrows together in consternation would undoubtably lead to permanent lines in her face.

Yes, she would have to enforce more control over her thoughts and feelings, but she never imagined she would find herself in this mess. The situation was completely beneath her estimable virtue, but unfortunately, nature had taken its course. It couldn't be helped.

She smiled when she recalled the beautiful words he'd spoken to her that magical afternoon.

"I adore you. I can't live without you."

Those words had filled her with a sense of worthiness. With him, her life would be complete. He could give her everything she wanted. She'd have status in the community, not that she didn't have that already with her father's position with the railroad, and continued wealth—she was used to a certain standard of living—but the most important thing he could provide her with was freedom from the cloying control of her parents.

She would have it all.

That was why she needed to remedy the situation.

But this waiting was interminable. It made her jumpy and nervous, especially if she thought about the consequences of waiting too long. It took such an effort to try to put it out of her mind. There was so much at stake.

She forced a smile, and the transformation of her expression gave her some ease. All traces of any sort of wrinkle or blemish vanished. She pinched her cheeks to bring up their color.

Happy with the results, she carefully fingered the tendrils of hair that surrounded her face, neatening the wisps. She liked the way they further softened her alabaster complexion. She dotted some color onto her lips and then adorned her ears with her favorite emerald dangles.

Her heart had fluttered with excitement when that saloon girl had come to her with a message from him. He wanted to meet with her at midnight. The anticipation of a secret rendezvous now filled her heart with joy, replacing her earlier worries. He'd said he had good news. Perhaps it was news that would change her life.

But how could she sit here in her room and wait 'til then? She'd go early to their meeting place and wait there.

She chose her most flattering, deep-cranberry, velvet evening dress. It accentuated her hourglass figure, with its flat front, fitted bodice, and square, open neckline that highlighted her ample bust. Best of all, it brought out the color of her eyes.

She dabbed her fingers into the pancake makeup she'd procured from one of the working girls a couple of weeks earlier. She'd traded it for a bracelet given to her by a previous beau. She had been using the makeup to further enhance her near perfect complexion, but tonight, it served to cover the angry marks on her neck. She frowned at the memory of those fingers closing around her throat, the surge of fear that had overtaken her. She pushed aside the recollection and the tumultuous feelings that came with it. None of that mattered now.

Once properly attired, she pulled on her elbow-length gloves. Though it was late, and the night-air of the mountain valley was sure to be cool in late spring, she pushed aside the idea of a coat. She didn't want to mash the dress's silk bows and lace at the off-shoulder sleeves.

With one last look in the mirror, she smiled at the result of her efforts. He would be weak in the knees at her appearance, and it would surely help perpetuate her plan to secure him forever.

She turned the knob on the door as slowly and quietly as she could. She pulled open the door and slipped through, satisfied that the only sound emitted was the swish of her skirts. She closed the door behind her and headed for the stairs.

Her skin pricked as she felt a presence. She scanned the hallway and staircase landing, which were dimly lit with a glow from the glass sconces lining the walls of the hotel. There was no one there, but she couldn't shake the feeling that someone *was* there. She shivered, wondering if she should have worn the coat after all. Perhaps her own sneakiness had elicited a sense of being secretly observed.

She shook off the sensation and started down the stairs when she heard a noise. The distinct noise of human breathing. It was coming from behind her.

Something slammed into the back of her head, and blinding white stars exploded before her eyes. Her arms and legs went numb, and her knees buckled.

Crumpling over, she lost her footing and jettisoned down the stairs, crashing onto the landing below. She sucked in a lungful of air, then choked out a faint, whimpering cry. She struggled to call for help, but no words formed in her throat. Darkness shrouded her body in its icy veil and the blood in her veins froze.

It was in that moment she knew she would never utter another word again.

CHAPTER 1

TWO WEEKS EARLIER
NEW YORK CITY, NEW YORK

I stepped forward to take my final bow, and the crowd exploded with thunderous applause.

"Brava! Brava, Arabella!" Hundreds of audience members shouted my name, and my heart filled to bursting. The thrill of making people happy, of creating an invisible thread of connection with each and every person who came to see me perform was like a balm to a tortured soul or water to a parched body. It was a drug that made everything feel right in my world.

I turned to my cast members on each side of me, and they beamed at me with adoration, too. Well, most of them. There were always one or two people who succumbed to professional jealousy, but the pure love I felt emanating from the crowd could not be diminished.

This was my muse. My ultimate joy. My reason for living. This was what made me feel worthy to walk the Earth.

We left the stage and I headed for my dressing room. There, the quiet gonged like a church bell. My body still hummed with electricity, and although I was exhausted, I found it difficult to relax. I longed to sit down, but the late eighteenth-century costume, with its stiff pannier, stifling corset, and rigid bejeweled stomacher made it impossible.

A knock on the door signaled relief as my assistant, companion, and dear friend, Cordelia Danson, stepped into the room carrying my little Havanese dog, Bijou, under her arm. Cordelia was a few years my junior, and although she worked for me, I considered her like a younger sister.

"You were wonderful, Arabella! The toast of New York. The audience is still applauding!" She set Bijou down, grasped my hands, and planted a light kiss on each of my cheeks. "William would have been so proud."

A sudden wave of grief engulfed me. My late husband had been gone five weeks now, and never had I imagined the hole that would exist in my life without him.

Some might have thought it indelicate of me to have returned to the stage so soon after his death, but I simply *had* to work. It was my best consolation. And I considered it an homage of sorts to William. He had loved to watch me perform. So much so that he'd purchased this very theater for me and bestowed upon it his name: the Pryce Theater. He'd wanted me to have complete control of my productions, with of course, the help of our theater manager, Mr. Thomas Blackthorn.

"Thank you, darling. I tell you, I gave it everything I had tonight. That beastly Atticus Brooks will be hard-pressed to dim the light from *that* performance!"

The famed theater critic was determined to see me ruined, why I knew not. Well, actually, it may have had something to do with William, a man of great power and wealth, who had, after one too many of Mr. Brooks scathing reviews of my performances, seen to it that Mr. Brooks be fired from the *Stage Guild,* the most popular weekly entertainment newspaper of the decade.

Bijou agreed with a sweet round of enthusiastic yips. She then went over to her bed near my vanity and settled in.

"Let's get you out of this costume." Cordelia began to unbutton, unsnap, and untie the elements of the constricting dress and undergarments.

Once I had been released, I reached for my silk dressing gown and wrapped it around me. Finally coming down from the excitement of the evening, I found myself suddenly exhausted. I sank down onto the plush, red-velvet fainting couch.

Next to me, on a side table, sat one of my most prized possessions: my scrapbook. I picked it up and flipped through the pages. In it were all the glorious accolades of my performances, copies of theater programs from all my plays and postcards with various images of me painted on them. The book was a wonderful tribute to my success.

There was another knock at the door, and I let out a groan. I wasn't quite ready to receive visitors yet.

"Tell them I need a few minutes, would you, darling?" I asked Cordelia.

She went to the door to do so, but an insistent male voice emanated from the other side. Before I knew it, Matthew Tisdale, my late husband's lawyer, pushed his way into the dressing room. Cordelia raised her hands in a silent apology.

"Hello, Mr. Tisdale." I closed the scrapbook and put it aside. "I did not realize you were coming. Did you enjoy the performance?"

He was a tall and wiry man who reminded me of a grasshopper, his movements alternating between quick and still. He wore a monocle.

"I did not see the performance, Mrs. Pryce. I am here to discuss your husband's will."

"But it's all been settled, hasn't it?" My voice came out tight and constricted. We had already had a brief meeting after the funeral. I hadn't wanted to face the business side of my husband's death. It seemed so impersonal, so cold. And discussing it further would only dredge up the feelings of loss I had wanted to ignore. That I *still* wanted to ignore.

"There is a matter that must be tended to." He settled his hands behind his back.

"Now? Can it not wait? I am due at the afterparty within the hour. I can't let down the guests. How would it look? They are celebrating *me,* after all."

He stiffened. "With all due respect, madam——"

I flinched at the word *madam.* I despised it. It only served to remind me that I was soon approaching my thirty-seventh year. *Madam* was a word for someone's elderly aunt or a woman who ran a brothel, not a celebrated and still quite youthful actress.

"Mrs. Pryce will suffice." I gave him a sweet smile, hoping I got my message across.

He sighed impatiently. "With all due respect, *Mrs. Pryce,* there is some urgency in the matter."

"Urgency? What sort of urgency? He's left me everything. What else is there to know?"

"Well, mada——"

Irritated, I cleared my throat loudly to remind him of his gaffe.

I did not want to discuss this now. I didn't want the heaviness of my grief to encroach upon the balm I had experienced onstage. I wanted to remain in my cloud of contentedness.

"Pardon me," he said. "Mrs. Pryce, there is a caveat to his leaving you everything."

I blinked. *A caveat?* I had known nothing of this. It had always been understood that I would inherit the lot. William had no family other than me.

"Make yourself plain, Mr. Tisdale."

"Your husband owns a hotel in the Southwest. In La Plata Springs, Colorado, to be exact."

"Yes, I am aware of that fact. He named it for me. The Arabella."

Several years ago, he had left New York for quite some time

to oversee the design and building of it. More recently, he'd been out to the dusty Colorado town for almost half the year to "take some time away." He loved that hotel. He likely would have stayed there longer had he not become ill with an ailment of the chest and returned to New York roughly four months before he died.

"What of it?" I asked. I was growing impatient with this conversation. I had only a few minutes to get dressed for the party. "What is this caveat?"

He removed his monocle and put it in his breast pocket. Then, from the interior pocket of his jacket, he pulled out a folded document. "In order to inherit the entirety of the estate, you must go to La Plata Springs and live there, in the hotel, for one year."

"What?!" I sprang up from the couch. That was the most absurd thing I'd ever heard. "You can't be serious!"

"I am, mada—Mrs. Pryce."

"This must be some kind of mistake. He was leaving everything to me. The manse, the theater, all his holdings. There were no conditions."

Mr. Tisdale ran his fingers across the crease of the document that was pinched between them. "He was in bed for several weeks before he passed, Mrs. Pryce. He had quite a lot of time to think."

"To think about what?" I did not understand.

He handed me the letter. "You should read this for yourself."

I snatched it from his hand and unfolded it.

My dearest Arabella,

I want you to know that my life with you has been a great joy. You are like a vibrant and brilliant, blooming rose that makes the world a brighter place with your talent. I am proud to call you my wife.

Although we did not come together because of love—I needed an heir I could trust, and you needed an escape from your overbearing mother,

God bless her—I did come to love you, my darling, and I hope that you, too, came to have a fondness for me.

What you are about to read, my dear, may cause you some distress. I have grown concerned about your complete and utter immersion in your art. While it has made you an actress of unparalleled talent, it has also fostered qualities that will not serve you. I worry that your unhealthy desire for admiration and adoration from your devotees will do you harm.

You see, my darling girl, the public is fickle and forgetful. The kind of adulation that you so crave is not lasting. It will fade, and I am afraid that will leave you empty, like a wilted flower that has given every ounce of energy to shine for the world, only to wither and turn to dust.

Since you were a young girl, you have known nothing but the theater, and my dear, there is a whole world for you to explore. It is time for you to experience something radically different, something other than the world of pretense and glitter. Something with substance.

That is why I have created a stipulation to our agreement. You will have everything that I have spent decades building, and you will want for nothing for the rest of your life, if you choose to live wisely.

The proviso is thus: You will leave New York and go to La Plata Springs, Colorado, where you will live and oversee the management of the Arabella Hotel for one year. You will be provided a monthly stipend with which to live and run the hotel. At the end of a year's time, you will inherit the entirety of my estate and you may live your life as you wish.

I know this seems an unfair and unjust requirement; however, I have every confidence it will open your eyes to a richer, more fulfilling life.

Forever yours,
William

P.S. One more little provision, or rather request, dear Arabella. If you choose to sell the hotel after the obligatory time, please see that it does not fall into the hands of the Archer and Archer Mining Company.

. . .

Stunned, I lowered the letter and sank down onto the couch. I looked up at Mr. Tisdale, who held his hand out for the letter.

"I don't believe it," I said, my heart wilting in my chest. "How could he do this to me? Without my theater, without my public, I am nothing. How can he so callously rip everything that matters to me from my hands?"

I glanced over at Cordelia, who had taken a seat in my vanity chair. Her heart-shaped face had grown quite pale, highlighting the sprinkle of freckles across her pert little nose.

I returned my attention to Mr. Tisdale. "And what if I don't agree to this stipulation?"

He raised his shoulders in a shrug. "Everything goes to charity."

"This is outrageous!" I shook my head in disbelief. The gamut of emotions crashing around in my mind and body were hard to reconcile. I had known poverty before my mother had given me over to the London stage. I had worked my whole life to provide for us. And then I'd met William. He had been my ticket to never having an empty belly and inhospitable lodgings again. He married me and brought me to America. I could not go back to a life of want. I would not.

"Shall I make the arrangements?" Mr. Tisdale asked.

I closed my eyes to stave off the pinpricks of tears, wishing that when I opened them, this would all have been some wild hallucination. The grief that I hadn't wanted to face had now been compounded with the shock of this impossible demand, a cold, hard reality staring me in the face.

The mere idea of living hand to mouth once again, of living in obscurity, sent a shudder of fear through me. I couldn't be without my theater. I had poured everything I had into it and my career. I couldn't lose that.

I opened my eyes and glared at him, punishing him for bringing this devastating news. "I suppose I have no choice in the matter."

CHAPTER 2

M AY 27, 1885

The sound of metal screeching against metal pierced the air, and I was thrown forward so hard I almost fell out of my chair head-first. The train came to an abrupt stop, sending the tea service on the table next to me smashing to the floor of the private rail-car. I leaped to my feet as the tea penetrated my fine satin skirt, petticoats, drawers, and chemise. The layers thankfully had provided a barrier to the scalding hot liquid and it had not burned my skin.

Bijou jumped from her bed and barked at the fallen items with alarm.

"Arabella, are you all right? What's happened?" Cordelia, who had been napping on the divan under the window, sat up. She put a hand to her strawberry-blond hair and with an upward motion smoothed the wisps that had come from the knot at the back of her head.

"Aside from the tea stain on my dress, I think I'm fine." I

brushed at the offending spot to no avail. My efforts only spread the mess. "Are you?"

Cordelia nodded, and I gingerly tiptoed around the scattered tea service and ventured over to the divan. I sat next to her to look out the window. The landscape, a verdant green meadow with groves of shimmering aspen trees, was like nothing I had seen before. The backdrop of majestic, craggy-peaked mountains, which were blanketed with pine trees under an azure sky with cottony-white thunderheads, reminded me of something I once saw in a picture book of fairy tales.

"Do you suppose we've arrived in La Plata Springs?" Cordelia asked.

"I'm not sure. I don't see a town of any sort or even any dwellings."

I walked over to the other side of the car to look out that window, hoping to see some sign of civilization, but instead I found a sheer wall of granite.

There was a knock at the door, sending Bijou into another chorus of barking. Cordelia rose to answer it.

A small man with round-rimmed spectacles and a mustache resembling a broom stepped into the car. It was the porter. He had been assigned to our car for the week-long journey.

"Is everything all right, madam? Are you injured?" he asked me.

Madam. That word!

I was about to chastise him but thought better of it. I had mentioned to him several times that I preferred to be called Mrs. Pryce, but he had not seemed to hear my request.

"No. We're fine," I replied. "What's happened?"

He pushed his spectacles farther up onto the bridge of his nose. "There was a rockslide, and some boulders have landed on the tracks."

"Oh dear. How terrible. How far are we from La Plata Springs?"

"About two miles, madam."

"What's to be done, then?" I asked, trying not to grind my teeth in frustration at the term. "How long 'til we can resume?"

He shook his head. "I'm afraid it will be some time. Hours. A couple of days, perhaps."

"Days?" I gasped. "Are we to sit here for days?" It was bad enough I had been banished to the hinterland of the American Southwest—which, by all accounts, was full of outlaws and heathens, a place removed from elegance and civility—but now I must endure more days in this cloister of a railcar?

"I'm afraid so, madam." He blinked at me. "Is there anything you require in the meantime?"

Exasperated, I sighed. "I'm afraid the tea has created quite a mess on the carpet."

"I will see that it's cleaned up . . . again."

I scowled at his sardonic tone. Poor little Bijou could not help herself. She was used to being let outside to take care of her business at least once every two hours. That had been impossible on this infernal journey, so she had to go somewhere. Wasn't cleaning up after the passengers part of the staff's job?

"Is there anything else, madam?" He stared at me blankly.

Irritated at his insistence on the offensive moniker but not wanting to give him more reason to be annoyed with me, I gave him a slight shake of my head.

"Very well. I'll send someone to take care of the carpet. Again." He turned on his heel and left.

"Days!" I threw my hands in the air. "We cannot sit here for days," I stated matter-of-factly. "I will simply lose my mind, Cordelia." My voice wavered, and I felt on the verge of tears. I still did not understand why William had done this to me.

Cordelia regarded me with a mixed expression of apprehension and concern, but she remained quiet. She often did when I became excitable. Which, in my defense, was not often, but this was just beyond the pale.

"This won't do," I said, my anxiety rising. How could I sit there on the railroad tracks for *days?*

"It's going to be fine, Arabella," Cordelia said softly. She smiled at me in that reassuring way of hers. "Please do try to relax."

I took a deep breath, placing my hands against my waist, suddenly feeling the claustrophobic constraint of my corset. "I need to get out of here. I can't breathe."

"I'm sure you could ask the porter if you could step outside," she said in an effort to placate me.

"Who knows when he is coming back?" I whined. My fingers and toes tingled, threatening to go numb. "It's not like the train will leave without me. You heard the man. We could be here for days! No, I am not waiting. I need fresh air."

"I can open the window." Cordelia pointed to it.

"Don't bother. I'm stepping out. Come, Bijou. You need fresh air, too."

I didn't want to give the sour-faced porter any more reason to scowl at me. My little *chouchou* probably needed to relieve herself yet again.

I took up her leash and attached it to her collar.

"Do be careful, Arabella." Cordelia blinked up at me. Her brows peaked above the bridge of her nose as they often did when she was concerned about something.

"I am only stepping outside, dear," I reminded her.

She peered out the window again. "The terrain looks quite rocky."

"I'm wearing my boots. I'll be fine."

"But what about the wildlife? There are Ursidae in this region of the United States."

I heaved a sigh. "Ursi what?"

"Ursidae. Bears. The American black bear resides here, I believe. Quite large, quite unwilling to share its space." She pointed a finger at me. "And then there's the brutal sun and the thin air. I understand we are now at an elevation of six thousand five hundred feet. Our bodies are not yet acclimated, and we must be careful of altitude sickness."

"Really, Cordelia," I quipped. "All the reading and researching you've done has quite addled your brain. A little fresh air might do you well, too. Are you coming?"

She gave me a pathetic frown. "I feel a headache coming on."

Cordelia had become prone to horrible migraine headaches, often brought on by distressing situations. She really was a dear, and I don't know how I'd get by without her, but she did have a delicate constitution, which, at times, I found mildly bothersome. I often wanted to tell her to buck up but refrained as I knew my impatience often caused her that duress.

"I'm sorry to hear that. Shall I get you your headache powders?" I asked.

"It's all right," she said. "I'll get them if it gets much worse."

"Very well. When someone comes to clean up the mess, order more tea and rest up. Who knows what horrors we'll encounter when we finally arrive at godforsaken La Plata Springs."

I say *finally* when, in actuality, it had only taken a week to plan and pack for this unthinkable move and then a week of traveling. That was a relatively short period of time to completely upend one's life, but I did not want to waste a minute getting to the beastly burg so I could start my year of incarceration. And now we were delayed.

Stepping down from the platform, I was immediately consumed with the roar of the river that ran alongside the train tracks. I surveyed the area. The late-afternoon sun glowed on the landscape, and with its descent, the summer air had become crisp and smelled of pine. The aspen leaves shivered on their delicate branches, and the sun shone through them, giving them a glittering effect.

I set Bijou down, and she immediately set about sniffing the ground. In her enthusiasm, she tugged on the leash, and I let her lead me to her next fascination.

"My, my!" A deep male voice rose over the sound of the water, sending a shiver up my spine. I knew that voice.

I turned to see Atticus Brooks, the renowned theater critic, standing near the platform smoking a ridiculously fat cigar. My body tensed.

What in heaven's name is he doing here?

"Arabella Pryce," he declared. "You are the *last* person I thought I'd see in the wilds of the West." His thick lips, hovering over a wide and rather flat chin, turned up with amusement.

"I could say the same. Looking for more professional reputations to destroy?"

The man had attempted to, once and for all, topple my career with a scathing review of one of my previous shows two years ago. It was the review that had gotten him fired. Apparently, he didn't appreciate my altering the ending of Anton Chekhov's play, *A Marriage Proposal,* to give it a more feminist conclusion. In my rendition, the heroine, Natalia, rejects the proposal, coming to realize her fiancé merely wanted a wealthy nursemaid, not a wife.

"Oh dear. I didn't realize you had such thin skin," he said with a frown of mock concern.

I tightened my jaw and raised my chin. I knew better than to confront a critic, especially one who seemed committed to ruining me.

"Enlighten me, my dear. What brings you out West?" He lifted his brows.

I hesitated. Anything I said to him could end up in the papers. "I'm here to check on one of my properties: the Arabella Hotel."

Technically, it wasn't mine just yet—I had to endure a year of exile first—but he didn't know that. I could not show my true feelings. The man would undoubtedly pounce on the opportunity to further disparage me. No, I would not give him any reason to publish something unfavorable.

Little did he, or anyone else, know that I had arranged with the editor and owner of the *New York City Times,* Mr. Theodore Rankin—he had been a dear friend of William's—to have a story, or perhaps a series of stories, written about me and my extended "holiday" at my "luxurious" hotel. I could not afford to be absent from the public eye, lest everything I had worked for be forgotten.

Mr. Rankin had been reluctant when I'd first proposed the idea, but I'd reminded him that he owed my late husband a debt of gratitude for investing so heavily in his newspaper. We had agreed that Cordelia would conduct some research and provide notes for his story, or stories, God willing.

"It's the finest hotel in the area, and dare I say, the Western states," I continued, "affording every luxury for its guests. I am paving the way for sophistication and refined culture in the wilds of the frontier. And, pray tell, what are you doing here?"

My answer to his entreaty might have been a little, well, exaggerated, as I had never seen the hotel, but I couldn't imagine William owning any building or business that wasn't of the highest standard or best quality.

"I'm working on a story. Or rather, several stories. About life in the West," he said with a condescending smile.

"But you are a theater critic. Or shall I say, gossip columnist? I thought your repertoire only consisted of tearing down individualistic and experimental artists. Surely, you are out of your element."

I knew I must curb my sarcasm, but I just couldn't help it.

He gave me a smirk. I realized I was being trite, but the man had attempted to ruin my standing in New York. And now, as a widowed woman, my reputation was all I had. Even when I did finally inherit, it remained a fact: no amount of money could fix a sullied name.

Thank goodness for my adoring and loyal fans. I hoped they would not soon forget me.

Mr. Brooks's lips twitched in irritation. He took a deep breath and then bestowed upon me another one of his patronizing smiles. "I'm expanding my repertoire. One needs a distraction, to grow, to improve one's skills. Don't you agree?"

I gritted my teeth. Was he implying that *my skills* needed improving? Oh! The nerve of this . . . creature!

Bijou pulled on the leash again, leading me toward the river.

"Sorry!" I called back at him. "Can't hear you!" The din of the river gave me the perfect excuse to evade the question.

"Madam?" Another male voice bellowed from the platform. It was the spindly, bespectacled porter.

Afraid he would request that I get back in the train, and eager to get away from Atticus Brooks, I shouted back, "I'm going for a walk! Won't be long!"

And with a withering glance at Mr. Brooks, I began walking. Bijou, happy for the forward momentum, continued sniffing the ground like a terrier in search of a rodent.

I took in the views. I hated to admit it, but the landscape was glorious. Surrounding me were magnificent mountains, colored in deep purples and blues, with caps of snow at the highest peaks.

With a loud flutter, a large bird took wing from the bushes, and Bijou started a round of high-pitched barking and surged forward at a run, forcing me to step up my pace. The bird landed on a large boulder jutting into the rushing river, and we came to a stop. But Bijou's barking continued at a more frantic volume.

"Bijou, quiet!"

Ignoring me, she moved dangerously close to the water, yanking me with her. My boot got stuck in my skirts, and the next thing I knew, I was tumbling headlong into the river. The icy torrent enveloped me, ripping the breath from my lungs, and I hurtled downstream like a child's wayward sailboat, my skirts billowing out around me.

"Help!" Sputtering and gasping, I finally managed to make my voice work. "Help!" I screamed again, hoping that someone from the train would hear me or Bijou's furious barking, which was quickly fading as I sped down the river.

After what seemed like an eternity of struggling for air and being sloshed through the frigid water, the current slowed and the denseness of the canopy of trees covering the river opened up, revealing a verdant meadow. Up ahead, to my extreme relief, was a man leaning over a small fire. His horse grazed nearby.

"Help me!" I yelled again.

He raised his head to see me coming toward him. He stopped what he was doing and waded into the water to await my arrival. When I was close enough, I stretched out my hand to grab on to his, but I missed. Terrified I'd lost my chance at rescue, I let out a wail but was then abruptly tugged backward. Somehow he had managed to grab hold of my skirt and was dragging me backward toward the bank. Had I not been so terrified, I would have been completely humiliated.

When we neared the bank, I tried to stand, but my legs would not cooperate. Hooking his hands under my arms, he hauled me out of the water like a soggy bag of potatoes. Now that I was out of danger, he released me and I fell onto my back, gulping for air.

He plopped down beside me, sitting with his knees propped up and his arms wrapped around them, catching his breath.

When I had sufficiently collected myself and could breathe without gasping like a beached fish, I sat up.

"Are you okay, ma'am?" he asked, flipping his wet hair off his forehead to reveal startling blue eyes. Crow's feet at his temples indicated he was nearing middle age, but the years seemed to have served him well. He was fit and as strong as any younger man.

"Does anything hurt?" he asked.

"I don't think so," I managed. I looked down to survey my body and was shocked to see my skirt hiked well above my knees and stuck to my thighs, revealing my petticoats, stockings—which had torn—and my now ruined boots. I scrambled to pull the fabric down to cover my legs.

Embarrassed, I glanced at him sideways to see that his face had split into a devastating smile. He was laughing at me.

Taken aback, I glared at him. "I hardly think this is funny."

He continued to chuckle and had I not been so irritated at him, I might have thought him quite handsome. His face was cut in angles, like a deftly chiseled marble bust, but his eyes were soft and large and the most captivating hue of sea-swept blue.

He raised a hand in apology. "I'm sorry. It's not funny. This is not the friendliest of rivers and you were headed for a waterfall just a half a mile down the way." He handed me my sodden hat. He had managed to pull it, too, from the rushing water. "Had I not been here—"

"Oh my goodness." I shuddered at the thought of hurtling over a precipice into oblivion. And then I remembered Bijou. Had she fallen in the water, too? Was she headed for the waterfall?

"Did you see my dog? I'm afraid she might have fallen in the water as well."

"I saw no dog. But I have to ask," he continued. "What were you doing in there? You hardly look dressed for a swim. And it's getting dark."

He asked the question as if I'd had a choice in the matter, and the comment about my attire was beyond the pale. I hardly knew what to say.

"I'm traveling here from the East Coast. The train is detained by boulders on the tracks. I stepped out for some fresh air and . . . found myself in the river. Are you sure you didn't see Bijou—er, my dog?"

"I'm sure," he said. He chuckled again. "The East Coast, huh? Sounds like you're from somewhere else. Is that a British accent?"

I gave him a tightlipped smile. "I'm originally from London, but I've lived in this country for some time."

He reached down and took hold of one of his boots, pulled it off, and turned it upside down to drain the water from it. He put it back on and did the same with his other boot. He then stretched out one of his long legs. "Where are you headed?"

"La Plata Springs."

A breeze rustled through the trees, and I shivered.

He got to his feet and went to his horse. I had hoped he would help me up. My legs were so shaky I wasn't sure I could stand.

He took something from one of the saddlebags. When he returned, he was carrying a canteen and a blanket. He held the canteen out to me.

I hadn't realized it 'til then but I was terribly thirsty. I took the canteen and drank. The water was sweet and pure. It was the best water I'd ever tasted. I wanted to drink it until the last drop, but that wouldn't have been very mannerly. The man had saved my life after all.

"I'll get you to town," he said.

"But I should go back to the train. All my belongings are there. And I'm worried about Bijou. If she didn't fall in the river, then I'm afraid she'll get lost. She's not used to the outdoors."

He shook his head. "She's probably fine. But there's no easy way back to the train from here. We'd have to get to the road, and it's a fair bit away. It's getting dark, and you're soaking wet. It can get mighty cold in these parts once the sun goes down. I think it's best we get you to town. Do you have a place to stay?" He draped the blanket around my shoulders. But he had not yet offered to help me remove myself from the mud puddle my drenched skirt had created.

Clutching the blanket tighter around me, I managed to get myself to my feet, but once I was upright, the world spun. I swayed, and he caught me by the elbow, steadying me.

"You should have sat awhile longer," he said, his grip on my arm strong and comforting. "Tumbling through the river like that would make anyone wobbly."

"I'm fine," I said, not wanting to admit that indeed I was not. My clothes, soggy and cold, clung to me. My trembling turned to a near-violent shiver, and a headache was threatening to form at the edges of my eyes.

"Do you have lodgings?" he asked again.

I straightened my spine. "I'm the owner of the Arabella Hotel."

He raised his eyebrows. "You're the widow Pryce?"

The widow Pryce?

He'd said it as if I were merely an overaged appendage to my late husband. Did I look so ancient in my rumpled state as to be referred to as an elderly matron? This country bumpkin obviously had no idea that my name had renown in its own right.

"*My name* is Arabella." I wanted to add *famed actress, known and beloved throughout the nation*, but I refrained. It would not have been dignified.

He thrust out his hand, apparently not impressed in the least. I clenched my jaw at his indifference, reticent to shake his hand. The man was clearly uncultured.

"Funny. You don't look anything like your portrait."

"My portrait?"

"Yeah," he said with a grin. "There's a portrait of you in the saloon at the hotel."

"Oh?" William had mentioned nothing about this. The only portraits I'd sat for were hanging in the lobby of my theater and our Fifth Avenue mansion.

"I'm Clayton Marshall. Sheriff of La Plata Springs."

I finally took his hand and gave it a firm shake to show that, indeed, I was no wilted flower but a woman of accomplishment. Although, at that moment, I admittedly felt less than polished.

"Lord, your hands are cold," he said, giving my palm a squeeze. "And your lips are turning blue. We need to get you to town."

I may have come from very humble beginnings—thus my early, and daresay, forced foray into theater at the tender age of ten—but despite our poverty, and my mother's lack of a nurturing nature, she had known her manners and had passed them on to me. And one of the most important rules was *never* to comment on a lady's appearance unless it was in the most glowing of terms. I scowled at his ignorance.

"Come on, then." He gave a shrill whistle, and his horse picked up its head from where it was grazing and then trotted over to us. Although I didn't care to let on, I was impressed.

The horse came up to him, and he reached out to stroke its forehead. "This is Queenie. Best horse I've ever had."

"She's . . . certainly obedient," I said, struggling with what to say. *How do you do, Queenie,* seemed inane.

Taking the reins, he pulled the horse up alongside us, and before I knew what was happening, Sheriff Marshall had wrapped his hands around my waist and hoisted me up onto the saddle. I let out a squeak of terror, and my legs, dangling over the side of the horse, tensed to the point of cramping.

Sheriff Marshall laughed in the most infuriating way and then climbed up behind me, sitting astride. It seemed I was a never-ending source of amusement for him.

His arms came around me as he picked up the reins. I tried to make myself smaller to shrink from his embrace but to no avail. To my further embarrassment—and yes, I'll say it, annoyance—he let out another low chuckle, clucked twice to his horse, and we were off.

CHAPTER 3

Queenie settled into a slow, rhythmic walk. I wished the animal would walk faster. Not only was I wet and cold with my corset seeming to grow tighter by the minute but utter humiliation nettled deep into my gut. Why had I not stayed on the train? Now I had to arrive in town looking like a drowned cat. Thank goodness it was growing dark.

And to make matters worse, Atticus Brooks might see me. Did he plan to stay in town for more than a night? Hopefully, once the train was freed, he would continue on his way to wherever it was he was going to "expand his repertoire." I did not need him to witness my lack of experience running a hotel. A pit of dread settled in my stomach at the thought. But I wouldn't think about it now.

Misery hung over me like a dark cloud. I wanted nothing more than to get to the hotel so that I might sit in front of a warm fire. As soon as we arrived at the hotel, I would send a coach to the train to retrieve Cordelia, Bijou—my heart lurched —if she'd been found, and my things. How I wished I had not been so impulsive. I shook my head in irritation with myself. It was indeed fortuitous that Sheriff Marshall had found me.

"You okay?" he asked, bringing the horse to a halt.

"Yes," I answered quickly, embarrassed that my thoughts had displayed themselves so visibly. I cleared my throat. "Thank you."

"Yep." He clucked to his horse, and we continued to walk on in silence.

I wondered at his lack of conversation. Was he just a man of few words, or was he annoyed at having to rescue me?

I had to say, despite my frigid and wet attire, and the way I was twisted in the saddle with my legs dangling over one side, Clayton Marshall's sturdy arms encircling me was oddly comforting. I couldn't remember being in such close proximity to a man, even William, for quite some time. Unless it was on the stage, and that was an entirely different matter.

The pink glow of the sky morphed into lavender as the sun dipped below the mountains. A town came into view. Nestled in the valley between an expanse of two mountain ranges, it ran alongside the river.

There wasn't much to it, I thought to my chagrin. The main thoroughfare was crowded with several buildings in a variety of styles and stature. Some were Romanesque, others Italian Renaissance, and there was even a building in the French style, complete with dormer windows. Settled between the larger buildings were smaller wooden structures that looked shabby in comparison. The largest structure at the south end of the street near what appeared to be the train station was grand and built in the American Victorian style, complete with red bricks and embellished with white carved stone. It's illuminated grandeur shone with brilliance. The Arabella, no doubt. I recognized it from a photo William had once shown me.

Despite my discomfort, a sensation of pride for my late husband washed through me, even though at the moment I was furious at him for sending me to this provincial borough. I had to admit that my feelings for William were not of the passionate sort, but I had cared for him a great deal and indeed had come to love him in my own way. I had basked in and deeply appreciated his admiration and respect for me. A wave of grief swept through me, and I blinked back tears.

I tried to focus on the town again. Another street, this one running parallel to the main avenue to the east and lined with two rows of trees, and it sported large and small dwellings of Victorian design. Homes, I reckoned.

Although quaint, a town of this size was not for me. Already, I missed the bustle of the city streets, the trolley bells, my theater, and my adoring audience. How would I survive an entire year here? It seemed an eternity. And I was not off to a great start in my new, if temporary, life.

As we neared the town, my stomach knotted. People milled about the streets. They would get their first glimpse of me in this humiliating state. I longed to tell the sheriff to turn around and take me back to the train. A few days on the tracks now didn't seem so bad. But I knew what his answer would be.

All eyes were on us, much to my great embarrassment. Heat crawled up my neck and into my face, I'm sure turning me red as a hothouse tomato.

I usually reveled in being the center of attention, but today, in my sullied and sodden state and atop a beast between the arms of a rough and uncultured stranger, shame washed through me. This was hardly a proper introduction for Arabella Pryce, esteemed actress and lady of utmost sophistication and style, to the townspeople of La Plata Springs. What would they think? This was the impression that would be stamped in their memories forever!

I drew in a deep breath, trying to steady my rising anxiety.

"Hey, Sheriff!" An older man with bowed legs and filthy beard called out. "Guess you caught a big one today!" He laughed, and several others passing by joined in.

My mortification was complete.

The sheriff merely tipped his hat to the man, and we walked on in silence, for which I was grateful.

Finally, we reached the hotel. The sheriff dismounted and

reached up to help me down when a dog came rushing toward us. He crashed into the sheriff, knocking him off-balance, and before I knew it, I was pulled from the saddle with a ferocious yank. I landed squarely on top of Sheriff Marshall with the dog circling us and barking happily, drawing even more attention.

This was awful!

"Whoa! You all right?" Sheriff Marshall asked, calm as a Sunday afternoon, his nose mere centimeters from mine and his sea-blue eyes scanning my face.

Flustered and beyond disgraced, I pushed myself to my knees. I struggled to rise to my feet as my dress and the blanket were entwined around my legs. I attempted to stand, but my boot caught the hem of my skirt and I tumbled, landing squarely on top of the sheriff again. Heavens but this was horrifying!

"Seems you can't get enough of me," he said with a chuckle.

I scrambled clumsily but was finally able to get to my knees again. To my relief, Sheriff Marshall untangled himself from me, got to his feet, and helped me up. I shook off his grip on my arm, appalled at his impertinence.

I glared at him. "I beg your pardon."

"My apologies." He held up his hands in surrender. "I was just trying to make light of the situation."

"There is nothing *light* about it!" I said through gritted teeth.

Now, not only was I wet but I was covered with dirt from the street. When would this indignity end?

Just then a coach pulled up. The driver brought the horses to a stop, and a very large, barrel-chested man stepped out. He had the appearance of one who commanded respect—and attention. To my utter dismay, Atticus Brooks came out of the coach behind him and stepped onto the street, his face lit with surprise.

"Mrs. Pryce!" he called out. He might as well have shouted from the rooftops. When he saw my appearance, he frowned. "I am so glad to see you in one piece. I was so worried when you did not return to the train."

"Ah!" the large man said in surprise. "Arabella Pryce. At last, we get to see you in the flesh. Archibald Archer, owner of the Archer and Archer Mining Company. But you can call me Boss. Everyone else does." He bowed low at the waist, sweeping his hat off his head.

Boss? How ridiculous. I made a mental note to never call him *Boss.*

"But you must be freezing, my dear," he continued. "Why are you so wet?"

"I—I fell into the river."

His eyes widened with surprise. "Oh, no, my dear lady. How did you get out?"

"Sheriff Marshall assisted me." I nodded toward the man.

Mr. Archer smiled widely. "Oh, but of course! Our own local hero."

The sheriff cleared his throat, clearly uncomfortable with the accolade. Did I sense some tension between the two men?

"When the rockslide was brought to my attention, I immediately sent a coach for you and my dear friend Atticus," Mr. Archer continued.

So Mr. Brooks knew Mr. Archer. Did this mean the theater critic was a guest of the mining tycoon? Would he be staying in La Plata Springs for an extended period? I swallowed my trepidation and tried my best to focus on Mr. Archer.

His face took on a serious demeanor. "But then he told me that you had gone missing. I have some of my men out in the area looking for you. I shall have to call them off."

"My. How very kind," I said with a lift of my chin, sizing up this larger-than-life figure. I remembered William's letter then, and I found myself curious as to why he had been so against this man purchasing the Arabella. At first blush, he seemed charming and accommodating, and he was obviously cultured.

"Let's get you inside, my dear," he suggested. "No need for you to be standing in the street."

My sentiments exactly.

He held his arm out to me and then ushered me through the impressive beveled glass and wood front doors and straight to the reception desk.

"Mr. Pettyjohn!" he called out.

A bespectacled man with a thick but neatly trimmed and waxed mustache, and equally polished fat eyebrows, peered around a doorway situated behind the counter and stared at me aghast with scrutinizing, dark eyes.

"This is Mrs. Pryce." Mr. Archibald patted my hand, which was still resting on his arm. "Please see her to her rooms."

While I appreciated Mr. Archibald's attentiveness, I nevertheless found it a bit presumptuous for him to be ordering one of the hotel staff—well *my staff*—around as if he owned the place. Besides, I was completely capable of doing so myself.

I turned to him. "Thank you for your kindness, Mr. Archer. I'll be fine now. I mustn't detain you any longer."

"Very well, my dear." He gently took my hand from his arm and brushed his lips against my knuckles. "I hope to see you again soon."

He departed, leaving me standing before the desk clerk as he blinked at me from behind his spectacles.

"Please do get me to my room and send someone to fetch my assistant and my belongings," I said to Mr. Pettyjohn. "The train is detained two miles away. It might be some time before it is in working order again." I tried to ignore the guests who walked by gawking at me.

"Yes, madam."

I flinched, bristling at the offensive title, but decided to let it pass . . . this time.

He cocked his head, looking at me with some curiosity. "I would never have guessed that you were Mrs. Pryce. You look so different from your portrait."

There was that portrait again.

I must see this portrait.

But later. I held my hands out in a gesture that indicated he should take a good look at my dampened state. "I'm not quite myself, as you can see. Now . . . my rooms?"

He cleared his throat. "Of course, madam."

For heaven's sake!

"Please, call me Mrs. Pryce."

He opened a drawer under the key cubbies and pulled out a ring of keys. "I will escort you." He rang the bell on the desk twice, and a bellhop appeared from around the corner.

"Clarence Hays, this is Mrs. Pryce."

The boy, eleven or twelve years old judging by the gangly structure of his body, eyed me up and down, clearly caught off guard by my appearance.

The desk clerk snapped his fingers at the boy. "Get Mr. Ellis to take the wagon to the train. It has been detained two miles down the tracks. Tell him to gather Mrs. Pryce's things and her assistant—"

"Cordelia Danson," I provided.

Mr. Pettyjohn nodded to me before continuing. "Miss Danson, and bring them to the hotel at once."

"And my little dog," I added, hoping that my sweet Bijou had not been lost in the wilderness.

"Yes, sir. Yes, ma'am." The boy nodded, still looking confused, then tipped his cap to me and was off.

"Thank you," I said to the desk clerk. "Mr. Pettyjohn, is it?"

"Forgive me," he said with a slight bow. "Yes, my name is Mervin Pettyjohn. The hotel manager, Mr. Bledsoe told me you would be arriving today. I just didn't expect—"

"Neither did I," I quipped.

"Would you like me to notify him that you are here?"

I looked at him aghast. "Absolutely not. I would hate to meet him looking such a spectacle. Now, if you please . . ." I longed to hide myself away from the possibility of encountering any more scrutinizing eyes.

"Of course. Right this way." He led me to the staircase.

As we ascended to the first landing, I noticed the wear on

the wooden balustrades. They looked like they hadn't been varnished in an age. We reached the landing and turned the corner to continue to the next. Looking down at the carpeting covering the stairway, I was further concerned at its appearance. It was frayed at the edges and obviously well-trodden.

"Your rooms are on the top floor," Mr. Pettyjohn explained, "and Mr. Bledsoe's—in addition to some of our more esteemed, permanent residents—are on the third. When he is not in residence, we offer Mr. Bledsoe's rooms to other distinguished clientele."

"I see. And our—my rooms? Did you offer them to distinguished clientele, as well, when my husband was not in residence?"

He did not respond, and I wondered if he had heard me. "Mr. Pettyjohn?"

"No, mada—"

I narrowed my eyes at him, silently warning him not to finish that word. "Why not?"

We rounded the next corner to climb to the third landing. My eyes drifted to the hallway lined with doors. Between two of them, the wall looked somehow marred. I squinted to see better. It appeared the wallpaper had come loose at the seams, leaving an unsightly gap.

This lack of attention was deplorable. I recalled what I had told Mr. Brooks, that the Arabella was a luxury hotel, and my stomach twisted. Surely, he would call me out on this, looking for any way to diminish my reputation. Why had the hotel manager not attended to these things?

I would have to see them fixed as soon as possible.

We continued up the stairs, and I wondered why Mr. Pettyjohn had not yet answered my question.

Finally, he stopped and turned to look at me. "Your husband didn't tell you?"

"Tell me what?"

He sighed. "No one, other than Mr. Pryce, has stayed in your rooms since—"

"Yes?" I asked, growing impatient.

"Since Mr. Percival Blank, his partner, the architect who built your hotel . . . well, he died there."

"Died?"

William had mentioned nothing of this to me, but then again, he did not often share the details of his business matters with me, nor did he talk about his colleagues or associates much.

"Yes, mada—Mrs. Pryce. It was a rather suspicious death, but foul play could not be proven."

"So you believe Mr. Blank was murdered?"

"That is the rumor." He continued up the stairs, and I followed.

"I see." But I really didn't see why that had any bearing at all on whether or not our rooms were let out. My late husband had not come to La Plata Springs often, and until now, I had never availed myself of our rooms at the hotel. It seemed such a waste. And if they were let out, more money could be made.

"Mr. Pettyjohn," I said between heavy breaths. I couldn't seem to get enough air. "People die all the time. I'm sure many have died in hotels."

Finally, we reached the top landing. I pressed my hand against my corset, fighting for breath, surprised I'd become so winded.

He turned to face me. "There was another death in the hotel. A year ago. Very mysterious. The townspeople have come to believe that— Well, there have been reports of noises—clunking and screeching in the night—and . . . some of the staff have had the experience of . . . I myself have . . ."

"What is it, Mr. Pettyjohn?" I asked, wishing he would get to the point.

He looked at me over the rims of his round spectacles. "You see, Mrs. Pryce, the hotel is haunted."

CHAPTER 4

Haunted. The word quickened my pulse. Not that I was frightened. I wasn't. Just surprised. I had been privy to this kind of phenomenon before. Meaning that, at times in my life, I have been able to see and communicate with otherworldly spirits. But it was only on rare occasions.

I had seen my first spiritual being when I was ten years old. One of my playmates, Oliver Shrewsbury, had died from the influenza, and he appeared to me only days after the funeral, at a picnic in the English countryside with Mother and some of her friends. Having no other children to play with, I had grown bored of their conversation and wandered to a small grove of trees. That's where I had seen him. He'd said he recovered from his illness and had been waiting for me.

When we had returned home, I'd gone to Oliver's parents' house and, not knowing any better, mentioned to them that Oliver was indeed alive and well, and that I had spoken to him only hours before. Little did I know the upset this would cause. Mr. Shrewsbury had marched me back to my mother and delivered a tirade.

My mother, exceedingly ambitious to make me the most sought-after theater phenom in London—to the extent of making me feel like nothing but a performing puppet—had been quite disturbed, yet surprisingly open-minded about the matter. She had told me I must have inherited the trait from my grandmother. According to my mother, my grandmother and I were "sensitive types" who had unusual abilities.

She had gone on to tell me that these abilities must be suppressed, if not completely squelched. If word had gotten out that I talked to ghosts, my days as an accomplished child thespian would be over and I would likely be committed to an insane asylum. So she had ushered me off to a spiritualist who had taught me how to close myself off from such visitations.

I had been successful until a few years after my husband had purchased the theater for me. It occurred during a particularly stressful time. I had lost my lucky ring, a Forget-Me-Not ring given to me by my father when I was young. I always wore it on stage and felt that it had bestowed upon me my talent, which of course wasn't true, but at the time I'd been devasted at the loss. I eventually got it back, but I supposed the fact that I was vulnerable at that time broke down the barriers I had learned to build up against such spiritual phenomenon. It was then I'd met Leticia Crookshank, the theater's ghost, a deceased actress who told me her heart had failed her. She gave me comfort and had taken it upon herself to coach me through that trying time, and I credit her with my meteoric rise to fame.

"Mr. Pettyjohn!" a female voice sang out from below, shaking me from my reverie. "Oh, Mr. Pettyjohn, we'd like a word."

Mr. Pettyjohn visibly flinched. We turned to see a portly woman and a reed-thin man with a balding head and enormous beard mounting the stairs to meet us on the fourth-floor landing. Coming up behind them was a strikingly beautiful young woman. I guessed her to be in her early twenties.

"Yes?" Mr. Pettyjohn asked as they reached us.

I lowered the brim of my hat to better conceal my face.

"Mr. Pettyjohn, there is still the matter of our rooms. Why

have we not been attended to?" the older woman asked, her voice clipped with annoyance.

The man, who I assumed was her husband, shrank into his finely made suit. The young woman fixed her eyes upon me, giving me a look of disdain, obviously put off by my appearance. Oh, if I could just get to my rooms!

The older woman continued. "There is still an awful smell coming from our fireplace. This is the third time I have complained, Mr. Pettyjohn. I even took the matter up with Mr. Bledsoe, but he obviously paid me no mind. I demand you take care of it. Now!"

There was something in her tone of voice that was familiar, causing the sensation that occurred when one ran their finger-nails down a schoolroom blackboard. The voice was much like my mother's, in fact, giving me the urge to flee.

Before Mr. Pettyjohn could respond, I intervened. "I'm sorry to hear that, ma'am. I will see to it that this situation is remedied."

She looked over at me, astonished, as if she hadn't even real-ized I was standing there.

"And who are you?" the younger woman snapped, eyeing me up and down.

Mr. Pettyjohn cleared his throat. "My apologies. This is Mrs. Pryce, the owner of the hotel. Mrs. Pryce, this is Mr. and Mrs. Horace Platte, and their daughter, Narcissa. They are long-term residents of the Arabella. They live on the third floor."

The young woman smirked. "So *you* are Bill's wife. He's told me about *you*. I see you've slimmed down. Good for you."

Bill? My husband had never referred to himself as *Bill* in all the time I'd known him. The familiarity with which she spoke of my husband sent a jolt through me. And what did she mean by my slimming down?

"Excuse me?" I shook my head, completely confused and actually quite vexed at this conversation.

She blinked at me with her wide eyes. They were an unusual

shade of green, like the color of a wave as it crested over the shore. She gave me a condescending smile. "You must tell me who your dressmaker is." She continued with glee. "And your hair . . . Well!"

I pulled in a sharp breath, aghast at the young woman's rudeness. "If you must know, I nearly drowned in the river today. Thank you for your concern."

"I thought Bledsoe was co-owner of the hotel," Mr. Platte said dismissively.

I tore my gaze from the beautiful young woman to look at him. He was still not making eye contact with me. "I don't know where you've gotten your information, Mr. Platte, but Mr. Bledsoe is the hotel's manager. My late husband has entrusted the hotel to me." I raised my chin, offended by Mr. Platte's tone.

The young woman's face paled, and I thought I detected a slight quiver of her chin. "*Late* husband?"

Mr. Pettyjohn and I exchanged a glance.

"Yes. He passed away two months ago. He had been ill . . . " I informed them, not able to finish because of the lump rising in my throat. But did I own them any kind of explanation?

Narcissa grabbed on to the railing of the staircase and pressed a hand to her stomach. Mrs. Platte, taking notice of her daughter's distress, wrapped an arm around her.

"What is it, darling? Are you not well again?" She pressed a hand to Narcissa's forehead.

The young woman waved off her mother's concern. "I'm fine, Mother. Please stop fussing."

Eager to be rid of this annoying couple and their daughter, who now stared at me with a blank expression on her wan face as if lost in a thousand thoughts, I turned to the desk clerk. "Mr. Pettyjohn, please show me to my rooms. I will deal with the problem of the Plattes' fireplace as soon as I can." I nodded to the three guests. "I apologize for any inconvenience. Now, if you will excuse us, I'm dying for a hot bath and some privacy."

"If this isn't taken care of by the end of the day, we will take our business elsewhere," Mrs. Platte huffed.

One of the benefits of being an actress was having mastered the skill of displaying one emotion on the face while feeling something quite different in the heart, and still getting the point across.

"Perhaps that is for the best," I said, pulling up my most sincere smile.

"Oh!" Mrs. Platte narrowed her eyes at me. "Well, I never!"

I did not know much about the town of La Plata Springs, but I did know that the Arabella was the nicest hotel in this little burg. There was one other somewhat respectable hotel owned by the railway company—it was called the General or some such—but William had told me it paled in comparison to the Arabella. It was a rooming house for the miners and had no amenities. The other lodgings in town were boarding houses with tiny rooms, outdoor facilities, and spotty, if any, heating. The Plattes did not strike me as the sort of people who cared to live without the finer things in life.

"Come now, Pretencia." Her husband took her by the arm. "Let's let Mrs. Pryce get settled. I'm sure she will see to our fireplace in good time. The smell can wait."

"It's unbearable!" Narcissa chimed in, seeming to have found her strength again. Her voice had the same shrill quality as her mother's.

"Let's go." Mr. Platte gathered his women together and directed them down the stairs to the third floor. I could hear Mrs. Platte grumbling all the way down to the lower landing.

When I turned to look at Mr. Pettyjohn, he was pinching the bridge of his nose between his thumb and forefinger.

"Are you quite all right?" I asked.

His eyes popped open. "Yes, ma'am. My apologies for the Plattes. They are—"

"No need to explain." I laid a hand on his arm. "I quite get the picture."

And I did, but I was still a little mystified at the young Miss Platte's reaction to the news of my husband's death. Had they been closely acquainted? Mr. Pettyjohn led me down the hallway to a set of double doors. With his jangling set of keys, he opened one of them. He then handed me the key ring. "This is your set of keys, Mrs. Pryce. Mr. Bledsoe and the maid also have a set, as well as me. There is a key for every room."

I took the key ring, which weighed as much as a stack of scripts, and we stepped into the room.

It was a parlor room with a fireplace flanked by two chairs. A large sofa sat under a large bay window, occupying the left side of the room. On the opposite wall sat a large writing desk and chair. A strange odor assaulted us.

"Oh my!" I said, holding my hand over my nose. Perhaps the Plattes had a point if this was what they smelled in their rooms.

Mr. Pettyjohn rushed to the windows and threw them open. Another doorway on the other side of the room indicated a second room. Mr. Pettyjohn hurried through that doorway to, I assumed, open more windows. I started to follow him when something caught my eye near the fireplace.

Lying on the floor in front of it were two large, decomposing rats. I let out a yelp and quickly covered my mouth.

Mr. Pettyjohn rushed back to the parlor. "Oh dear," he exclaimed. "I'm so sorry, Mrs. Pryce. I don't understand."

"Get them out!" I demanded.

I am not usually so dictatorial, but the fact remained that I was still cold, and wet, and filthy, and if I was being honest, quite at my wit's end. I shuddered thinking back on the humiliation of riding through town like a half-clothed Lady Godiva in the intimate embrace of a man I didn't know from Adam. The distress was compounded by my worries about poor little Bijou. I prayed that someone from the train had found her. Then, having met the charming Plattes, and now faced with decomposing rats in my fireplace, I was near tears.

All I wanted in that moment was to get out of my sodden clothes and into a warm bath.

"I will f-find the maid, m-madam," Mr. Pettyjohn stammered.

"Thank you," I said. "And please don't call me madam!"

CHAPTER 5

I took in a deep breath and let it out, determined not to let the events of the day, or the rats, get the best of me.

I continued my perusal of the place. Despite the odiferous assault, the parlor was neatly appointed. The two armchairs, Louis XVI in design and upholstered in gold damask, were set in front of the fireplace with a round accent table placed between them. To my left, under the large bay window, the Queen Anne–styled parlor sofa looked plush and comfortable with a generously tufted, dusty-rose velvet back. An ornately carved coffee table with a marble top sat in front of it. To my right was a large, carved oak desk with leather inserts covering the top and on the face of the drawers.

I caught my reflection in the gilt-framed mirror that hung above the desk and gasped. I looked far worse than I had imagined. My skin was blotchy from the cold, my hair hung in strings about my face, and my hat rested at an absurd angle atop my head.

Exhausted and overwhelmed, I tossed the limp thing on the desk and plopped my damp and unkempt self down in the accompanying chair. The smoothness of the leather beckoned to be touched, and I ran my hand over the surface of the desk. A stack of stationary rested in a leather letter box. Next to it was a tray with several fountain pens, and next to that was a small bottle of ink. I pulled open the narrow center drawer and smiled at the neatness with which the items within it had been arranged. So like William. I closed the drawer, and then rose to complete my tour of my new—albeit temporary, I comforted myself once again—lodgings.

The bedroom next door was complete with a canopied, walnut bed covered with a fussy, if not garish, floral print bedspread that strikingly clashed with the equally busy wallpaper. It struck me as odd that my husband would have chosen such a combination. The more spartan decor of the parlor most suited his taste. But perhaps he had arranged this for me? We had not shared a bedroom in New York, so why would we here?

I walked over to the matching walnut bureau. On one corner, a porcelain washbasin and pitcher sat atop a finely crocheted lace doily. On the other corner was a silver tray holding an engraved silver hairbrush, comb, and hand mirror. Absently, I picked up the brush. Strands of blond hair entwined themselves within the bristles. Strange. William's hair had been dark.

"Hello?" a small voice behind me startled me out of my thoughts. I whirled around to see the maid standing in the doorway.

When we made eye contact, she furrowed her brow as if I was not quite what she had expected. Could this have to do with my dampened state, or was it about the portrait everyone kept mentioning? My curiosity about the painting was bursting, but I had other things to attend to at the moment. At least the young woman had the decency not to say anything.

She rearranged her face to deliver a welcoming smile. "Mrs. Pryce, I'm Maggie Mae Freeman. But everyone just calls me Maggie. It's so nice to meet you, ma'am. I've disposed of the rats. I'm so sorry that happened."

She was a pretty girl with delicate features and eyebrows that turned up at the bridge of her nose, making her look perpetually quizzical.

"Hello, Maggie," I said. "Thank you. It was a bit of a rude welcome. But it is of no consequence now. As you can see, I've had quite a day." I looked down at my wilted attire. "I long for a warm bath. With any luck, my luggage, along with my companion, Miss Danson, and my dear little dog will be here shortly. Could I prevail upon you to help me in the meantime?"

She nodded, holding her clasped hands at her waist. "Yes, ma'am. Mr. Pettyjohn said you'd fallen into the river. I took the liberty of bringing this." I hadn't notice before, but she had something draped over her arm. She held it out for me. It was a dressing gown.

"Will you or your companion be staying in this room? There is another room just beyond the bathing room.

"Bathing room?"

"Yes, ma'am. This is the only set of rooms with a water closet and fixed tub. Your husband and Mr. Blank devised a way to plumb water up here."

The news filled me with joy. I'd had grim visions of sitting in a small tin basin while the maid poured water over my head.

"Wonderful." A warm, luxurious bath would be a glorious end to this most taxing day.

Maggie crossed the room and opened another door that led to the bathing room. It was small but satisfactory with black-and-white honeycomb floor tiles. A square, carved walnut cabinet housed the water closet and another rectangular cabinet held a copper bathing tub.

"This will do," I said brightly. "But where do the used water and waste go?"

"It travels down a pipe to the river."

"I see." Leave it to my William to assure himself his creature comforts.

"What about the guests in the other rooms. Where are their privies?"

"All of the rooms have commodes that require emptying every day, but there is also a three-storied outhouse on the back side of the building. One for each floor, other than this one of course. That waste, too, is sent to the river."

I fought back an impulse to gag. I had just spent time in that river, although, mercifully, the sheriff had pulled me out upstream, before I had neared the hotel.

"We also have two copper tubs," she continued. "If a guest wants to bathe, we take one of the tubs to their room and bring the hot water."

"Ah." It seemed they had quite a system of hygiene at the Arabella, crude as it was.

We passed through a door at the other end of the bathroom that led to a much larger bedroom. It was dark, the curtains closed, and Maggie quickly went to them and threw them open. The warm light of evening filled the space. The room was appointed with yet another canopied bed, a large bureau, a stately desk and chair, and behind the desk, a large and absolutely stunning, ornamented, gold gilt mirror.

This room had a much more masculine feel than the other, and I quite preferred it. It also provided more privacy as it was farther from the parlor, more spacious, and less audacious with that horrid wallpaper.

"I'll stay here," I told her, walking up to the mirror. It really was quite captivating. "Where did this come from?" I asked her.

"I believe the architect, Mr. Blank, had it sent from Europe when he and your husband—er, your late husband—were building the hotel. Mr. Pryce was quite taken with it so he wanted it for this room."

"And Mr. Blank was the last person to stay in these rooms?" I asked.

"I don't believe so, ma'am," she said, averting my gaze. "I think it was . . . Mr. Pryce to stay here last. And there's been no one else since Mr. Blank . . . well, you know."

"Yes." I thought it strange that William had never

mentioned Mr. Blank by name, only as "the architect" who was helping him to build the hotel. He also never mentioned that Mr. Blank had died in these rooms. But, to be fair, I hadn't been interested in his business affairs much outside of the theater.

"I'll start your bath, ma'am. I'm afraid the water is quite cold. I'll bring some hot water up to warm it for you." She laid the dressing gown on the bed. "And this will keep you toasty until the bath is ready. We often keep a spare dressing gown for just such an occasion. Laundered, of course."

"Of course," I replied. At this point I didn't really care. I just wanted out of these clothes.

Before she left the room, she lit the three gas sconces that were affixed to the walls, suffusing the darkened room with a satisfying glow.

Smiling and then sinking in a half curtsy, Maggie left the room. I quickly removed my dress and then my corset. What a blessed relief to get them off. Shivering, I slipped into the dressing gown.

It took quite some time for Maggie to fill the tub with hot water. She had enlisted the help of Clarence, the bellhop, and in about thirty minutes, there was ample warm water for me to bathe.

When I emerged from the bathing room, warm, clean, and utterly exhausted, I was relieved to see that Cordelia, Bijou, and our trunks had arrived.

"Thank goodness you are here," I said to Cordelia. "Oh, and you, too, Bijou! I'm so glad you are safe!"

Cordelia's face was flushed, and her pinched expression indicated that her headache had gotten worse. I had developed one, as well.

Bijou gave a joyful bark at seeing me. I took her from Cordelia's arms and held her tightly against my chest, showering her little head with kisses. She returned my affections by happily licking my chin.

"You have bathed already?" Cordelia asked, confusion on her face. "And where did you get that dressing gown?"

"I fell into the river." I set Bijou down and went over to one of the trunks. "The maid brought me hot water and an extra gown. Quite the service you'd expect from a finer hotel." I looked down at the frayed sleeve of the dressing gown. "It's a bit worn, though. I'll have to see about ordering some new ones."

"Oh my goodness, Arabella!" Cordelia's mouth fell open. "That river is a torrent. You could have drowned. How did you ever get out?"

Not wanting to regale my humiliating ride through the street and my falling on top of Sheriff Marshall like a rag doll—twice—I waved a hand at her.

"I'll explain later. Now I just want to go to bed."

"I know what you mean," she said, absently pressing her fingers to her temple.

A loud knock on the door startled us both.

"Oh, what now?" I groaned. I wanted nothing more but for this day to end and to start anew tomorrow. Hastily, I went to answer it.

A daunting figure of considerable largess and the stern demeanor of a schoolmarm stood on the other side of the door. Her shiny raven hair was piled neatly on top of her head, and her dark eyes appraised me from head to toe. She carried a wooden platter with a small loaf of bread and an equally small block of cheese.

"Good evening, Mrs. Pryce," Her voice had a kind quality about it, but her face remained void of any emotion. "I'm Kitty Carlisle. I run the saloon."

"Ah, yes, hello," I said, hoping my own voice didn't betray my impatience.

"I understand you had a bit of trouble today," she said. "I won't keep you. I just wanted to bring you this, seeing as you didn't come down to the saloon for dinner."

Cordelia joined me at the door. "How thoughtful of you," she said.

"This is my companion, Cordelia Danson," I said, making the introduction. The two bobbed their heads in greeting, and Miss Carlisle handed Cordelia the platter.

"You just holler if you need anything more, Mrs. Pryce. I'm usually at the saloon late. I hope the noise won't bother you too much. The miners and other menfolk can get a bit rowdy in there."

"I thank you for your kindness," I said, giving her a smile. "I believe we are both so tired, nothing could wake us."

"Good night, then," she said with a nod and left.

I closed the door. "Well, she was certainly an interesting figure."

"Yes, it was nice of her to bring us something to eat. Would you like some?" Cordelia held the platter out to me.

It did look appetizing, but all I wanted was my bed.

I shook my head. "No, thank you. Only sleep for me."

She gave a faint smile of relief. "I will bring you your nightdress."

"Bless you, dear."

Once I had brushed my hair, which was now nearly dry, I removed the dressing gown, pulled on my nightdress, and climbed under the heavy covers. I had scarcely put my head on the pillow before I fell into a deep sleep.

It seemed only mere moments after I had fallen into that peaceful slumber that a bone-chilling scream woke me.

CHAPTER 6

I sat up in bed, trying to assess where the noise had come
from. The screaming continued, and I quickly put on the
discarded dressing gown and accessed the door in my bedroom
that led to the hotel hallway, so as to not awaken Cordelia, had
she managed to sleep through the horrible screams.

The noise was coming from the stairway below. I made my
way down the stairs and past the third-floor landing but stopped
when I reached the next one. Narcissa Platte was sprawled on
the second-floor landing, her body crumpled next to the nearby
plant stand. Her head lay in a pool of blood. A woman and a
man, guests of the hotel, stood over her, the woman visibly trembling from head to toe, her face white as a sheet, and tears
streaming down her face.

"Oh my goodness!" I hurried down the stairs to Narcissa. My
stomach wrenched at the sight of her lifeless body.

A shriek from above nearly made me jump out of my skin. I
looked up to find Mr. and Mrs. Platte staring down upon the
body of their daughter. Mrs. Platte started another round of
horrified screaming. She sank to her knees, and her husband
caught her in his arms.

I pressed my fingers against Narcissa's wrist, looking for a pulse but finding nothing. I laid my head against her breast, listening for a heartbeat. There was none.

"What happened?" I asked, looking up at the shocked couple, my own heart thrumming in my chest.

Cordelia, in her nightcap and robe, had joined the Plattes. "Oh my. What on earth is this? What's happened?"

"We don't know." The man held his wife in a comforting embrace. "We were coming up the stairs to go to our room when we saw her lying there."

From down below, Mr. Pettyjohn appeared in a robe and leather slippers.

"What's all this noise?" His voice was gravelly from sleep.

"She's dead," I said softly. I took in a deep breath to try to still the trembling in my hands.

"It looks like she fell down the stairs," Cordelia said.

I gazed at Narcissa's face, placid and beautiful as if she were sleeping. It was then I noticed a slight redness on the visible side of her neck, and a dark bruise had formed on her throat.

I raised my gaze to Cordelia. "I'm not so sure this was an accident." I turned my attention to Mr. Pettyjohn, who had shoved his hands into the pockets of his robe. "Fetch the Sheriff, would you?"

He nodded. "I'll get Doc Tate as well." Then he fled down the stairs.

Down the hallway, someone emerged from their room on the second floor. To my utter chagrin, I recognized Atticus Brooks rushing toward us. He wore a hideous paisley smoking jacket. It reminded me of a molting peacock.

Mrs. Platte released herself from her husband. "It was the ghost, I tell you! It's the ghost of Mr. Blank that's killed my daughter." She went on with another round of keening.

"A ghost?" The woman who'd found poor Narcissa looked up at her husband, her eyes wide and her chin quivering. "There is a ghost here?"

"Please." I held up a hand as if I could catch this air of

hysteria and close my fist around it. "I can assure you, you will come to no harm from any ghost," I said with confidence, which was, again, acting on my part. I had no idea if the rumors of the ghost were true.

"It was him, I know it!" Mrs. Platte wailed.

"What do you mean?" I asked. "Why would a ghost want to harm your daughter?"

She rounded on me, her eyes aflame. "Or more likely it was YOU!"

I pulled my chin back and gasped. "Me? Why on earth—"

"You were jealous! You have come to enact your revenge. Everyone knows your husband was pursuing my Narcissa. And why wouldn't he? She was perfect! She said he left La Plata Springs to return to New York to leave you."

A searing-hot dagger pierced my heart. That couldn't be true. William had said nothing about leaving me. Although, he'd been quite ill by the time he'd returned from Colorado. Perhaps he'd been waiting until he recovered . . . which of course, he did not.

"Oh, my beautiful Narcissa!" she wailed.

I snapped out of my shock and confusion. "How dare you accuse me of such a thing! I knew nothing of your daughter before I set foot in this hotel. And William would never—"

My gaze slid over to the small group clustered next to the body. Atticus Brooks regarded me with pursed lips. I imagined him licking those lips with that wolf's tongue. I half expected him to produce a pad and pencil from that ridiculous smoking jacket.

Suddenly, I remembered the blond hairs in the brush. I gazed down at Narcissa's golden waves. Could it be true? Had William betrayed me? I had always known him to be a man of honor. I couldn't imagine . . . But then again, I had been preoccupied with the theater and my career. For years.

"Now, now," Cordelia came to my rescue, addressing Mrs. Platte. "This has been a terrible shock. Why don't you go to your rooms? We will handle this."

Mrs. Platte balled her fists at her sides. "And that ghost. That ghost! He killed that man last year. He wants us out of this hotel. All of us!"

Swallowing down my outrage at the horrible accusation that I had murdered her daughter and the declaration of my husband's supposed infidelity, I settled my gaze again on the bruise at Narcissa's throat. How would a ghost, who had no physical body, cause a bruise like that? If, indeed, the killer had caused the bruise.

"Oh, this is awful! Why, why, why?" Mrs. Platte cried. "My girl . . . My lovely girl!"

Mr. Platte made no move to comfort his wife but simply stared down at the lifeless body of his daughter.

I brought myself to standing and approached the grieving woman. My practical nature, and the realization that I was responsible for the hotel and the goings on in it, kicked in, overtaking my defensiveness. With some effort, I stuffed my anger, hurt, and humiliation aside. I would deal with that later.

"Mrs. Platte, I am sorry for what happened to your daughter, but rest assured, I did not do this heinous thing. Let's get you to your rooms," I said stiffly. There was no need for her to continue to see her daughter like this. The shock must be overwhelming.

Snuffling into a handkerchief, Mrs. Platte let me guide her to the open door of their rooms, and I ushered her inside. Cordelia followed.

I led the distraught woman to a chair by the fireplace where smoldering embers breathed their last and tendrils of smoke wafted up the chimney. Remembering what she had said earlier about the odor in their rooms, I gave a sniff but could smell nothing save for the sweet pine smoke.

"Cordelia," I said, indicating for her to enter the room and come over to us. "Would you sit with Mrs. Platte? I'd like to be there when the sheriff and the doctor arrive."

"Of course." She took the chair opposite Mrs. Platte on the other side of the hearth and looked on while Mrs. Platte continued to sob into her handkerchief. Raising her head, the grieving woman howled with despair. Not one to succumb to emotional displays herself, Cordelia shot me a look of panic. I didn't envy her the task I'd set for her, but it was my responsibility to see to the matter on the stairs.

"Thank you," I said, by means of encouragement.

Mrs. Platte let out another blood-curdling wail. She'd wake the entire hotel if they weren't awake already, but how could I tell her to be quiet? Her daughter was dead. Although I did not like the woman, or the accusation that I had killed her daughter, my heart twisted for her.

The mere idea that I had been jealous of the young woman was preposterous and, quite frankly, insulting, but I couldn't help but feel a responsibility to find out exactly what had happened to Miss Platte. I owned the hotel, and didn't the safety of the guests and residents fall to me, or at the very least to the hotel manager who'd been here for more than just mere hours?

My gaze traveled to Mr. Brooks who was taking a closer look at the prostrate body, and a sinking feeling hit my stomach. He'd write about this, and this sort of tragedy could damage the reputation of the hotel, and thus mine. If the hotel went to ruin during my tenure here, that would mean I had failed. Failure went against everything in my being. My mission in life, as my mother had often reminded me, was to succeed, for success meant security.

The duties of overseeing and running a business in which I had absolutely no experience suddenly weighed heavily upon me. *How could William have done this to me?* I thought for the thousandth time. He knew I would be completely out of my element, and the unfairness of it all only added to my resentment of the situation.

How I wished I had never come to this damnable hotel.

As I left the Plattes' rooms, heavy footsteps and male voices echoed from below.

Mr. Pettyjohn, the sheriff, and someone who I assumed to be Dr. Tate, climbed the stairs to the second-floor landing. When Sheriff Marshall saw me coming down from the third floor his face registered surprise.

Suddenly feeling self-conscious at parading around in my nightclothes, with my waist-length hair unbound and falling over my shoulders, I pulled my dressing gown around me and secured it with its sash.

The man with Sheriff Marshall was small in stature with delicate features. He was stooped with age, yet his gray eyes bore a keen and alert intelligence. Carrying his black leather bag, he knelt down next to the body.

"Does anyone know what happened?" he asked, examining Narcissa's blood-soaked head.

Mr. Platte, who had been standing in the very same spot he had been before I took his wife into their rooms, took in a gulp of air, as if he'd been holding his breath the entire time. "She wasn't feeling well, so she retired early. Earlier than usual. We figured she'd gone to bed. We didn't hear her leave our rooms."

"How long do you think she's been dead?" the sheriff asked the doctor.

Dr. Tate pulled his pocket watch from his vest pocket. "It's midnight. From the temperature of her skin and the stiffness in her face, I'd say two hours or so."

"So she died at around ten o'clock?" the sheriff confirmed.

"Yes, I'd say definitely around that time."

"That woman said something about a ghost," the lady who'd found the body spoke up in a trembling voice. Her husband wrapped a comforting arm around her shoulders.

"Did you see anything?" Sheriff Marshall asked them. "Was there anyone else nearby?"

The woman shook her head. "No."

"Yes," the man said, his eyes wide with remembrance. "There

was someone, a man, headed down the hallway toward the back staircase."

"What did he look like?"

The man pressed his lips together. "I don't know. All I saw was the back of him. He was wearing a buckskin jacket and a hat."

"So not a ghost," the sheriff said with a sardonic tone. "Was there anything else?"

The man then repeated what he had said to me and Cordelia. That he and his wife had been going to their room when they'd found the young woman on the landing.

"Do you require anything more of us, Sheriff?" the man asked. "My wife is distressed, and we'd like to go to our room."

Sheriff Marshall gave them a nod. "You are free to go. Thank you for your time." He then addressed Mr. Pettyjohn, Mr. Brooks, and me. "You too. Dr. Tate and I have got it from here. You can go back to your beds."

The man guided the woman down the hallway. She kept muttering about the ghost, and her husband did his best to assure her there were no such things as ghosts. They disappeared into one of the rooms. Mr. Pettyjohn, too, took his leave but Mr. Brooks remained, obviously eager to sink his teeth into this tragedy.

"My poor darling girl," Horace Platte croaked. He placed a hand over his mouth and squeezed his eyes shut, his shoulders shaking.

"Come, Mr. Platte," I said. "There is nothing more you can do at the moment. The doctor and the sheriff will take care of things here. Go be with your wife. You need each other right now."

Just then, Mrs. Platte came bursting down the stairs, Cordelia on her heels. She was shaking a finger in my direction.

"She did it, Sheriff! I tell you, it was her! She was jealous. Oh! What am I going to do without my Narcissa?" she cried.

Sheriff Marshall and the doctor swung their heads to look up at me. Mr. Brooks stood by with a smirk on his face. To my dismay, he *did* have a small notepad and pencil at the ready. Did he sleep with them?

I tried to keep my voice even, steady. "This accusation is absurd. Mrs. Platte is distressed and jumping to conclusions." I looked straight into the sheriff's blue eyes. "Just a second ago she was claiming that a ghost killed her daughter."

Sheriff Marshall and the doctor exchanged a knowing glance that sent my heart to the pit of my stomach. So it was true? My husband had had a relationship with this girl?

"You don't really think that I—"

"Oh, my Narcissa!" Mrs. Platte wailed.

Cordelia gathered Mr. and Mrs. Platte together and led them back up to their rooms. In moments, she was back.

"We'll discuss this tomorrow," Sheriff Marshall said. "Dr. Tate will examine the body, and we'll know more after that."

Cordelia reached out and took me by the hand. "I think they will stay put now. The sheriff is right. It's out of our hands for the moment."

"Let's get her to your infirmary." The sheriff nodded to Dr. Tate. "I'll go fetch the wagon." Without another glance at me and Cordelia, he bounded down the stairs.

The doctor stood up from his kneeling position. "You ladies can go on back to bed now. There is nothing more you can do here."

I wanted to stay, to protest my innocence, but I knew it would fall on deaf ears tonight.

Cordelia took me by the elbow. "You need to get some sleep, Arabella," she said.

Although I didn't want to go, I couldn't argue with her. I let her lead me up the stairs, wondering if I would ever sleep again.

CHAPTER 7

The following morning, Bijou, who had been curled up by my side, awakened me with her usual morning kisses, letting me know she wanted to go outdoors to take care of her business.

"One moment, darling," I said, stroking her golden head. She blinked at me with her dark, button eyes and then let out a round of short barks.

Cordelia peeked her head into my room. She was fully dressed and looked as if she'd been up for hours, which I did not doubt in the least. She was always an early riser, usually eager to stick her nose in one of her books.

"Morning," she said, her face all seriousness. "Did you sleep well?"

I yawned. "Not really. You?"

She nodded. "I slept for a few hours. That was a horrible shock last night."

I heaved a sigh, remembering the appalling accusation that I had killed that poor young woman. And the insinuation that there had been something going on between her and my late husband. It was all so very confusing.

"Yes, it was. And to pin her death on me?"

"The woman was out of her mind with grief. She'll see sense today," Cordelia tried to assure me.

"Let's hope so."

"For all we know, Narcissa tripped while going down the stairs and cracked open her head," she said with a shrug.

"I suppose it's possible, but there is the matter of the bruises on her neck."

"True," she acquiesced. "But we don't know if that is what killed her. She could have suffered the bruises at an earlier time."

"Right." She did have a point. As I recall, Narcissa had been wearing a high-necked blouse earlier yesterday. The bruises may have already been there.

"I have coffee and some pastries for you in the drawing room. I found a little bakery down the road."

"You are a godsend, my dear," I said, stretching.

Bijou jumped off the bed and scurried out the door with Cordelia. I continued to lie there, staring up at the ceiling, recounting the terrible events of last night. A young woman dead in the hotel. My hotel. I shuddered. I hoped Cordelia was right and that the supposition that I had done this young woman harm would vanish into the air.

I recalled Cordelia's earlier thought: this could have been some kind of accident, despite the bruises. Yet, Mrs. Platte had immediately jumped to murder the moment she had seen the body. Did the young woman have enemies? Is that why her mother assumed she had been murdered?

The grieving mother had at first implicated "the ghost," Mr. Percival Blank. If he did indeed exist, was he a killer? I prayed he was not. From what Mr. Pettyjohn and Mrs. Platte had said, there was only a rumor that he'd killed before.

A hotel with a murderous ghost. That story was no better than a hotel with a murderous proprietor. My stomach clenched at the image of Atticus Brooks, pencil and pad in hand, writing furiously to put the final nail in the coffin of my now neglected career.

I made a mental note to remind Cordelia to jot down some of the more positive attributes of the hotel and the town for Mr. Rankin's stories of my "exciting adventure" in the Southwest.

The sound of someone clearing their throat startled me. I opened my eyes, expecting to see Cordelia, but she was gone and had closed the door behind her. My gaze traveled to the mirror where I saw the reflection of a dark-haired man in a smoking jacket standing in my room.

I sat bolt upright in bed, my heart in my throat. I glanced toward the door, but there was no one there. Then it dawned on me. My sudden alarm waned ever so slightly, although I was still unsettled at the idea of a strange man intruding upon my privacy.

"You're the ghost," I said matter-of-factly.

"I prefer the word *spirit,*" he said, crossing his arms over his chest.

"I'm sorry. You must be Mr. Blank."

He was quite handsome, with dark, wavy hair, luminous chocolate eyes, and an attractive cleft in his chin. His voice was smooth and soft, like butter churned to creamy perfection.

He cocked his head at me. "Why are you not afraid? I usually send people out of the room screaming as if I were carrying an axe with which to chop them up."

I sighed. "I'm not unfamiliar with ghosts—er, spirits."

"You are a spiritualist?"

"Not exactly. I prefer the word *sensitive.*"

"Who are you?"

"I beg your pardon," I stated, quite affronted. "I would like to get out of bed. Please turn your back."

He gave a half smile and rolled his eyes but proceeded to comply.

I slipped into my dressing gown.

"May I turn around now?" he asked.

"Yes." I stepped closer to the mirror to get a better look at him. There was a Byronic and moody quality about him, which I quite liked, and his smoking jacket looked to be of the finest quality, if not a tad flamboyant.

"I am Arabella Pryce, owner of this hotel."

A captivating smile crossed his face. "So *you're* the actress. Your husband spoke very highly of you."

"Did he?" I was surprised at this declaration. Of course, I knew my husband thought well of me, but he was not the sort of man to throw about compliments. He was, first and foremost, a businessman. I believe he purchased the theater for financial reasons but also to keep me occupied so he could travel about finding other worthy investment opportunities. In truth, we spent little time together. The previous assertion of his alleged feelings for another woman intruded upon my thoughts, but I chose to ignore it.

"Yes, he did," Mr. Blank continued. "And I must say, you are every bit as beautiful as he described. Your portrait does you no justice." A faint smile crossed his full lips. I blushed at the compliment and the reassurance of William's feelings for me. But I really must see this portrait.

"Thank you," I said under my breath, appreciating the senti- ment. And then an uneasy thought struck me. "Are you always there, in the mirror, or do you travel about?"

Was he going to be a permanent guest, allowing me no privacy?

His sly smile turned into a devilish grin, making my insides swirl. "This room is one of my favorite haunts—pardon the pun —but I do occasionally move throughout the hotel. When it's necessary."

"Necessary?"

"Yes. Some of the guests, and residents, are not to my liking."

"So you try to chase them away?"

He shrugged in mild agreement.

Leticia Crookshank had been a shy ghost. In fact, I had owned the theater in New York for four years before I became aware of her presence. There had been no rumors of a resident ghost there. But, Percival didn't seem shy in the least.

"Have there been many not to your liking?" I asked, growing a little concerned about the reputation of the hotel.

"Some. Not many. It takes a great deal of energy to reveal myself to those who are not as sensitive as you are."

I recalled Leticia saying something similar.

"And that is why no one, except my late husband, has occupied these rooms since you died?"

That smile again.

"And you never leave the hotel?" I asked, curious about the life of a ghost. To my knowledge, Mrs. Crookshank had never left the theater, but I had encountered Oliver out of doors.

"I do on occasion. I have a favorite spot down by the river."

"Ah. I see. Did you murder one of the guests last night?" I figured I'd just come out with it, take the proverbial bull by the horns.

"What?" His brow creased, and his mouth hung open in chagrin.

I set my lips in a hard line. "You heard me. A young woman, Miss Narcissa Platte, was found dead on the second-floor landing. Did you kill her?"

He shook his head in confusion. "Why on earth—"

"Did you also kill a man in this hotel a year ago?"

He put a hand over his heart, his face contorting in hurt and disappointment. "Mrs. Pryce, you wound me."

I could not tell if he was sincere or in jest, as I had only just met the man—er, ghost.

"I'm sorry, but I simply must know the truth." I crossed my arms at my waist and looked him dead in the eyes. Or, rather, looked into his dead eyes.

He sighed with resignation. "I thought you said you'd encountered a spiritual being before."

"I have," I stated resolutely.

"Then you must know it is very difficult for me to kill. I have no physical form. I cannot have direct contact with anything in the physical realm, save for the contents in my mirror, or the other mirrors in the hotel."

I did not recall seeing a mirror on or near the stairwell where we'd found Miss Platte.

He continued. "The person, or thing, must be in the reflection of the mirror, in essence *with me,* for me to make contact with them or it."

His explanation sent a shiver down my spine. He had been here while I'd slept. If what he said was true, he could kill me this very instant because I was "with him" in the mirror and would be "with him" while I resided in this room. Unless I had the mirror removed, an idea that had presented itself quite strongly in that moment.

"Arabella?" Cordelia knocked and then came into the room. Mr. Blank vanished.

I spun around, feeling somewhat like I'd been caught doing something I shouldn't. "Yes, dear? I—I thought you'd left."

"Just getting ready to. Did I hear voices in here?"

"Oh, it's just me," I said with a nervous twitter.

"Very well." She scanned the room, uncertainty in her expression. "Bijou and I won't be long."

I smiled sweetly at her, frozen in front of the mirror. She closed the door, leaving me alone. I had hoped Mr. Blank would come back because I had more questions, but there was only my reflection.

I waited for several minutes. When he did not reappear, I commenced with getting dressed. It took me a little longer than usual. Cordelia typically helped me get into my corset and fasten the many buttons on my sleeves, but I managed. I was just arranging my hair when Mr. Blank popped into the mirror again, sending my heart into spasms.

"Mr. Blank!" I gasped. "Don't do that! If you are going to insist on sharing this room with me, we are going to have to establish some ground rules, and rule number one is you mustn't sneak up on me."

"I apologize." He placed his hands behind his back. "That was rude."

"Thank you," I said, finishing with my hair. "But I'm actually glad you've returned. I have some more questions for you."

"I hope I have some answers," he said gently and smiled. He really was quite charming.

"Was the man who was murdered last year in the hotel in this mirror?

"Ah," he said. "Man by the name of Valdez. Gambler. Rake." He heaved a sigh of irritation. "The man was exceedingly boorish and quite duplicitous. I did not like him, but no, he did not reside in this room, and no, I did not kill him."

"Do you know who did?"

"No idea." He raised his arm from the elbow, curled his fingers over his palm and proceeded to examine his fingernails. I had the feeling he had more to say about Mr. Valdez but it didn't seem he was going to elaborate.

"How many other mirrors are there in the hotel?"

He lowered his arm. "There are twelve others. Two in these rooms, one in the saloon which I never frequent—too many people, too noisy—one in Mr. Bledsoe's parlor room, seven others in some of the nicer rooms, one more is cracked and safely stored in the attic, and two in other rooms I never occupy."

"Really, why not?"

"They are in the Plattes' rooms. One in their parlor and a small one on the young woman's vanity. I do not like their company."

"And, you have not tried to run them off?"

He scoffed. "It would require too much effort. Hard as bricks, those three."

"The other guest rooms in the hotel do not have mirrors?"

"They are quite costly, Mrs. Pryce, and difficult to come by in these parts."

My thoughts returned to the matter of the disturbances Mr. Pettyjohn had mentioned. "Mr. Pettyjohn said people have heard things—clunking and screeching in the night. Are you responsible for that?"

He raised a shoulder in a half shrug. "That is entirely possible. I may have, on an occasion, made a bit of a ruckus within the mirrors of the hotel. Especially the one in the attic. So many interesting things up there: furniture, trunks, crates. All manner of noisy things. Sometimes I like to rearrange the furniture, particularly in these rooms." He held his arm aloft, indicating the area around me. "But I cannot physically touch, injure, or kill a living being unless they are in the mirror," he repeated. "I can prove it if you want."

He reached out and set the tip of his finger against my shoulder, and indeed, I felt it as if he were as solid and alive as I was. An icy chill sparked down my arm, and I sucked in a breath. He gave a smug smile and pulled a pipe from his jacket pocket. With a flick of his fingers, a red glow filled the bowl of the pipe.

"And the odiferous rats?" I crossed my arms, refusing to let on that his touch had elicited such a visceral response.

He puffed deeply at the stem of the pipe, making the bowl of it glow crimson again. Then he gave me a wicked grin. "I may have lured them to the chimney with a scrap of food I picked up in the mirror in this room. Sometimes the maid, Maggie, has a piece of bread or a sweet with her when she cleans. She also makes a habit of setting out strychnine to keep the place clear of infestation. I was only helping her out."

"You must cease the mischief, Mr. Blank. The reputation of the hotel is paramount to its success." And mine, as well, I thought.

"How exactly did Miss Platte die?" he asked, ignoring my request.

"You did not see anything?" I asked.

He shook his head. The sweet aroma of burning tobacco filled the room.

"I don't know how she died." I raised my chin. "But Mrs. Platte has the preposterous notion that I might have—" I could barely form my lips around the words "—killed her."

"I see."

"And that Miss Platte and my late husband—"

He dipped his chin and looked at me from under brows that were full and fractionally asymmetrical, one hiked higher that the other.

"You know something," I stated.

He shrugged. "I've seen her up here with your husband. Once."

Remembering the hairbrush, I swallowed down the lump that had formed in my throat. "Oh? Doing what, pray tell?"

"They were in the parlor. They were discussing something."

"Discussing what?" Why was he being so cagey?

"I haven't the slightest." He puffed again on his pipe and then pulled it away from his mouth. "Well, come to think of it, it might have had something to do with travel. Frankly, the conversation was boring and I didn't much care to eavesdrop. I moved on."

Travel? Had this been what Mrs. Platte had referred to, that William was coming back to New York to tell me he was leaving me? Or had he and Narcissa been planning to go away together? I shook my head, telling myself I was jumping to conclusions. It couldn't be true. William had adored me. And he was a man of principle.

I did my best to ignore the niggling of doubt in the back of my mind. "Is that the only time you've seen her in these rooms?" I asked.

He nodded. "But I'm not here all the time. I come and go." He took another mouthful of smoke from his pipe and exhaled it slowly. "So you don't know if Miss Platte was killed, or if this was some kind of accident?"

He stepped through the mirror and the bureau below it to stand next to me. His form instantly changed, and a radiant glow surrounded him. The air around me cooled, sending a river of chills down my back, and I gasped at the sensation.

Up close, he really was quite dashing, even though he had become as semitranslucent as a dragonfly's wings. His dark eyes were soulful and sad, and his strong jaw contrasted with the fullness of his lips. My eyes were drawn to the cleft in his chin, and then I raised them to meet his gaze. It seemed to go right through me, taking my breath away.

"N-no," I stammered. "The doctor took the body to examine it further. I assume he will have an answer today."

He reached out to push a stray lock of hair out of my eyes, but it didn't move. Instead, the sensation of a cool breeze passed over my forehead and a faint tingling flooded my body.

"See?" he said quietly. "When I am not in the mirror, I cannot make even a wisp of hair on your head move. Do you believe me now?"

My heart hammering in my chest, I backed away from him. This encounter was much different from the encounters I had experienced with Oliver Shrewsbury and Leticia Crookshank. Yes, I could see them and hear them, but I couldn't *feel* them like I felt Percival Blank. And even more unsettling, there was something about him that gave me the sense I had known him always. Like there was a thin thread between us that wove us together in a most inexplicable way. The sensation was most unnerving.

"Yes," I said firmly, trying to disguise the fact I had been completely caught off guard by the intimate gesture. However, I did concede there was no conceivable way he could push someone down the stairs. He would move right through them.

"Fine. I believe that you did not kill Miss Platte. But are you sure you did not see anything? Anything at all? The couple who found the body said there was a man in a buckskin coat nearby. Did you see him?"

He shook his head. "I was out."

"Out? Out where?"

He gave me an indulgent smile. "Are you now my keeper?"

I shook my head, embarrassed. "No. No, I'm sorry. I didn't mean to—" What had prompted me to ask the question? Of course it was none of my business where this spirit chose to roam. Perhaps he had a phantom lady friend in a nearby dwelling.

Flustered, I returned to my previous inquiry. "And you don't know how Mr. Valdez died?"

Mr. Blank gave a shrug. "I do not. Apparently, he was found dead in one of the rooms. I believe he was staying in Mr. Bledsoe's rooms to be exact."

Mr. Blank had mentioned a mirror in Mr. Bledsoe's parlor.

"So he was occupying Mr. Bledsoe's rooms?" I repeated for clarification.

"Yes. He was found in bed."

"I see," I said. So no mirror present. "Well, it's rumored that you did it, and now Mrs. Platte is saying that either you or I killed her daughter."

Mr. Blank frowned. "Indeed. The woman is probably quite beside herself with grief. The Plattes, intolerable as they are, adored their daughter. Quite doted on her, especially Mrs. Platte. Almost to the point of smothering her. It's no wonder Narcissa had a rebellious streak."

"Rebellious, you say?" Having a domineering mother myself, I could relate.

"Yes. The woman treated Narcissa like a trophy of sorts. It was as if she pinned all her own hopes and dreams on the girl."

I sighed. Yes, I could commiserate with Narcissa all too well.

"At any rate," he continued, "the accusation against me is unacceptable. Something needs to be done about this. I should not like to have my name further besmirched in such a distasteful manner."

I could see his point, but did it really matter? He was dead. I had more at stake than he did.

"But I'm alive," I argued. "I cannot have my impeccable repu-tation here and abroad sullied by the goings on in this hotel. I agree, something must be done."

He took another puff from his pipe. "It sounds like you'll have to find out exactly what happened, then. If Miss Platte was murdered, you'll have to find her killer."

"Right." With any luck, Miss Platte's demise would be ruled an unfortunate accident and I could go about repairing the repu-tation of the hotel. But something told me it wasn't going to be that easy.

CHAPTER 8

I left Mr. Blank and went to the parlor. Maggie had just entered carrying a small stack of wood in her arms, a pail dangling from her elbow.

"Miss Danson said I could come in. I'll build you a fire if you like," she offered.

"A fire would be nice, thank you."

I watched the young woman as she pulled some newspapers from under her arm, scrunched them into loose balls, and placed them beneath the logs. After that, she took smaller pieces of wood from the pail and placed them on top of the papers. She then produced a box of matches from her pocket and lit the paper on fire. Soon the kindling caught.

"That should do it," she said, raising herself from her knees.

I gave her an appreciative smile. "Thank you."

Suddenly, her face contorted in anguish, and I could see she was trying to keep her emotions reined in.

"Are you quite all right?" I asked.

Pressing her fingers to her trembling lips, she nodded and looked up at me with sorrowful eyes brimming with tears.

Just then, Cordelia and Bijou came back from their walk. Cordelia's face was pink from the cool morning air and exercise.

At seeing me, Bijou emitted a joyous bark and pranced around my feet. I bent down and picked her up to quiet her.

"The fire looks lovely." Cordelia crossed the room to place her hands in front of it. When she glanced at Maggie, her countenance darkened. "Oh dear," she said, meeting my gaze.

The maid covered her face with both hands and sobbed. I assumed she'd heard about Miss Platte.

"Goodness, Maggie. Come and sit down." I led her to the love seat under the bay window.

"I'm sorry," she said, shaking her head. "You must think me terribly unprofessional." She swiped at the tears on her cheeks, which had bloomed red with embarrassment.

"Not at all," I said. "Were you close?"

"What?" Her face registered confusion.

"With Miss Platte. You were friends?"

She huffed. "Hardly. The woman was the most vain and conceited creature I'd ever met." Her features hardened. "She could be extremely cruel."

From what I'd experienced in my brief encounter with Narcissa Platte, the idea of her being cruel was not unfounded. "Then what is troubling you?" I asked.

"Oh, it's nothing." She waved a dismissive hand. "Please forgive my outburst. I must go. I have so much work to do—" Her voice hitched, threatening to unleash another round of sobs.

I looked over at Cordelia, and she shrugged, holding her hands out in question. I turned back to Maggie. "I can see that it is not 'nothing.' Please tell me what is the matter."

"Really, I have to—"

"Nonsense. Surely you can take a moment to collect yourself. The other maids can cover you for a bit."

"Other maids?" she squeaked. "There are no other maids."

"No?" I asked. "Not even one other?"

She shook her head. "No, ma'am. I'm the only one." She sniffed.

Cordelia had left the room and came back with a handkerchief. She handed it to Maggie.

"Surely not," I said indignantly. "How many guest rooms does
this hotel have?"

"Not counting the long-term guests on the third and fourth
floors, twenty-five. And then there's the annex on the eastern
side, where some of the miners and their families live, and
Kitty's girls, but I don't have to cater to them. They keep their
own house." She pressed the hanky to her cheeks and chin.

"Kitty's girls?" I asked.

"Yes, ma'am. Kitty runs a brothel from some of the rooms in
the annex."

"What?!" I could scarcely believe what I'd just heard. Had
William known about this? If so, how could he have condoned
it? That kind of business enterprise was completely inappropriate for the type of hotel he, and now I, wanted the Arabella to
be. I wondered how well I had known my husband at all. If word
got out about this . . . Anxiety gripped my stomach as Atticus
Brooks's smarmy face popped into my mind.

"Oh my stars," Cordelia said, wide-eyed. "However do you
manage?" she asked the maid, changing the subject, probably
afraid of what I would say next.

But really? A brothel? If people found out that I was associated with a den of ill repute, I would be ruined. In that moment,
I wanted to fly away from that ball and chain of a hotel like a
bird on the wing, but alas, I was caged. For an entire year.

"I'm so sorry," Maggie repeated. "There is just ever so much
work. I never seem to get caught up. We've had to turn guests
away because I have not been able to get to all the rooms for
cleaning, which vexes Mr. Pettyjohn. And sometimes, even after
the rooms are cleaned, there is some kind of mess when the
guests arrive, like the rats in your fireplace. We've had a terrible
problem with the vermin. The guests complain, and then Mr.
Pettyjohn scolds me. He's even withheld my wages on occasion."

I pressed my lips together in an attempt to keep myself from screaming to the rafters. After all, it wasn't the poor girl's fault that I now owned a haunted, rat-infested bawdy house where now three occupants had come to their demise. Instead, I channeled my acting skills, put on a serene expression, and held my voice steady. "What does Mr. Bledsoe have to say about all this?"

He, as hotel manager and permanent resident, should have seen to these problems. Surely there were young women in want of jobs—respectable jobs—in this town. And why hadn't Mr. Bledsoe seen to the problem of the rats and the malodorous situation in the Plattes' rooms? I remembered the peeling paint, bubbling wallpaper, and frayed carpet on the staircase. I shuddered to imagine the state of the rest of the hotel.

"He tells me he will hire more help, but it never seems to happen. I am so sorry I can't keep up with the work. I can't lose this job, Mrs. Pryce."

"Dry your tears, my dear," I said, perhaps a bit harshly. I couldn't abide such a display of emotion any longer. I softened my voice. "You shall not lose your job, I assure you."

"I'm ever so grateful," she said with a sniff and rose from the love seat. She managed a smile. "Is there anything else you require?"

"Yes. Please inform Mr. Bledsoe that I request his company at lunch today. There is a dining room in this hotel, God willing?"

"Um . . ." Maggie blinked at me again.

"Yes?" I asked, waiting for her to speak.

"There isn't a dining room."

"No dining room? But—"

"Just the saloon. Only beef stew and bean chili on the menu."

I heaved a sigh, my stomach turning at the thought.

"Well, I best be going," Maggie said, gathering up her pail. "I have lots of work to do."

"Yes," I agreed. "But take heart, my dear. I will find more help."

"Thank you, ma'am." She bobbed her head and left.

I took a look at myself in the parlor mirror to check my appearance, confident that Mr. Blank would not materialize with Cordelia present. In light of the circumstances of my less than glorious arrival yesterday, and now with the possibility of my name being tainted with an accusation of murder, I wanted to make sure I looked my best. I needed to give a favorable impression to the people of the town for several reasons, but the most important was to assure them that a person of my standing and reputation would never stoop to a crime so devious and heinous as murder. If Miss Platte had been killed in the first place. I needed to elicit their trust in order that I may find out more about her—and her relationship with William. Thirdly, I wanted to gird myself against the reality that I was the proud owner of a "hen house" and fortify myself for the immediate rectification of the state of the hotel and its operation immediately.

As I was finishing the last of my pastry in the parlor, I heard a whooshing noise at the door. Someone had jettisoned a note into the room.

Cordelia closed the book she was reading. "I'll get it."

She got up from her chair, went to the note, and picked it up.

"It's from Daniel Bledsoe. It says, *Meet me in the hotel saloon for lunch. Now. Bring your friend.*"

I frowned at the impudence of his demand. He expected me to jump at his bidding? The man most definitely needed a reminder of who worked for whom. After all, *I* had been the one to summon *him* to lunch. I looked at the watch pendant I wore on a chain around my neck. It was eleven twenty-five.

"Really! Of all the cheek!" I took the note from Cordelia. I hoped her erudite way of speaking, which sometimes came off as cold or detached—of which she was neither—was the reason for the perceived tone of the note. I scanned the jagged scrawl. Indeed, Cordelia had not misrepresented the missive.

"Very well," I said. "But we will wait thirty minutes. I will not be summoned like a common servant. How dare he?"

My welcome to the town had, so far, been seriously lacking, and my desire to leave it grew with each passing breath.

Thirty-five minutes later, Cordelia and I left our rooms.

CHAPTER 9

An odd feeling crept over me when we set foot on the second-floor landing. A young woman had taken her last breath here. I shuddered at the memory of her body lying there, pressed against the rectangular plant stand.

Maggie had done her best to clean the bloodstain, but there remained a darkened scar on the carpet, and the plant stand was still askew from the impact of Narcissa's body crashing into it.

An urge to straighten it overtook me. I set it parallel to the wall, and when I moved it, something glittery was revealed. I knelt down to observe it more carefully. It was a shard of thick glass about an inch tall and half an inch wide.

"What is it, Arabella?" Cordelia asked.

I held it up to the light. "A piece of glass."

"I wonder where it came from," she said.

I set it in my palm. The break had been clean with no jagged edges, and its thickness reminded me of the bottom of a whiskey tumbler. "How strange that it is here, near where Narcissa's body lay," I mused, wondering if it might be some kind of clue to her death.

"Could be a coincidence," Cordelia said. "You heard Maggie.

She's having trouble keeping up with her duties. That piece of glass could have been there for some time."

"True. Just as well, I'm going to keep it." I put the shard in my skirt pocket.

The sound of boisterous piano music and a cacophony of gay voices greeted us as we stepped from the hotel lobby through the wooden and etched glass doors of Bella's Saloon.

I took in a sharp breath at the name. William had often referred to me as "Bella," a nickname I could barely stomach. My mother, when she was at her most narcissistically charming and manipulative, had used the name when she was trying to convince me of something or wanted something from me.

Also, the name distinctly rang of a brothel. I curled my lip in displeasure. But why shouldn't the saloon be named something suitable for a sporting house with Miss Carlisle's side business in operation? I swallowed my annoyance as the list of things I intended to change at the Arabella multiplied.

I stepped down into the room and took in the decor. Garish, red velvet and gold lamé wallpaper in a fleur-de-lis design added to the heavy atmosphere of the room. Dark wood furnishings crowded the place, and the floor was littered with the shells of boiled peanuts. Behind the bar, a large man with arms the size of Sunday hams opened a bottle of whiskey. His voluminous black beard added to his air of menace. He poured a round of drinks and slid them to his thirsty clients.

I thought it a little early for such libations, but things here seemed to operate at quite a base level.

At the corner of the bar, a slender girl with delicate features and an ample bosom pushed up to her chin, draped herself across the shoulders of a man whose face I could not see.

"Mrs. Pryce." Kitty Carlisle appeared at my elbow. "Welcome to the Bella."

"Hello," I said, my voice tight. I needed to speak with her about her enterprise but couldn't fathom the right words. I would have to rehearse something later.

She shook her head and let out a chuckle. "You sure don't look anything like your picture." She tilted her head toward the front of the saloon.

Above the beveled glass door that led to the street was a framed portrait of a plump nude reclining on a divan, smiling at the room. A dog lay at her feet.

The portrait!

I gasped. The image was nothing like me. And I had never posed for such a portrait! My mortification froze my tongue. I glanced at Cordelia, who had pulled her lower lip between her teeth. Her eyes were wide as carriage wheels.

"What can I do for you?" Kitty Carlisle's voice pulled me out of my stupefaction, but I couldn't take my eyes off the offensive creation.

"Um. Yes. We . . . we are meeting with Mr. Bledsoe for luncheon," I said.

"Luncheon?" She gave another snort. "No tea and crumpets here. It's beans, rice, and—you're in luck today—chicken. Are you two and Mr. Bledsoe meeting about the death of the Platte girl?"

I blinked at her in surprise. "You heard about it?" I wondered if she'd also heard that Mrs. Platte had accused me of the horrible deed. Had Mr. Brooks been circulating the allegation? My stomach tightened.

She nodded. "There's not much that happens here that I don't know about."

"I see," I said, scanning her face. There was an honesty and practicality about her I quite liked. "Did you know Miss Platte well?"

She shrugged. "We weren't friendly, if that's what you mean. She and her mother made it quite clear they were above the rest of us here at the hotel. Narcissa snapped at us like we were her personal servants."

"So she wasn't well-liked?"

She gave a snort. "Uh, no, she wasn't."

"What did you know of her relationship with my husband?" I asked.

Miss Carlisle cleared her throat, caught off guard by my bluntness. I saw no point in beating about the bush.

"I saw them together, on occasion, but I don't know if they were—romantically involved."

I couldn't tell if she was sugarcoating her response, but it gave me some comfort. Clearly, William and Narcissa had some kind of familiarity, but to what degree?

"Look, Mrs. Pryce—" her face softened "—This is a small town. Rumors abound and get all twisted up. Your husband was a kind and decent man."

Indeed he was. But, had he been beguiled by Miss Platte and turned his affections toward her? Emotion welling up inside me. I couldn't respond for fear of my voice cracking.

Cordelia, sensing the reason for my hesitation, laid a comforting hand on my arm and gave it a gentle squeeze.

Kitty Carlisle then pointed to a booth at the back corner of the saloon. "That's Mr. Bledsoe's favorite table. I'm sure he'll be here in a minute."

My melancholy shifted to irritation. He hadn't arrived? Yet, he dared to command me to come immediately. And, if I had, would I have been cooling my heels for thirty-five minutes? I gritted my teeth so hard my jaw ached.

"Thank you, Miss Carlisle," I finally managed.

She nodded. "You just let me know if there's anything I can do to help," she said.

Cordelia and I squeezed through the crowded saloon and made our way to the booth.

I looked over my shoulder at the distasteful portrait. Did everyone truly think that was me? How appalling! And what was the thing doing there at all? Had William done this? I wanted to shrink inside myself, then run for the door and back up to my rooms.

Well, there was nothing to it. The thing was coming down —immediately!

Recalling Kitty Carlisle's mentioning of rumors abounding in the town, suddenly I felt all eyes on us as we walked to the back of the room. The sensation it produced harkened back to my grand and water-logged entrance into La Plata Springs. Had that been spoken about?

I got the impression then, and now, that people were looking down their noses at me, or laughing at me, which sent a pang of anxiety straight to my stomach.

We settled ourselves in the booth.

"I'm so sorry, Arabella," Cordelia whispered, obviously picking up on my embarrassment and perhaps even my angst.

"What was William thinking with that portrait?" I snapped.

She shrugged her shoulders.

From my vantage point, I could view the entire saloon. To my relief, people had gone back to the business of eating, drinking, smoking, and conversing. I spied Miss Carlisle go over to address the man who had the saloon girl draped across his shoulders. When he turned around, I was shocked to see it was Sheriff Marshall. Granted, I did not know him well—rather I did not know him at all—but the sight of him in such an intimate situation with the saloon girl made me feel disconcerted in a way I could not reconcile.

He rose from his seat and headed toward us. Reflexively, I patted the coils at the back of my head to assure they were in place—not that I cared what the sheriff might think of my appearance. Not in the least.

"Mrs. Pryce," he said in greeting when he reached the table. His startling blue eyes slid over to Cordelia. I made the introductions.

"May I have a word?" he asked me.

"Of course. Please, join us." I gave him my most dazzling smile.

"Perhaps you'd prefer a place with more privacy? It's about Narcissa Platte."

I raised my chin. "I don't know why. I have nothing to hide."

"Okay." He slid into the booth next to Cordelia, who had moved over for him.

The thin and willowy saloon girl approached the table with a glass-laden tray in hand. Her bustier was brilliant pink, as was the enormous feather in her brown hair, which had been pulled into a loose topknot at the crown of her head. Her skirt, in shiny black satin, rose well above her knees. The woman was dressed to garner attention, and she made the other two saloon girls look like nuns in comparison. Obviously, these were Kitty Carlisle's "girls."

"Here's your beer, Clayton," she said sweetly. Curling tendrils of hair framed her face and her large brown eyes were for no one but the handsome sheriff.

Finally, her gaze shifted to me. "Can I get you something? Sarsaparilla? Or something stronger? Whiskey?"

"Sally, this is Mrs. Arabella Pryce," the sheriff said.

The girl batted her large brown eyes at me, but she did not smile. "Hello. Sally Dean, at your service." She sank into an awkward curtsy. The gesture was charming but excessive.

"I'll have a cup of Earl Grey, please." In my estimation, it was far too early for alcohol. And where the devil was Daniel Bledsoe? I looked at my watch pendant again. Twenty more minutes had passed. How long was I supposed to wait for him?

"Earl, who?" The young woman furrowed her brow at me with a smile of confusion.

Lord, was I speaking a different language?

"Tea?" I pressed. "I'll have some tea."

"Oh." She giggled. "We don't have any tea. They serve tea down the road at the bakery, but we don't have any here."

Of course not, I wanted to say. Any respectable hotel had a tearoom for goodness' sake. But I just nodded, adding yet another item on my list of things to rectify in the hotel. I had my work cut out for me.

"Coffee, then?" I asked.

"We have coffee." She turned to Cordelia. "And you, miss?"

"I'll have the same."

With another adoring smile at the sheriff, Sally Dean left us to go get our beverages.

"I need to speak with you about last night," Sheriff Marshall said after taking a large swallow of his beer.

I sighed. "Yes. It was dreadful. Has the doctor done his examination?"

Just then a tall man with a small, stout woman on his arm approached the table. He was the most finely polished person I'd seen in the town thus far. He outshone the woman next to him to the degree that one could not take their eyes off him. She seemed a mere appendage.

His clothing, a dark suit and crisp white shirt, were of the finest quality. His nearly jet-black hair was carefully pomaded to control thick waves, and his closely cropped mustache was perfectly groomed. But there was something else about him. There was a heaviness to his posture, as if he carried a burden that was too large for his shoulders to support.

"I apologize for my tardiness," he addressed me. "I'm Daniel Bledsoe. This is my wife, Prunella."

On closer inspection, the woman's pinched expression gave her the appearance of a dried prune. I wondered if she'd been that way as a baby, and thus, her name. A strong floral fragrance filled the space around us. What was it? Jasmine? Whatever the scent, it was overbearing.

"How do you do?" I held my hand out to her. She took it in her gloved hand and weakly squeezed mine.

I looked to Mr. Bledsoe to greet him in turn, but his attention was riveted to something else in the saloon. I followed his gaze only to have it land on the barmaid—and lady of the evening—Sally Dean. She was busy fawning over a male customer whose mustache hung down to his collarbone. A quick glance at Mrs. Bledsoe revealed that she, too, had become aware of her husband's distraction.

She cleared her throat loudly, snapping the man out of his trance.

"Ah, forgive me, Mrs. Pryce. I was somewhere else." He focused his intense gaze on me and gave me a smile that would melt the hardest and coldest iceberg.

"Of course," I said, mustering a well-rehearsed and equally charming smile. He had kept me waiting and nothing irritated me more. It took every ounce of control I had to not comment on his rudeness.

The couple exchanged greetings with Cordelia.

"Please, sit," I said.

"I'll go." Cordelia was about to rise to offer them her place in the booth, but Mr. Bledsoe raised a hand to stop her.

"Don't get up. Prunella was just leaving to do some shopping."

The woman's eyes flared in surprise, and her face hardened. Mr. Bledsoe turned to her, and she gave him a prim smile that I daresay did not reach her eyes. She nodded a terse farewell to both Cordelia and me, and then left the saloon.

I scooted to the far end of the booth near the wall so Mr. Bledsoe could sit down.

He did so, looking at me with a curious expression. "It's a pleasure to meet you at last, Mrs. Pryce. You don't at all resemble—"

"The portrait," I cut in. Really, this was beyond the pale. *"That woman"*—I pointed to the dreadful objet d'art—"is not me. I have no idea where that has come from or why it is there. I would like it removed please."

Mr. Bledsoe and the Sheriff exchanged a glance.

"I'll see what I can do," Mr. Bledsoe said after a moment.

"Very well," I replied, eager to be done with the subject.

"Sheriff Marshall was just about to tell us about the doctor's findings concerning the death of Miss Platte."

"Ah, yes. I've just spoken with Mr. and Mrs. Platte. Terrible tragedy." Mr. Bledsoe fixed me with a strange look. Did he, too, believe I killed her?

"What did the doctor find?" he asked.

"He's not completely finished with his examination," the sheriff said, "but so far he has ruled out an accidental death. The injury to the back of her head was not consistent with a fall down the stairs. The wound was deep."

"And the marks on her neck and throat?" I asked.

Mr. Bledsoe's complexion took on a ghostly hue.

"Happened close to the time of death," the sheriff said.

"So it was murder?" Mr. Bledsoe asked, directing his gaze at me. I imagined Mrs. Platte was persisting with her theory that I had done the deed.

I narrowed my eyes at him, affronted at his silent accusation.

"Yes." The sheriff took another sip of his beer.

"What could have caused the injury to her head?" Cordelia asked. "In one short story about Sherlock Holmes, *The Adventure of the Abby Grange,* a cudgel, or poker, was used as the murder weapon. Perhaps a fireplace poker?"

"We don't know." He gave her a patient smile.

I pulled the piece of glass from my pocket. "I found this on the floor this morning, near where Miss Platte's body was found."

Sheriff Marshall took it from my open palm and examined it.

Mr. Bledsoe leaned in to get a better look at it, as well. "Where was her body found?" he asked.

"The second-floor landing," the sheriff said.

"Ah. There was a bit of a scuffle there about a week ago," Mr. Bledsoe said. "Two of the male guests got into an altercation over one of Kitty's girls in the saloon. I tossed them both out but didn't know that one of them had pocketed a whiskey bottle. They continued their brawl on the stairs on their way to their rooms. The one with the whiskey bottle crowned the other with it. Made a terrible mess."

I shook my head. Public brawls in the hotel? In what kind of uncivilized place had I landed?

The sheriff handed the piece of glass back to me. "Well, that answers that."

"I suppose so." I placed it back in my pocket until I could properly dispose of it.

The sheriff laced his fingers together on top of the table. "Mrs. Pryce, I'd like to search your rooms."

My mouth fell open. He really didn't believe that I'd committed the crime, did he?

"I beg your pardon?" I said with indignation.

"Look," he said, his hands raised in placation, "we just need to rule you out."

My jaw clenched, sending a spike of pain up into my temples. "This is quite insulting," I said, trying desperately to keep myself from shrieking. "I did not kill that young woman. I had no idea of her existence until I met her yesterday. If it's true, that she and my husband were . . . were carrying on, I had no earthly idea about it. So, I ask you, were they lovers?"

Both men pulled back their chins, obviously taken by surprise by the boldness of my question.

Mr. Bledsoe raised a shoulder in a half shrug. "I'd seen them together."

"Where? Doing what?" I fired back.

He blinked at me. "Here in the saloon."

"Is that all? How often did you see them together?" I challenged. He seemed to shrink the slightest bit.

"Well, alone, just the once."

I turned to face the sheriff. "And you? Did you see them together?"

"We don't know what went on behind closed doors, Mrs.—" he started, but I cut him off.

"Did you see them together?" I demanded.

"I saw them on the street. Walking. Talking."

"Often?"

"No. Just once."

"Does this mean they were having an affair?" I looked him straight in those arresting blue eyes.

"No," he said quietly.

I straightened my back, satisfied that I had made my point clear. "It seems to me that before making accusations of any kind, we need to find evidence. *Hard evidence* of this alleged affair, and of who killed Miss Platte. Am I right, Sheriff?"

His eyes dropped to his half-consumed beer. "Yes, ma'am," he said. Then he raised his gaze to me. "I still need to search your rooms."

I pursed my lips in annoyance. "Be my guest!"

CHAPTER 10

We arose from the table just as Sally Dean returned with our coffees.

"I'm sorry, Miss Dean," I said to her. "Something has come up and we must leave. But we will return for lunch. We have business to discuss. Isn't that right, Mr. Bledsoe?"

Once this silly charade of searching my rooms was over and I was exonerated of this intolerable accusation, I wanted to get down to the business of hotel matters.

Mr. Bledsoe gave me a thin-lipped smile.

"Oh." Miss Dean looked up at the sheriff with big brown eyes. "See you later?"

He gave her a slight nod but did not verbally respond. I wondered at their relationship. She seemed completely enamored with him, yet he was much more reserved in regard to her. Although I did not know him well, what I had observed about him so far was this detached reservedness to any circumstance, or person, including myself. It left me curious.

The four of us entered into the lobby of the hotel. As we passed the reception desk, Mr. Pettyjohn silently watched us go by, a frown of confusion on his face.

I led the small group up the four flights of stairs, my breath becoming more labored at each landing. The air was so thin here, I found it difficult to drink it in.

Finally, we reached my rooms. I pulled the ring of room keys from my pocket and opened the door for the sheriff.

I gestured with an outstretched palm for him to enter. "Do what you will."

He ducked into the room and began perusing the place. He went directly to the fireplace and examined the iron tools hanging on a matching iron rack. He turned to look at me.

"There's no fireplace poker here. Just a shovel, a brush, and a dustpan."

"So?" I queried.

My heart fell to the pit of my stomach, recalling that Cordelia had suggested the blow to the back of Miss Platte's head could have been delivered with a fireplace poker. And the one in my rooms was missing. That didn't bode well. But I had never even picked up the thing. Maggie was the one who might have used it.

"You'll have to ask the maid about that," I said with nonchalance. "She takes care of the fireplaces in the rooms." And everything else, as I remembered from our earlier conversation.

Could Maggie have killed Miss Platte? She'd made it clear she didn't care for the woman at all; however, from what I'd learned so far, she was not alone in her dislike of our murder victim. But Maggie seemed docile, meek. I found it hard to believe she could do something so evil. However, with the right provocation perhaps everyone was capable of murder.

Thinking of Maggie and her state of overwork, I mentally added hiring at least one more maid to my list. Again. I looked over at Daniel Bledsoe, who seemed to have found some fascination with his shoes. Was he always so quiet?

"Why is Maggie the only maid in the hotel?" I asked him. "The poor girl is run ragged."

He cleared his throat. "We are cutting expenses. She manages fine."

"Does she?" I said. I wanted to say more but thought it prudent to wait until our meeting at lunch. Now was not the time, nor the situation, as Sheriff Marshall felt the need to search my rooms as if I were a common criminal.

The sheriff passed through the door that led to the room Cordelia occupied. I followed, leaving Mr. Bledsoe with Cordelia in the parlor. Sheriff Marshall immediately went to the bureau and commenced opening and closing the drawers.

He turned to me again. "So do you believe the hotel is haunted by the ghost of Percival Blank? Do you think he—or it —could have killed Narcissa Platte?"

I stiffened at the questions and then blew a half-hearted puff of air through my nose. The deep-seated admonishing of my mother in regard to communicating with the beings grabbed hold of me. How could I explain to him what Mr. Blank told me —nay, *showed* me—that he was not capable of physical contact unless a person was with him in the mirror? Add to that the fact that there were no mirrors present where Miss Platte had been killed. How could I convey this knowledge without seeming completely barmy? It wouldn't do to have people think I'd lost all reason, or thought of me as some kind of witch—like one of my former relatives had been accused of—especially now when I was being falsely accused of murder.

"There are no such things as ghosts," I said dryly.

"No," he agreed. He moved through the bathing room and into the larger bedroom that I inhabited. I wondered if Mr. Blank was lurking in the mirror or if he was off on some ghostly excursion? A quick glance assured me that no, he was not present.

Through the bedroom wall I could hear muffled voices coming from the parlor. It was clearly Mr. Bledsoe and Cordelia, but there was a third voice that I couldn't make out.

The sheriff approached the large armoire and opened the doors. My stomach clenched as he handled my corsets, underthings, and dresses. The act felt so intimate. Not usually one to blush, I was appalled to feel heat crawl up my neck and into my cheeks.

Suddenly, there was a crash next to the bureau. We spun around to see that a porcelain vase, which had been sitting in front of the mirror, had fallen from the bureau and onto the floor. It had splintered into a thousand pieces. I stifled a gasp. Mr. Blank had made himself known.

"Oh dear!" I said, rushing over to the mess. "I shouldn't have placed that vase so close to the edge." I hoped the sheriff hadn't noticed its position earlier.

Sheriff Marshall came over to join me as I picked up the broken shards.

"Ouch!" I yelped. In my agitation, I had tried to gather too many of the pieces in my hand and one of them had cut my palm.

Sheriff Marshall knelt down next to me. He was so close I could smell his woodsy scent. I tried to ignore the flutter in my stomach.

"You've hurt yourself. Let me see." He took my hand and gently removed the offending piece of vase. A streak of blood oozed over the center of my palm. He reached into his vest pocket and pulled out a red kerchief.

"Luckily, the cut is superficial," he said, raising his blue gaze to meet mine.

A spark of electricity zinged through my body, and heat returned to my neck and rose to my face once again. The feeling intensified when he grinned at me and made those indigo eyes dance.

Strangely unable to speak, I swallowed. I found my reaction to him disturbing, yet moderately pleasurable at the same time. The sensation was quite different from the one I'd felt with

Percival Blank. That heightening of my senses was something more akin to wonder. This was something like physical attraction. But that wouldn't do. I didn't have time for such things.

He refocused on his task and gingerly wrapped the fabric around my hand. "There." He secured it with a knot. "You might want to visit the doc. To make sure there are no slivers left in the wound." He helped me to my feet.

"Thank you," I managed.

The sheriff perused the bureau further. He ran his hand over the front edge of it and then studied the mirror. I gulped, wondering if Mr. Blank would make himself seen in an attempt to scare him. But Sheriff Marshall seemed undisturbed. He went to the window and bent down to examine the sill, running his fingers over it.

"The vase falling from the dresser was a bit strange," he mused, indicating the mess on the floor with a tilt of his head. "But we do have earth tremors around here on occasion. And then there's always the explosions from the mines. Can rattle you down to your bones sometimes." He straightened and turned his attention to me.

"Of course," I said. I gave him the most pleasant smile I could muster. He held my gaze for several moments. I could not tell from his expression what was going on behind his eyes, but the intensity with which he looked at me produced another flutter in my stomach.

I cleared my throat and looked away. "Are we finished here?"

"Think so," he said. He moved past me to go back through the other rooms and to the parlor.

Another quick glance in the mirror revealed a very smug-looking Percival Blank. He leaned against the reflection of the armoire, his arms crossed over his chest and his hand cradling the bowl of his pipe. I narrowed my eyes at him. I would deal with him later.

I followed the sheriff back to the parlor where, to my utter dismay, Mr. Brooks had joined Cordelia and Mr. Bledsoe. How dare he enter my rooms without an invitation!

"What are you doing here?" I asked him.

"I'm following a lead, darling." He grinned at me. He wore an outlandish, paisley-print ascot and a red velvet coat. He looked ridiculous.

I gritted my teeth. "I thought you were after a story of the Western frontier."

"I am. But how could I ignore a murder on my very doorstep? As a journalist, I would be remiss."

I glanced over at Cordelia, who rolled her eyes at his declaration.

"Well," I said, "as a *theater critic,* you certainly have a flair for drama." I ran my eyes up and down the length of him.

The sheriff stood at the desk, going through the three file drawers on the right-hand side and then the two drawers on the left-hand side. Finding nothing, he opened the narrow drawer in the middle of the desk. He pulled out a piece of paper and read it.

He raised his gaze to meet mine. "It's a letter to your husband," he said. "From Narcissa Platte."

"What? What do you mean?" I went to the desk. There had been no letter there before.

I took it from him. It was written in a unique hand, with the slope of the letters tilted toward the left margin of the page.

Dear William,

I have received the train ticket and will wait for you at the station. I am counting the days until we will be together and anxiously await the time when mine will be the only arms to comfort you.

Thank you for the lovely emerald earrings. I will wear them every day to remind me of you.

Forever yours, hugs and kisses,

Narcissa

· · ·

My mouth dropped open, and I looked up to see Sheriff Marshall staring at me intently. "This letter was unfolded," he said evenly. "Did you see this? I thought you said you knew nothing of the girl."

"I don't! I mean, I didn't!" My mind reeled with the hard reality that had been written in the bold letters. My husband had been unfaithful. He'd had an intimate relationship outside of our marriage. I couldn't make sense of it. It was true ours was not a passionate union, but it had been a relationship based on mutual respect and a deep caring for each other. Or at least I'd thought it was. This was completely out of character for the William I knew.

He took the letter back from me.

"I never saw this before now, I swear it," I said, remembering how everything was so neatly laid within the drawer. "It wasn't there yesterday."

He turned to Cordelia. "Did you see this here?" He held up the letter.

The color had drained from her cheeks. "No."

"Someone must have put that there!" I said, then wondered how. Whenever I left the room, I made a point of locking the door. Whoever placed the letter in the drawer must have had a key. My gaze traveled to Mr. Bledsoe who, again, seemed to be contemplating his shoes.

He'd been late for our meeting at the saloon. Had he put the letter there? But why would he do that?

The sheriff's gaze slid over to Mr. Bledsoe. "Who has keys to the rooms?" he asked as if reading my mind.

"Myself, Mr. Pettyjohn, and the maid. And, now, Mrs. Pryce," he answered resolutely.

"Where were you before our meeting?" I blurted. "You were quite late."

"Mrs. Pryce." The sheriff raised a hand to quiet me but kept his attention on Mr. Bledsoe.

"With my wife," Mr. Bledsoe answered. "We were in our

rooms. I was late because, well, we were having a discussion."

"A discussion?" I blurted. He had demanded I meet him immediately and then kept me waiting while he'd had a conversation with his wife?

"Well, an argument, if you must know." He glared at me. "It simply needed to be resolved."

"And then you went directly to the saloon?" the sheriff asked.

"Yes. Well I stopped a few moments to speak with Mr. and Mrs. Platte in the lobby. They told me what had happened to their daughter."

It struck me that Mr. and Mrs. Bledsoe had not been present last night when the body had been discovered. Surely, they would have heard the commotion. "I am surprised you did not hear the screaming woman who'd found Narcissa on the landing," I said. "It woke several of us."

"We spent the night at our house. It's about two miles from here. We arrived at around eleven twenty this morning. I had Clarence deliver my note to your room."

"And at what time did you see the Plattes in the lobby?" the sheriff asked.

Mr. Bledsoe rubbed his chin, thinking. "Around ten minutes or so after twelve?"

"All right," Sheriff Marshall said, standing up. "Mr. Bledsoe, would you mind fetching the maid please? And Mr. Pettyjohn?"

"Certainly," he said, and with a nod, he left.

Sheriff Marshall turned to me. "You came to the saloon at around noon as I recall."

"Yes. To meet Mr. Bledsoe," I answered.

"And you had not left the room before then?"

Cordelia stepped forward. "I went to the bakery at around nine thirty, but Arabella stayed here."

"I did," I confirmed.

Just then, Maggie appeared at the door. She must have been cleaning nearby. The sheriff asked her about the letter.

"No, sir, I did not put that there. I don't open drawers, Sheriff. Mr. Bledsoe has a strict policy about that. He says what's in the guests' drawers is their business."

"But you were here this morning?"

"Yes, sir. But in the company of Mrs. Pryce and Miss Danson."

"I see." The Sheriff ran a hand along his angular jaw. "Oh, and Maggie, the fireplace poker is missing. Do you know anything about that?"

She pulled her lips between her teeth and gave a quick shake of her head. My stomach clenched at her denial. I had hoped she would have had an explanation for the missing item.

"All right," the sheriff said. "Thank you, Maggie."

She bobbed a slight curtsy and left just as Mr. Pettyjohn entered the room accompanied by Mr. Bledsoe.

"You've requested my presence?" he asked Sheriff Marshall.

"Yes. Mr. Pettyjohn, where were you this morning at around noon?"

"I was at the reception desk," he said. "Then I accompanied Mr. and Mrs. Platte back to their rooms. They had locked themselves out. Understandable, given their state of mind."

"Thank you, Mr. Pettyjohn," the sheriff said. "That is all."

Mr. Pettyjohn excused himself to go back to reception.

The sound of scratching pulled my attention away from the sheriff. Atticus Brooks was furiously scribbling on a notepad.

"Don't you dare!" I marched over to him and ripped the pad from his hands. "You cannot write about this."

He gave me a patronizing smile. "Sounds like you have a motive for murder, my dear."

I pulled in a breath at his infuriating tone. "You have no proof that I killed that girl. It would be irresponsible of you to print this."

"She's got a point, you know," the sheriff came to my defense. "Best keep your notes to yourself."

Mr. Brooks raised his nose in the air. "Very well. We'll see how this plays out." He held his hand out to me for the notepad. Reluctantly, I slapped it into his palm, my fury at the situation reaching a boiling point. If this beastly man was truly intent on ruining me, he certainly had a running head start.

CHAPTER 11

"Well?" I lifted my chin and addressed the sheriff. "Are you going to arrest me?"

He folded the letter and put it in his vest pocket. "No. The letter proves nothing. Only that Miss Platte and your husband had some kind of relationship."

"It shows she has motive." Atticus Brooks tapped his pencil on his notepad.

"Mr. Brooks," I said, keeping my voice as composed as possible but shooting daggers at him with a pointed stare, "I am tired of your company. Please leave."

He looked to Sheriff Marshall and Mr. Bledsoe for some kind of support, but they remained silent on the subject. To my utter delight, Mr. Brooks cleared his throat and then left the room.

I turned to the sheriff. "I did not commit this crime. You must believe me," I implored him calmly.

"She's telling the truth," Cordelia added, her voice strong and resolute, which was unusual. She rarely spoke passionately about anything except her books. "Arabella would never do something like this."

I gave her an appreciative smile.

Sheriff Marshall nodded, regarding me with reserved sympathy, but sympathy nonetheless. Mr. Bledsoe remained curiously quiet.

"I'll take that under advisement," the sheriff said. I sensed that he believed me but didn't want to go so far as to admitting it. "But don't leave town."

My jaw tensed, and I raised my chin. "Why would I? I have nothing to hide, and certainly nothing to run away from. I will prove I did not do this."

He pressed his lips together and shook his head in disapproval. "Best leave the crime solving to me, Mrs. Pryce. I have already started to question the guests."

"And?" I inquired. I tried my best not to be distracted by those startling blue eyes.

"Nothing conclusive."

"What of the gentleman who found Narcissa? He'd said he saw someone in the hallway. The person with the buckskin jacket?" I asked.

"I'm considering all possibilities, Mrs. Pryce."

"Don't you think that whoever killed her knew her? It seems unlikely that a random visitor to the hotel would do so."

He was about to retort when there was a faint knocking on the doorframe.

"Mr. Bledsoe?" It was the young bellhop, Clarence. "Boss Archer is here. He's asking to see you. Wants to see Mrs. Pryce, as well. Oh, hey, Sheriff," he said, and nodded to Sheriff Marshall. "I was supposed to look for you next. He wants to see you, too."

"Very well, thank you, Clarence," Mr. Bledsoe said. He turned to Sheriff Marshall. "Do you require anything more of us here?"

"Not for the time being," the sheriff said.

We all followed him out of the room. Cordelia, the last to leave, closed the door behind us.

We descended the stairs and when we reached the lobby, we were greeted by the imposing figure of Mr. Archer and a much younger man who bore a resemblance to him but, despite the fact that he stood a few inches taller than the older man, lacked the air of authority Mr. Archer possessed. He was a good-looking young man, with a head of thick, sandy-blond hair. A sprinkling of freckles covered the bridge of his nose and spilled out onto his cheeks. His golden, leonine eyes had a faraway quality to them, as if he lived in a persistent dream.

Mr. Archer greeted us with a look of grave concern. "Good afternoon, Daniel. Mrs. Pryce." He turned to the young man. "This is my nephew, Andrew."

"Hello." I gave him a friendly smile, and he returned the greeting with a slight nod of his head. I introduced them both to Cordelia.

"Sheriff," Mr. Archer greeted Sheriff Marshall. "Terrible business here at the hotel, I understand. I ran into Atticus Brooks earlier who told me of the dreadful news."

My jaw clenched. So the busybody critic was already at work.

"Let's go into my office, shall we?" Mr. Bledsoe said. "No need to discuss this out here."

He led us to a door, and then we proceeded down a narrow hallway. Once at the end, we stepped through another doorway and found ourselves outside under a portico. Rows of small dwellings stood on each side of me—I counted four on each side —all with three steps leading up to small porches. This must be the annex Maggie had mentioned. The condition of the porches left much to be desired. The paint was chipped, and several of them had various items piled up on them, including stacks of wood, small box crates, and other sundry things. On some, clothing hung from rope strewn between their timbers.

More items to be repaired and restored added to the list . . .

We entered the dwelling closest to the hotel on the left.

"Come in." Mr. Bledsoe opened the door for us, and we stepped inside.

I took in the spartan decor: a desk, two filing cabinets, two armchairs positioned in front of a wood burning stove, and a bookshelf. In the back corner was a single sleigh bed.

"Do you stay here?" I nodded toward the bed. "I thought you had rooms upstairs." I was very confused about Mr. Bledsoe's living arrangements.

"On occasion," he said. "When I want to stay in town and my rooms on the third floor are rented out. "

"And Mrs. Bledsoe?" The bed hardly looked like it could accommodate two people.

"She rarely stays at the hotel. She prefers our home outside town."

"A beautiful home, I might add," said Mr. Archer. "Prunella Bledsoe has quite the eye for architectural style." He gave me a broad grin.

"I see," I said. So Mr. Bledsoe had three different dwellings at his disposal. How convenient for him.

"But to the business at hand." Mr. Archer's jovial tone gave way to seriousness. "Sheriff Marshall, do you have any leads on who might have done this horrible thing to Miss Platte? Atticus said it was murder."

The sheriff pressed his lips together and crossed his arms over his chest. His gaze briefly flitted over to me, but then he resumed his stoic demeanor.

"No solid leads," he said stiffly.

"What about you, Bledsoe, do you know what happened?"

Mr. Bledsoe shook his head. "I'm sorry," he said. "I don't."

His eyes shifted over to Andrew, whose fists clenched and unclenched at his sides. The young man's face had mottled pink, and the way he glared at Mr. Bledsoe was alarming. I gathered the two did not get on.

"That's a lie and you know it," Andrew said between gritted teeth.

"Now, son—" Mr. Archer leveled a finger at him "—hold your tongue." He turned to me and Cordelia. "You'll have to excuse my nephew. You see, he and Miss Platte were engaged to be married."

"Oh my," Cordelia whispered, pressing her hand to her heart.

"I'm so sorry for your loss," I added.

The young Mr. Archer finally turned his gaze from Mr. Bledsoe and gave me and Cordelia another curt nod. Then his stare returned to Mr. Bledsoe. "I can't listen to this."

He stormed from the room.

"My goodness," I said, surprised by his outburst.

"Pay him no mind," Mr. Archer said. "He's distraught. As am I. I've raised Andrew since he was a boy. His parents, God rest their souls, passed on when he was just five years old."

"That was kind of you," Cordelia replied.

Mr. Archer clasped his hands behind his back and slightly thrust out his chest. "It was my duty. I wanted to do right by the boy and my deceased brother."

"It is commendable," I added. "You must be a great comfort to him at this time."

"I hope so," he said with an endearing smile.

"Mr. Archer," I continued, wanting to get to the business at hand, "do you know of anyone who would want to harm Narcissa?"

He cleared his throat. "She was a lovely girl."

Interesting. That's not what we'd heard so far. At least not from Maggie and Miss Carlisle.

Mr. Bledsoe addressed Mr. Archer. "There was some speculation on the part of her parents that either the supposed ghost we have in the hotel or Mrs. Pryce here could be the culprit."

I darted a look at him. Why did he feel the need to bring that up? I glanced at the sheriff, who met my gaze with those sober, cobalt eyes.

"Are you serious, man?" Mr. Archer asked, his white eyebrows pressing down on the bridge of his nose. "That's absolutely ridiculous."

"Exactly!" I exclaimed, absently placing my hand on his arm, relieved that I had found an ally in this godforsaken place. "Ridiculous!"

"It simply isn't true about Arabella," Cordelia chimed in. Again, I was grateful for her support.

"Of course not." Mr. Archer patted my hand, pulling it closer to his side. Embarrassed that I had been so bold, I gently pulled it away.

"But we can't have people thinking there are murderous ghosts in the hotel," he continued. "Or in the town for that matter. It's bad for business. This town is becoming a tourist attraction, thanks to the mines, the nearby Indian ruins, and the railroad. We've put La Plata Springs on the map. It simply won't do to have bad press."

"I agree, sir," I said. I wanted to mention the threat of Mr. Brooks spreading ill will but thought I should reserve that for later, if need be. The two were friends, after all. I could only hope that Mr. Brooks would heed the sheriff's warning about writing of the murder before there was solid evidence.

"We simply must find the killer," I went on. "I aim to find out exactly what happened to Miss Platte, not only for the reputation of the town but to clear my name and set the record straight."

"A woman of conviction," he said, smiling at me with twinkling eyes. "I like that."

I turned to Mr. Bledsoe. "And what of the man who was killed at the hotel a year ago? What do you know about that?"

He and Mr. Archer shared a glance, which I found curious. The sheriff remained quiet.

Mr. Bledsoe tucked his hands in his trouser pockets and jutted his chin forward as if his collar irritated him. "Fellow from Mexico named Valdez," he said. "The rumor floating around that he was murdered is just that Mrs. Pryce. A rumor. The man was found dead in his room."

"Your rooms, I believe?" I added.

He pressed his lips together. "Yes. My rooms. He'd been drinking and gambling the night before. He got very drunk and a little sideways with a few men at the card table. He got mad and left the game. That is all I know for sure."

Drinking and gambling and women of the evening seemed to cause quite a bit of trouble in the hotel, I thought, recalling what Mr. Bledsoe had said earlier about the two men fighting in the stairwell. The problems I faced suddenly felt insurmountable. A flock of nervous, caged birds fluttered in my chest. I took in a deep breath to calm them.

"What did the doctor say?" Cordelia asked.

The sheriff finally spoke up. "Doc Tate wasn't here at the time. We had no doctor."

"Did you investigate?" I asked.

He shook his head. "There was nothing to go on. No signs of foul play."

I supposed what Mr. Bledsoe had said was true, that the death of Mr. Valdez was just that simple. He could have died in his sleep, perhaps from excessive alcohol. And with no one to examine the body, it could not be proven otherwise.

"The town needed a doctor, so I brought Dr. Tate on at the expense of my company," Mr. Archer added. "But, that was only six months ago."

"I see. And what of the death of Mr. Blank? The architect and our alleged ghost?" I asked.

"Again, Mrs. Pryce, we don't know for sure," Mr. Archer answered. "It was just an unfortunate circumstance. We knew Mr. Blank had been ill . . ."

"Ill? With what?"

"He didn't really make it known."

"I see." I made a mental note to ask Mr. Blank about this myself. "So it's down to bad luck for the hotel?"

"Yes." Mr. Archer clicked his tongue in sympathy. "It seems you've inherited a bit of a mess. Not a very warm welcome, I'm afraid."

"No," I agreed, wishing again that William had not made this unbearable request of me. Life was so much simpler in New

York. I had my theater, my adoring fans, my lovely home. But now it all seemed like a faraway dream.

"Well, Mr. Archer, if there isn't anything else—" the sheriff uncrossed his arms and straightened his hat "—I need to get back to work."

"Of course, Sheriff Marshall," Mr. Archer said. "We must let you get back to the business of finding out what happened to poor Narcissa." He addressed the rest of us. "That will be all. Please keep me apprised of anything you might feel is important to this situation."

My, but he has an authoritative attitude, I thought. Did he always treat everyone as if they were his underlings? If so, I could see how that would chafe William. Perhaps that was where his dislike of the mining mogul had come from.

We filed out of Mr. Bledsoe's office, and he locked it behind us.

Something fell over the railing of the porch of the dwelling next door. It looked like a tattered blanket.

The sheriff walked over to pick it up. He was about to set it back on the railing when he raised his hand in the air. "Hold on."

He squatted down on his haunches and pulled something from underneath the porch. He swiveled on his feet to show us. It was a fireplace poker.

Cordelia and I gasped in unison.

"Odd place for this," he said.

We all crowded around him to get a better look. The tip of the curved part of the poker was caked with dirt. The sheriff pinched it between his fingers, and when he pulled them away, they were coated with something thick and dark.

Mr. Archer stepped closer. "Good heavens. Could that be coagulated blood?"

CHAPTER 12

I clutched at my chest as the sheriff stood up with the implement.

"Could be blood," the sheriff said in answer to Mr. Archer's question. "But it's a little hard to tell with all the dirt on it." He held it closer to his face. "It also looks like there's some kind of hair on it."

"Blond hair?" Cordelia croaked.

"Maybe. But they're awfully short."

"Do you think that is the murder weapon?" Cordelia asked.

"It's certainly worth considering," he said, his gaze shifting to mine.

My mouth went dry, and I found it hard to swallow. He didn't need to mention that the fireplace poker in my rooms was missing.

"Best not to jump to conclusions just yet," he said. "I'll take this to Dr. Tate. He might be able to tell what this substance is." He wiped his hand on his pants pocket.

"We might be onto something, here," Mr. Archer said with enthusiasm.

Just then, Clarence came through the hotel door. "Mr. Bledsoe, a message from your wife." The bellhop thrust a note toward him.

Mr. Bledsoe quickly perused it. A decided twitch played at the corner of his mouth. He crumpled the note and then turned his attention to me. "I'm sorry, Mrs. Pryce. It seems my wife needs me to take her home. Our meeting will have to wait."

"Is everything all right?" I croaked, finally able to find my voice.

"Yes, yes. Quite fine," he said.

"I would like to meet you with soon," I added, "to discuss matters of the hotel." I thought it best to put on a brave face, to show that I was not rattled by the appearance of this new development in the murder case. A development that could make me look guilty.

"Of course. Soon," he agreed but did not offer anything more.

We said our goodbyes to Mr. Bledsoe and Mr. Archer, and Cordelia and I went back through the corridor to the hotel lobby.

When we reached the reception desk, I grabbed on to it for support, finally succumbing to my shock at what Sheriff Marshall had found.

"Are you all right, dear?" Cordelia came up by my side.

"Yes," I said, waving my hand dismissively, trying to ignore the staccato of my heartbeat.

"That was certainly interesting," she said.

I nodded. "It doesn't look good for me, does it?" I raised a shaking hand to my temple. "Why is this happening?"

Cordelia set her hand on my shoulder. "That fireplace poker could have come from anywhere," she assured me. "Most of the rooms have fireplaces and the tools with which to make a fire, do they not?"

"Yes, they do."

"Then we will see. The evidence will prove conclusive,

Arabella. You did not commit this crime. That will be obvious in short order."

I straightened my shoulders. She was right. I took a deep breath. I would get to the bottom of this. But I didn't see the harm in reducing the *short* in *short order*.

"We have *got* to find out who killed Narcissa," I said. "And fast."

"There's the Arabella I know." She gave my shoulder a pat. "Now, are you hungry?"

"Not really," I said, still trying to quell the flittering birds in my chest. "You?"

"Actually, yes. And you really should eat something, too. One can't live on pastries and tea."

"All right," I sighed. "But I cannot stomach beans and rice. Or chicken. Or coffee. Or whiskey," I added with a modicum of disgust.

"The bakery might have something more to your taste. I believe I saw a ham and cheese sandwich in the window," Cordelia offered. "And they do have tea."

"Yes. Tea. Sounds delicious."

"Would you like me to bring it to you, or shall we go to the bakery? There are a few tables set up inside."

"Ah. An outing would be good. I'd like to see more of the town. And I'd like to ask some of the townspeople about Miss Platte. See what I can find out about her. Let's go to our rooms and get our coats and hats."

We climbed the first set of stairs and were about to turn on the landing to ascend the next when something at the end of the hallway caught my eye. A couple was locked in an embrace. I was about to turn away when I realized it was Maggie . . . and Andrew Archer.

"That's interesting," I whispered to Cordelia.

They must have heard me because they both turned their heads and then abruptly broke apart. Maggie smoothed her apron, and Andrew shoved his hands into his pants pockets after first holding one of them up in greeting. We nodded and continued up to our rooms.

Bijou met us at the door with several happy chirps.

"What did you make of that display of affection?" I asked Cordelia. "Didn't Mr. Archer say his nephew was engaged to Narcissa?"

"Yes," she said. "Maggie was upset earlier this morning. Perhaps he was comforting her? Or she was comforting him? He's just lost his fiancée."

"Hmm. Could be," I mused.

Bijou stood on her hind legs and hopped up and down, distracting me from my thoughts. She often did this little dance when she wanted attention. I bent down and picked her up, stroking her soft little head. With how busy we'd been since we'd arrived, the poor thing had been neglected. Her long white and golden coat was beginning to tangle.

"You need a good brushing, don't you, darling?" I said, resting my forehead against hers.

"I can do that later this afternoon," Cordelia offered.

"Yes, that would be splendid. I intend to take myself on a little tour of the hotel to assess its condition further. I fear we have a lot of work ahead of us. But for now, let's take her with us to the bakery. She could do with some fresh air as well."

Cordelia nodded. "I'll get her leash."

I put Bijou down and then made my way to my room to gather my things. When I passed through the bathroom, I noticed it had been tidied. And both our beds had been made. Maggie must have cleaned our rooms while we had been meeting with Mr. Archer, Mr. Bledsoe, and the sheriff. I appreciated her diligence. I would do everything I could to find the girl some help.

I went to the mirror to put on my hat and then remembered its inhabitant.

"Mr. Blank?" I asked into the glass. "Mr. Blank, are you there?" I wanted to ask him about his death. Perhaps his death, and even Mr. Valdez's, might be related to Narcissa's demise. It was hard to imagine a connection, though. One had most likely died of drink and the other of illness. What they had in common with Narcissa I couldn't imagine, but still, I was curious.

I looked from the top of the mirror to the bottom and on both sides. There was no sign of him, although the fragrance of pipe tobacco lingered in the room.

"Mr. Blank?" I ventured again.

Getting no response, I affixed my hat to my coif with two hat pins and then pinched my cheeks to bring up their color. I would summon him later. He was probably off on some other ghostly business. I wondered how often he left the hotel. He'd said he liked a spot down by the river. My list of questions for him grew.

Out on the street with Cordelia and little Bijou, I took in the tiny settlement. When I'd first seen it, I was as drenched as a cotton mop and it had been near dark. Now, with the bright sun, and in a different state of mind, I could see it with new eyes.

Smelling of fresh pine, the town fairly sparkled in the sunshine. The mountain air was cool and intensely clean. I drank it in, feeling instantly refreshed. My stomach settled down, and I was overcome with a sensation that everything was going to be all right. Eventually.

The hotel was situated toward the end of the main street on the southern side of town. Next to it was a butcher shop. The sign read ARCHER'S BUTCHERY. Farther down there was another, larger store, Archer's Dry Goods. Across from the hotel was the post office and Archer's Livery and Blacksmith. So what William had declared was true. "Boss" Archer aimed to buy up the entire town.

"Lovely day," Cordelia said. "The air is so crisp. I did some more reading, and I believe we are at an altitude of about eight thousand feet." She adjusted the strap of her leather satchel on her shoulder. She had become more studious over the past few years and carried the bag wherever she went. It was usually heavy, full of books and her diary.

Which reminded me . . .

"Cordelia, please be sure to add the beauty of the landscape in your notes for Mr. Rankin's articles. I want the town shown in the best light, and also that I am here to bring good tidings to La Plata Springs to help its public image. Mr. Archer said the town's tourist trade is growing, and obviously, it could only help to attach my name to its publicity."

I wasn't afraid to admit it. The public had to see me, and my foray into this new business venture, in a positive light if I hoped to maintain their favor, and their loyalty.

"Of course, Arabella," she reassured me.

Suddenly short of breath, I stopped walking and set a hand against my chest. "Goodness," I said. "Why am I so winded?"

"It's the altitude," Cordelia said. "I've noticed it, too. I believe that is why my head ached so on the train. According to what I've read, our bodies will adjust in time." She pointed down the next street. "The bakery is just this way."

I wondered if the bakery was also one of Mr. Archer's properties. We passed by a dress shop called simply *Cynthia's*. No *Archer* in the name.

I stopped to look at the window display. The tweed suit and high-collared shirtwaist were made in the latest fashion. The hat on the rack next to it was adorned with a charming plume of feathers. I was immediately impressed. I would have to inspect this shop more carefully, but the sudden growling of my stomach could not be ignored.

"Here we are," Cordelia said.

The sign above the bakery read GILROY'S BAKERS. Another shop without the Archer name attached to it.

We stepped inside to be greeted by the delicious aroma of baked goods. I eyed the pastries on the cake stand on the counter. A portly woman with a red face and kind eyes was on the other side of the counter filling another cake plate with delicacies. My mouth watered.

"Good day to you." She placed the domed glass cover over

the plate of goodies. "You must be Mrs. Pryce. We heard you'd be coming to town."

"That I am." I smiled at her. It always delighted me to be recognized, either by sight or reputation. I wondered, with a sudden pang of anxiety, if it had been known that I had been accused of Narcissa's murder. For that, I did *not* want to be recognized.

"I'm Betty Gilroy. Pleased to meet you." She gave me a warm smile, easing my fears.

"This is my companion, Cordelia." I raised my palm toward her.

"Oh yes. I know Miss Danson. She has kept me busy brewing tea for you, Mrs. Pryce."

"Well, I greatly appreciate it. Your pastries are lovely, too," I said.

Feeling neglected in the friendly exchange, Bijou gave a merry yip.

"Oh, and I've met Bijou, as well," Mrs. Gilroy said with affection. "What a sweet little dog."

"I hope you don't mind that she is with us," I said.

She batted a hand in the air. "Couldn't be half as dirty as them miners. They often stop in to grab loaves of bread for their wives at home after their shifts. What can I do for you?"

"Two ham sandwiches and some tea?" I asked.

"Comin' right up. What kind of tea do you like? I have black tea and dandelion tea."

"Dandelion tea would be smashing," I said. "I wasn't aware that black tea grew in these parts."

"It don't. My sister's husband works at the Pinehurst Plantation in South Carolina. That's where I get the black tea. The dandelion tea I grow myself in the warmer months. Old family recipe."

"Sounds delicious. Are you the baker as well?"

"My husband is the baker," she said with a smile. "I just manage the shop. Why don't you just sit a spell and I'll be right out." She nodded toward the table in the corner and then disappeared through a doorway.

Once we settled ourselves at the table, Cordelia pulled a small book out of her satchel. "It says here that the area is rich with metals. Silver and copper and gold." Her voice brimmed with enthusiasm. "From what it says here, the town was organized by the railroad about ten years ago. Archibald Archer was with the railroad at the time, but he'd heard of several veins of ore in the region and began to explore. He found the mountains around here rich with them. He left the railroad, although he still has a vested interest in it, and began a small mining company, and the rest is history. He's one of the wealthiest men in the American West, and La Plata Springs is on its way to becoming one of the most popular spots for tourism in the region."

Mr. Archer had quite an interesting résumé. And from what I'd seen so far, the man was industrious, enterprising, and charming. True, he was a little on the commanding side, but was that a bad thing? Other than that, I had trouble reconciling much of what William had said about him. I believe the words he'd used to describe Mr. Archer consisted of *blowhard* and *greedy,* among others.

"Here we are." Mrs. Gilroy carried a tray laden with a teapot and two teacups and saucers. She set them on the table. "Sandwiches are ready, too. Be back in a moment."

She returned with two plates. The sandwiches were a far cry from the tea sandwiches I was accustomed to. They were huge and served open-faced, and the bread was thick as a book. Still, they looked appetizing.

"Thank you, Mrs. Gilroy," I said.

She stood back with her hands on her hips, looking quite pleased with herself. "Are you enjoying our town, Mrs. Pryce?" she asked just as I had managed to get my lips around the brick of bread to take a small corner of it with my teeth.

I pressed one hand to my mouth while I chewed and held up

a finger with the other to indicate I couldn't speak until I had swallowed. I was also struggling to come up with something positive to say about this little burg. So far, it had been a place of my worst nightmares. My mouth burned with the spice of the mustard she'd generously applied to the sandwich, and I suppressed a cough. I washed the mouthful down with a sip of tea. The flavors mingled on my tongue, causing great confusion for my taste buds, but it wasn't unpleasant. In fact, it was quite satisfying. Finally, I was able to answer her.

"It's very quaint. But this business with Miss Platte is alarming," I said in the hope that she might offer some information about the girl.

"Oh yes." She nodded. "Sheriff came in for his weekly loaf this morning and told me all about it."

"Did you know her well?" I asked.

She blew a puff of air through her lips. "Well enough."

"Oh? Did you not care for her?"

Her face hardened. "That woman was the most conceited, selfish, and cruel person I have ever laid eyes on."

That seemed to be the general consensus. There was certainly no love lost between yet another and Miss Platte.

"It is on account of her that my boy, Seth, left La Plata Springs just a few months ago. She gave him reason to believe she was calling it off with Andrew and that they could be together. But it was all lies. Then, out of the blue, she wouldn't give him the time of day. Broke his heart she did. I think she was using him to make Andrew jealous."

"I'm sorry to hear that," I said. "That must be difficult for you."

"I miss him terribly." Her lower lip quivered through the frown on her face, and she fluttered her eyelids to suppress tears. "I don't make a habit of wishing death on anyone—not even her —but I tell you, that girl had it coming. Now, if you'll excuse me, I must go to the back to help my husband. It was very nice to meet you."

After we finished our sandwiches and tea, we left the bakery, satiated and satisfied.

"Mrs. Gilroy certainly had strong feelings about Miss Platte," Cordelia commented as she set Bijou down on the boardwalk.

"Yes, she did," I agreed.

"Mothers can be fierce when it comes to their children. No matter how old they are."

"Yes," I mused, thinking of my own mother. When it came to my career, the woman was indeed fierce. But when matters concerned my well-being, it was entirely different. In that area I was on my own. I shuddered as I recalled the hours of reading scripts and memorizing lines, and the number of rehearsals she'd put me through. I hadn't had a real childhood. I'd worked from the time I was very young. I supposed that was what gave me my drive to succeed at anything I took on.

From what I'd learned so far, my relationship with my mother had distinct similarities to that of Narcissa and Pretencia Platte. Mr. Blank had mentioned that Pretencia had pinned all her hopes and dreams on Narcissa, much like my mother had on me. What would life be like for my mother if I were gone from this Earth? She had very little control over me at this point, but her identity was still wrapped up in my fame. Would she even know who she was anymore? Mrs. Platte must have felt so lost.

As I thought of my career, my chest tightened. Would my fame diminish by the time I returned to New York? I had to do everything in my power to see that my love affair with my fans stayed intact. I was eager for Cordelia to send the first install-ment of notes to Mr. Rankin at the *Times,* and more importantly, I needed to assure that the taint of a murder accusation gained no purchase.

I wondered if the sheriff had made any progress in his inves-tigation.

"Let's go see Sheriff Marshall," I said to Cordelia. Bijou yipped in agreement.

Just as we were about to step down onto the street, a woman

wearing a bright-yellow-and-black dress with a matching hat came scurrying toward us. She resembled a large bumblebee.

"Yoo hoo!" She raised a hand in the air, waving at us. "Is that you, Mrs. Pryce?"

I exchanged a glance with Cordelia, who was unsuccessfully trying to hold back a grimace. She had little tolerance for such overt gusto. She was such a quiet person.

"Mrs. Pryce! How good it is to meet you." The bumblebee rushed up and stood uncomfortably close to me. My eyes nearly crossed at the brightness of her dress and the contrast of colors. I expected her to fairly buzz, which actually, she did.

"I'm Constance Chatterley, owner, editor, and writer of the *La Plata Springs Herald.*" She shoved her hand toward my chest. She was a woman of mature years, plump and doughy with small, dark, deep set-eyes. Her hair, equally plump and shot through with gray, puffed out from under her hat.

"Oh, the town is talking about you, Mrs. Pryce. It's such an honor to have such an esteemed performer in our midst. I've read all your reviews. How wonderful that you have your own theater!" She beamed at me, and I rewarded her with a smile. She'd made no mention of my being a murderess. And neither had Mrs. Gilroy, come to think of it. My heart lightened.

"I was so sorry to hear about the death of your husband. He was such a dear man. He had many friends here. Some closer than others, of course." She raised her brows in a disconcerting way.

I cocked my head in question. What did that mean? *Some closer than others.* Was she referring to William's supposed relationship with Narcissa Platte? The thought curdled in my stomach like spoiled cream.

"He really cared about La Plata Springs," she rambled on. "And the Arabella! What a jewel in our little town!"

"Yes. He was quite devoted to his work," I said absently.

"But, oh!" She pressed her hands to her cheeks. "I've just learned about Miss Platte! Dreadful business, I say. Dreadful!

But I must say, I'm not surprised. You know, I don't like to speak ill of the dead, but she wasn't the kindest of women. In fact, I don't think there was a person in this town with whom she hadn't crossed swords. She and I even had words once. She said my paper was rubbish! Just a rag—a glorified gossip column! Well, I told her it's important for the people of La Plata Springs to know what is going on in their town. Wouldn't you agree, Mrs. Pryce?"

"Well, yes, I suppose—"

"And poor Andrew! You know, Andrew Archer? He and Narcissa were engaged to be married. Such a sweet boy. And so talented. Did you know he's quite an accomplished artist?"

"No, I—"

"I don't really think Narcissa deserved him. And she rather berated him for his art. Said it was just foolishness. A passing fancy. I'm afraid his uncle, Archibald Archer, feels the same and wants Andrew to take over the company business someday." She took a quick breath that sounded more like a gasp. "And you know, Narcissa was a terrible flirt. Had all the men in town eating out of her hand. Well, except for the sheriff. He really keeps himself to himself. You know, I heard he was married once. Yes, wife died, poor man. Anyway, Narcissa raised a few eyebrows when she started spending time with Mr. Bledsoe—"

"Mr. Bledsoe?"

I shot a look at Cordelia. Well, that was certainly interesting.

"Yes," Miss Chatterley continued. "Mrs. Bell saw them canoodling once—and him married and all."

"Mrs. Bell?"

"She's the town laundress. You know, so many of the miners are here without their wives. Need proper tending to, they do."

I was beginning to see the wisdom of Miss Platte's remark about the woman's paper being a glorified gossip column, but Constance Chatterley was certainly a good source of information. How accurate that information was remained to be determined.

"Yes!" She moved even farther into my personal space. "But back to Mr. Bledsoe," she said, her eyes wild with excitement. "You must know he has rooms at the hotel while his wife lives in their house outside of town. Beautiful home, it is. Prunella Bledsoe has excellent taste. Anyway, he was spending more and more time at the hotel, and—"

"Miss Chatterley—" I cut in. "Is it 'Miss'?" I hoped I hadn't committed a faux pas.

"Yes, dear. Never married. Engaged once, but that was long ago. I—"

"Miss Chatterley," I repeated. "May I ask you a question? It is of a personal nature but might have some bearing on the murder of Miss Platte." I neglected to add that it might have bearing on my closely guarded reputation.

She blinked up at me with a gleam in her eyes. "Of course, of course."

"Do you take any stock in the idea that Miss Platte and my husband . . ."

I had sufficiently stunned her to silence. She blinked at me as if trying to decide what, or how, to say what she wanted to say.

"I see," she said at length. "Far be it from me to gossip, and I don't mean to be indelicate, but I did see them together on a few occasions. Their conversations looked to be all seriousness. No frivolity. No flirting. I even saw her crying once, and it looked like he was trying to comfort her—with words, mind you, nothing more."

I nodded. "Thank you, that's helpful."

"You're welcome, dear."

"Miss Chatterley, do you know of anyone who might go so far as to kill Miss Platte?"

She blinked at me again. "Oh, there are a number of people."

"Really." I didn't pose the word as a question. This was consistent with Mrs. Gilroy's opinion. "Can you think of anyone specifically?"

"Hmm." She tapped her lace-gloved finger on her chin. "That

girl at the saloon—everyone's favorite—Sally Dean. Why, you know, I saw her and Miss Platte fighting in the street! Grabbed her by the hair Sally did. It was quite the spectacle. Good thing the sheriff happened by. He broke it up and marched Sally back to the hotel."

"Do you know what the row was about?"

"No idea, dear. I really don't pry into people's business. I just report the news. Oh, by the way, I understand we have another esteemed journalist in town? He arrived on the train with you?"

"Yes. Atticus Brooks," I said dryly, unable to conceal my contempt. "He's not really a journalist. He's a theater critic."

"Oh my. How exciting. I must meet him. It will be nice to rub elbows with a fellow writer. It's such a solitary business, you know." She batted her eyes at me.

Miss Chatterley struck me as anything but solitary. As for Mr. Brooks, I had no idea if he was a solitary sort, but it wouldn't surprise me. His solitude was probably brought on by the fact that no one liked him. How could they? Oddly enough, Mr. Archer had called him 'a good friend.' I wondered how they knew each other exactly.

"Why are you so interested in the murder of Miss Platte?" she asked me, pulling me out of my thoughts.

It took me a moment to come up with a reply. I didn't want to mention that I was actually trying to clear my own name. "It happened in my hotel. Of course I would be interested," I said after a moment.

She reached over and patted my arm. "Don't worry, dear. I have a nose for the truth, and I know you did not kill that girl. Despite what others are saying."

I suppressed a sigh. If Miss Chatterley thought she was comforting me with her declaration, she was dead wrong.

CHAPTER 13

Having received sufficient nourishment, Cordelia and I went to the jail in search of Sheriff Marshall. but he was not in.

We headed back to our rooms. We still had some unpacking to do, and I hoped that Mr. Bledsoe had returned. I wanted to continue our conversation about the hotel. It would keep my mind occupied until the sheriff received his report from the doctor in regard to the fireplace poker. I also wanted to further question Mr. Bledsoe about Narcissa Platte, now that I'd learned the two were friendly. He had given no indication of that earlier.

As we walked, I was struck with how the sky had changed. When we'd set out earlier, the heavens had been crystal clear, but within the hour, puffy white clouds had gathered over the mountains to the north, and to the west gun-metal thunderheads rolled over the landscape. Loud booming sounded in the distance. I wondered if it was the impending storm or the blasting at the mine the sheriff had mentioned before.

As we stepped into the lobby of the hotel, the sheriff was making his way toward the front door.

"Sheriff Marshall," I said. "Just the man. How is your investigation going?"

Before he could respond, Cordelia excused herself to go to our rooms, taking Bijou with her.

"I've only just started," he said. "But I've now questioned all the guests."

"All of them? Well, that was fast."

"There are only ten rooms occupied."

"Only ten?" I was astonished at the number. Less than half of the rooms occupied? I wondered if that was normal for this time of year. Surely, at that rate, the hotel would be losing money.

"There might be a few more guests on the train. I suppose they didn't want to brave the river like you did, Mrs. Pryce," he teased. His indigo eyes danced with amusement, causing my breath to catch in my throat, which was disconcerting at best. I attempted to ignore the sensation this man seemed to produce in me. I had to control my emotions. This was absolutely absurd.

I gave him a tight smile. "Very funny, Sheriff Marshall."

His boyish grin did not fade. "You can call me Clay."

I cleared my throat. "Perhaps," I said, knowing full well that I would not. I did not want to encourage any familiarity.

"Mr. Platte said he wired the railroad's head offices in Addison," he said, his tone more thoughtful. "A crew was sent out last night. Tracks should be cleared by the end of the day."

"Addison?" I asked.

"It's a city about ninety miles south of here. Quite the metropolis compared to La Plata Springs."

"And why would Mr. Platte be the one to wire the head offices?"

"He works for the railroad. He and Mr. Archer managed to bring the railroad here to La Plata Springs about ten years ago. Back then, this town was just a tiny settlement. Then Mr. Archer opened his first mine, and soon after, his second. Now, he has the majority stake in the veins of ore around here. People started coming from all over to work the mines."

This information was consistent with what Cordelia had shared from her book.

"Yes, so I understand," I said. "I imagine with the arrival of the railroad, tourism has grown."

"It has. People are fascinated by the West and its native peoples. There are several Indian ruins in this area. Most of the local tribes have been sent north to a reservation in Utah, but there are still a few of the native peoples left here. Mr. Archer has hired some of the Indians to give tours of their ancestorial dwellings."

"I see. Mr. Archer seems to be quite ambitious."

"There is no seeming about it," Sheriff Marshall said with that droll upturning of his lips. "Ambitious is his middle name. And then your husband came along and built the hotel. He helped build the town, too. La Plata Springs would be nothing without the Arabella."

"Yes." I smiled, remembering William's enthusiasm when he spoke of La Plata Springs.

I appreciated this little history lesson but wanted to get back to the murder inquiry. Also, the image of that damning fireplace poker had been niggling at the back of my mind since it's discovery.

"Any news from the doctor as to the substance on the fireplace poker?" I asked.

"Not yet."

"I see," I said on a sigh. "Did the guests offer any clues? Evidence? Insight?"

He shook his head.

"And what about the miners who live in the annex? Surely, they knew Miss Platte." I reiterated my theory that the killer was someone with whom Narcissa was familiar.

He shook his head. "I've checked with the miners' wives. They didn't offer anything that stood out. Most of them knew who Miss Platte was—they'd seen her around—but Miss Platte didn't really give them the time of day."

I remembered what Mrs. Gilroy and Constance Chatterley had said about Narcissa's feminine wiles. That she was a flirt.

"And the miners?"

"They're at work right now. But they stop in at the Bella after their shift. I'll talk with them then."

"What about Kitty Carlisle's girls?" I asked with some caution. I would have to do something about the madam's enterprise. The truth was, I couldn't care less what kind of occupation Ms. Carlisle chose. In fact, more power to the woman for running her own business, but I did not want it under my roof. The Arabella would be a respectable hotel. At least until I got it into the hands of a new owner at the end of my year-long sentence. Then, they could do what they pleased with it.

"Ms. Dean, for instance," I finished. The image of her delicate arms draped across the sheriff's broad shoulders resurfaced, clipping my words.

"Sally?" The sheriff crossed his arms over his chest. I couldn't say for sure, but I thought I detected an air of defensiveness.

"Yes, Sally," I said resolutely.

"Sally wouldn't hurt a flea."

"That's not what I've heard, Sheriff Marshall. I heard she had a row in the street with Miss Platte. There was hair pulling and everything." I blinked at him awaiting his response.

His lips pressed together, forming a grim line and then he took in a deep breath. "It's true. They were fighting in the street."

"And, you broke it up?"

"Yes."

"What were they fighting about?"

I wondered if Miss Platte had maybe turned her attentions to the sheriff. He obviously had an eye for pretty women.

The sheriff narrowed his eyes at me. "Why is it that I feel like I'm the one being interrogated here?"

I held his gaze. "I wasn't aware that you were interrogating me." I smiled sweetly. "You don't really believe that I killed Miss Platte, do you? I swear I didn't know anything about my husband

and Narcissa—if there was anything. We led quite separate lives."

He pressed his lips together, considering my statement. The effect was charming as it deepened the dimples in his cheeks.

"How do you explain the opened letter in the drawer, then?"

I shook my head. "I can't. All I can tell you is that I never saw that letter. Not until you found it."

"And the missing fireplace poker?"

I squared my shoulders. Now I was keenly aware that I was being interrogated. "Again, I can't explain it. But the one missing from my room is not the only fireplace poker in the entire hotel, Sheriff Marshall. There are many."

He continued to regard me with that sapphire gaze and his expression slightly softened, but I don't think he was ready to believe I was innocent. So I would just have to find proof.

"Sheriff?" a male voice broke in, severing our conversation. Dr. Tate strode up to us. "I've got a bit more information about Miss Platte," he said. "I think it might have some importance to the case."

"Oh?" I said, hoping it might be something to prove my innocence.

The doctor shifted his gaze to me, nodded a greeting, and then glanced back at the sheriff, as if to ask permission to speak in front of me.

"It's okay," Sheriff Marshall said.

The doctor tilted his head toward the staircase. "Not here in the lobby. It's a bit . . . sensitive."

We followed him to the foot of the stairs. He rubbed the stubble on his pointed chin and blinked at us from behind his spectacles.

"Well, what is it?" I could barely contain my curiosity.

He gave a furtive glance around the room. "It seems the girl was pregnant."

CHAPTER 14

"Pregnant?" Cordelia sank onto the loveseat in the parlor room.

I crossed my arms over my chest. "That's what the doctor said."

"How tragic. Two lives lost. I wonder who the father was," she said, biting a nail.

"You and me both. I also wonder who knew about it other than Narcissa. The doctor said she was about four months along."

Cordelia shook her head. "I never would have guessed."

"She concealed it well." I crossed over to the window and gazed outside. The leaden sky cast a gloominess over the town. Four months pregnant. She must have conceived around the time William had departed La Plata Springs to return home. Could he and she have . . . ?

No. I refused to believe it.

"Do you think this changes things? As far as the murder is concerned?" Cordelia asked.

"I don't know. I suppose it may depend on who knew about the pregnancy. Perhaps she had kept it entirely to herself. A young, unmarried woman in her condition had a lot to lose. Especially if her fiancé was not the father. But even then . . ."

"That poor child. It never had a chance." Cordelia's voice faded into the silence of the room.

Later that afternoon, I sat down at the desk in the parlor to write letters to my theater and household staff. The first letter was addressed to my theater manager, Thomas Blackthorn, telling him we had arrived safely in La Plata Springs. When we departed New York, I'd told him I was uncertain as to my return. I did not want him knowing that I had been sentenced to a year's absence and intended to run as much theater business from afar as I could.

With great disappointment, I knew another actress would have to be hired for the role I had been rehearsing. The show was to open in two months' time. I hated the idea of another filling my shoes. I *was* the Pryce Theater, after all. I hoped my fans would not forget it.

I also left a missive with Mr. Pettyjohn to give to Mr. Bledsoe, asking him to meet me in the saloon to discuss matters of the hotel.

As I started a letter to my butler, Delancey, a crack of thunder rattled the room, making me jump. A quick trip to the window revealed that the sky had grown even darker and streaks of jagged light danced over the mountains to the east.

I went back to the desk and continued with my correspondence while I awaited Mr. Bledsoe's reply.

A faint tapping at the window signaled the rain had begun. In seconds, the pitter-patter became a staccato drumming, the rain coming down in sheets. Another thunderclap rattled the doors. I reached above the desk to turn on the gas lamp that was positioned on the wall next to the mirror. It sputtered to life and then died.

"Drat!" I turned the knob again. Nothing.

"Mr. Blank?" I said into the mirror. "Mr. Blank, is this your doing?"

He appeared in the mirror next to me, smoking his pipe. Instantly, the aroma of spicy tobacco filled the room.

"I don't know what you are talking about," he said.

"Did you snuff out the light?"

He gave me that devilish smirk of his and then snapped his fingers. The sconce came to life with a brilliant glow.

"Thank you," I said with some aggravation at his mischief. Then I remembered I wanted to ask him about his death.

"Oh, Mr. Blank," I started.

"Percival, please."

"All right, Percival."

I wondered how to begin. The question seemed uncomfortably personal. Perhaps if I posed it in relation to the other deaths it would not seem so cheeky.

"I find it very disturbing that three people have died at this hotel—all in rather mysterious ways. I wonder if there is a connection. You say you do not know who killed either Miss Platte or Mr. Valdez?"

He removed his pipe from his mouth again. "That is correct."

"Well, then, how did *you* die?"

He placed his pipe back in the breast pocket of his velvet smoking jacket, and his dark and luminous, if not transparent, eyes regarded me with an air of consideration. "I don't know," he said at last.

"You don't know?" Surely, this was something he would have been keenly aware of. Oliver had known that he'd been ill, and Leticia Crookshank had said her heart had given out.

"I don't."

"Were you ill?" I asked, remembering what Mr. Archer had said.

He cleared his throat and unclasped his fingers forming them into a steeple. He tapped them together.

"Mr. Blank?"

"I came from a consumptive family," he said finally.

"I see. So did you . . . succumb?"

"I don't believe so. My health had improved after coming west."

I wondered how ill he had been. I had known of many people who had died from the "white death." Some had been taken quite rapidly while others had lingered. Going west was known as "the cure."

Mr. Blank seemed reluctant to discuss his illness, so I decided to change the subject, but I kept the information in the back of my mind.

"What is the last thing you remember?"

"The last thing? Going to bed."

"You died in your sleep?"

"Yes."

"But why?"

"I haven't the foggiest. I do recall I didn't feel well."

I furrowed my brow. "So you *were* ill."

"No. Not really."

I sighed. This conversation was like pulling toffee out of one's teeth. "What do you remember before that? Before going to bed?"

"I had come home from a party. At Archer's ranch."

"He has a ranch?" I asked.

"Yes. One of the largest ranches in Colorado."

"So you went to the party. When did you start feeling unwell?"

His lips curved up slightly in a curious smile. "You are an inquisitive one."

Growing impatient, I clenched my jaw. "Please answer the question. When did you decide to come back to the hotel because you weren't well?"

"I didn't decide exactly. Someone put me in a coach." His gaze shifted from mine.

"Someone— Oh, I see." I gave him a prim little upturn of my lips. "You were drunk."

"The wine and spirits were overflowing," he said by way of an excuse. "I believe it was young Andrew, as a matter of fact, who helped me up the stairs and got me into bed. It's all a bit foggy, you know. The next thing I remember was waking up, but I felt quite strange."

"You mean, you were suffering from your overindulgence the night before?"

"No. That's not what I mean. I felt perfectly fine. Divine, in fact. Better than I'd ever felt. My clothes were a rumpled mess so I went to change them. Getting them off was no problem, but when I went to the wardrobe to get clean trousers, I couldn't grasp them. My hand moved right through them. I tell you, it was an incredible sensation."

My irritation vanished as fascination set in. "I can only imagine . . ."

"Then there was a knock on the door," he continued. "I called out, saying that I would only be a minute, but Maggie Mae Freeman marched right into the room. I thought my scantily clad appearance would embarrass her, but she didn't flinch. And then, to my utter astonishment, she walked right through me! She shivered and ran her hands up and down her arms as if she were chilled and then went to the wardrobe, took out some fresh clothes, and hung them on the valet stand."

"Which was in the mirror."

"Yes." He held his hands wide. "I still wear them today. I have no need to change them. They don't get dirty. My body emits no odors."

I wrinkled my nose in distaste. "So you really don't know how you died?"

"I do not."

I sighed. From what he had told me, it was hard to make a connection between his death and the deaths of Mr. Valdez and Narcissa Platte.

"Thank you for sharing that with me, Percival," I said.

"You're welcome."

I opened the drawer for another sheet of paper to continue

my letter writing and cringed at remembering the offending billet-doux that had been placed there—a love letter to my husband from Miss Platte. And then, coming on its heels, the news that she had been pregnant made my stomach churn. William had wanted children. And I'd had every intention of granting him his wish. Someday. But I was so wrapped up in my career, the time flew by. And now I'd never have the chance.

"Yesterday, did you see anyone come into these rooms other than me and Cordelia?" I asked Percival.

"Maggie comes in to clean, of course," he said. "But I did see something unusual."

"Really? What was it?"

"I did not see him enter, but I saw him leaving. It was the bellboy. I popped in just as he was making his exit."

I sucked in a breath. "Clarence? Do you know why he would have been here?"

He shrugged. "No, but he shouldn't have been up here unaccompanied."

"Cordelia!" I called out. Percival vanished from the mirror.

"Yes?" She peeked her head around the corner.

"Please go find Clarence and ask him to come up here."

She scratched at her temple, her eyes bleary like they usually were after she'd been reading. "The bellboy? Why?"

I didn't want to go into it at the moment. How could I explain to her that the ghost of Mr. Blank told me the boy had been up here?

"I have a hunch. Please, quickly."

"All right." She grabbed her coat that was hung on a hook by the door, and Bijou jumped from her bed barking, obviously wanting to go out. Cordelia also grabbed the leash.

"Come on, girl." She attached the clip to Bijou's collar, and they were off.

I leaned against the back of the chair. Why would the boy come into my rooms unaccompanied? And how did he get the key? Mr. Blank was right. He shouldn't have been here alone. It was highly inappropriate for a bellhop to do so.

Then it came to me. Had he put the letter in William's desk drawer? It was more likely that Maggie had been in my rooms alone, but she'd claimed she didn't do it. I supposed she could have been lying, but something about her planting the letter didn't feel right—she'd been in my rooms many times since my arrival—but Clarence being here without consent was definitely suspicious.

Someone might have put the boy up to it. Someone who wanted to frame me for the murder. But who? Who would want to be rid of me and why?

Atticus Brooks came to mind. He was most definitely not my friend, and he would do anything for a sensational story. But I couldn't very well ask him about it. Confronting him would surely just add to my troubles. I'd have to tread carefully.

Granted, the man did not like me, but with me in prison, or hanging from a noose, how could he further torment me? I was his favorite subject.

Still, I couldn't discount the fact that it might have been him. But what if it was one of the townspeople, even someone at the hotel.

The notion sent a wave of panic through me. As much as I hated to admit it, I couldn't stand the idea of not being liked, or wanted, or valued—for any reason. That was why I longed to be back in New York, where I was largely adored. Of course, there were those who were jealous of my success. There was always that. But what could the people of La Plata Springs have against my success? Or me, for that matter?

The beating of the rain on the windows persisted, pulling me out of the whirlwind of my anxiety. Then a loud pinging sound seemed to come from within the room.

I spun in the chair and rose, my ears straining to listen. It was probably Mr. Blank up to his tricks again, I decided.

So I set my turbulent feelings aside and took up the pen once more, but I found myself still absorbed with the notion of someone wanting to abuse me in such a way. Even my rivals within my small community of actors had never done anything so mean. Being singled out for such evil intent left me feeling quite dejected. If it had been one of the townspeople, that meant I was being cast off by someone I hadn't even gotten the chance to know. Although, I couldn't fathom why I was so concerned about the people of La Plata Springs liking me or not. My stay here was only temporary.

Archibald Archer had given me the impression that he liked me. I recalled how he had firmly agreed that the idea of me killing someone was preposterous, and it gave me some comfort. At least someone in this town believed me.

Miss Chatterley had said she didn't think I'd killed Miss Platte, either, but her penchant for gossip gave me doubts as to her sincerity.

And then there was Sheriff Marshall. I found the man intriguing, and if I was not mistaken, there seemed to be a thread of connection between us. He hadn't indicated one way or the other if he thought me a murderess, aside from the fact that he'd requested I not leave town. I suppose he was reserving judgment until he had more information. But all the same, he did not give me full absolution, which I did not like to admit stung a bit. I could not gauge why it was so important to me to have his good opinion. I should not care about his estimation of me. The man was far from refined or sophisticated, and someone I never would have sought to befriend.

I shook my head to rid myself of thoughts of him. This strange attraction appealed to my baser self, and I could not tolerate that. Besides, he'd made it quite clear that he had not made up his mind about my innocence in regard to the murder. No, he would not do.

I turned my attention back to my letter to my butler but was interrupted by a knock at the door. It opened only wide enough for Maggie's head to poke through.

"Hello? Mrs. Pryce? Oh!" She startled when she saw me sitting at the desk. "I'm sorry to disturb you. I've come up to start your fire. The rain has brought with it a mighty chill."

I waved her in. "Of course, of course. Come in."

She entered with her pail, and behind her, a man in filthy clothes entered the room with a stack of wood in his arms. He gave me a brief nod, set the logs down, then tipped his hat to me and left.

"Who was that?" I whispered.

"That's one of the miners. Mr. Johns. Usually Clarence helps me, but I couldn't find him. Mr. Pettyjohn must have sent him on an errand."

"Perhaps. I sent Cordelia to look for him actually," I said.

"Is there something I can do for you, Mrs. Pryce?"

"As a matter of fact, yes," I said. "You can answer a question for me. Honestly, if you please."

Her brows knit with concern. "Of course, ma'am."

"Did you let Clarence into my rooms unattended? Did you let him use your key?"

Her head flinched back slightly. "Clarence? No, ma'am."

"You are certain?"

"Yes, ma'am."

I regarded her for a few moments, assessing her countenance. She seemed utterly sincere.

Just then, Cordelia and Bijou came in through the door. "I looked everywhere for him." Cordelia unhooked Bijou's leash, and the little dog ran to her bed. "Mr. Pettyjohn hasn't seen him, either. Not since this morning."

"Oh dear," I muttered. I would have to speak with him tomorrow.

"What is it?" Cordelia asked.

I waved a hand in the air. "It's nothing."

"Thank you, Maggie," I said. "You may tend to the fire. Oh, have you seen Mr. Bledsoe about?" I asked, wondering why he had not answered my request that he meet me for dinner.

"No, ma'am. Not since he went home earlier this afternoon."

"Right," I said. I hoped I would hear from him soon.

The plink-plinking sound became louder, followed by an echo of same sound at the other side of the room.

"What is that noise?" I asked, rising from the desk again. My gaze traveled to the ceiling. A long crack snaked its way across the plaster. Droplets of water descended and landed on the rugs, creating the irritating noise.

"The roof is leaking, ma'am," Maggie said as she lit the fire. "It's been that way for quite some time. I'll go fetch some buckets."

"Quite some time?" I placed my hands on my hips, my ire rising. "Why was this not attended to? I can't have the roof leaking all over me. It's unacceptable."

Maggie frowned and blinked her eyes rapidly, as if trying to hold back tears. "Yes, ma'am," she croaked. "I'm sorry, ma'am."

I was puzzled by her emotion. "I'm not blaming you, dear," I assured her.

"Yes, ma'am." She diverted her gaze. "I'll get those buckets."

She fled from the room, and I wondered at her nervous temperament. The young woman always seemed on the verge of a breakdown. I recalled the image of her and Andrew in the hallway earlier, as well as when she'd cried in my rooms. What could be troubling her?

"Arabella?" Cordelia came through the interior door from her bedroom. "The roof is leaking in my room, too. And I've checked yours. I'm afraid it is leaking over your bed."

"What?" I wailed. This was too much for me to bear. There was so much to be done at the hotel. Not only to prepare it for sale after my tenure but to *live* in it for the time being. For the life of me, I could not understand Mr. Bledsoe's remiss.

Why had William saddled me with such a heavy burden? Had he known the condition of the hotel when he'd most recently visited? Was this all a part of his plan to teach me a lesson about my "unhealthy desire" for adoration? Did he wish to make me a servant to the needs of the hotel?

Heat flushed through my body, and my muscles tensed. I clenched my fists. The Arabella had a manager who was responsible for the upkeep and running of the hotel, and it wasn't me. This situation had to be rectified, and it had to be done now.

This was the last straw!

CHAPTER 15

I would not wait another minute to have words with Mr. Bledsoe, and believe me, he would get an earful!

"I've placed some rags over your bed to protect it from the dripping," Cordelia said. "It will help for a short while, but—"

"This is completely unacceptable!" My voice sounded shrill even to my own ears.

Cordelia flinched at my outburst. "I'm sure once the rain passes, we can hire someone to make repairs," she said, using that voice she always used when trying to calm me down.

"I don't have time for this!" I exclaimed, my worries about the planted letter in the desk and the missing fireplace poker returning, making everything look even more grim. The last thing I needed to be concerned with at the moment was a leaking roof. "I'm going to go find Bledsoe myself if I have to walk miles to his house in the rain."

I rushed to the door and flung it open to find Maggie there with a stack of tin buckets in her hands.

"I've got the buckets, Mrs. Pryce," she said, her face turning ashen at the fury in my eyes.

"Yes." I let her pass through. "Set one under the leak above my bed first," I demanded. "Completely unacceptable," I repeated, muttering under my breath.

I hurried down the staircase to the lobby and approached the reception desk where Mr. Pettyjohn was helping a guest.

"Do you know where Mr. Bledsoe is?" I interrupted.

He gave me a startled look and then addressed the guest with a note of apology in his voice and said to him. "Excuse me."

He turned to me with an expression of irritation. I realized I had been rude in my abruptness, but I would not be deterred.

"Well?" I said. I didn't have time to apologize. "Where is he?'

"I believe he is in the saloon."

"The saloon? Did you give him my note in regard to dinner?"

"Yes."

"And he didn't bother to send a reply?"

"I suppose not, madam."

Argggh! That word!

Without thanking him, I flounced toward the door of the saloon. I flung it open and spied Mr. Bledsoe standing nearby talking with Mr. and Mrs. Platte. From her posture, I could see that Mrs. Platte was upset. Her husband laid a hand on her shoulder and she leaned into him, taking comfort from the gesture.

Their presence stopped me in my tracks. I couldn't very well rush up to Mr. Bledsoe and deliver a torrent without so much as a greeting toward the grieving couple, but I was itching to give Mr. Bledsoe a piece of my mind.

"Good evening," I managed. Mr. Platte gave me a nod, and Mrs. Platte looked at me with such sorrow in her eyes it nearly took my breath away. Her pain was palpable, and it filled the room.

"Mrs. Pryce," Bledsoe said with a patronizing smile.

My nails bit into my palms, my anger at him returning with such a vengeance it was quickly reaching a crescendo.

With an upturning of his palm, he gestured toward his favorite booth. "I just received your note. Shall we sit?"

"You have some explaining to do," I said through clenched teeth.

In the back of my mind, I knew my vehement feelings were about more than just the condition of the hotel, but I couldn't stop the torrent flooding through me. "Why is this place a shambles? Have you done anything at all to maintain it? There are rats in the fireplace flues, paint and wallpaper are peeling off the walls, the roof is leaking, a madam is running a bordello out of the place, and three people have *died* here! Mark my words, Mr. Bledsoe, I will be contacting my lawyer. I will not have my reputation as owner of this hotel sullied because you can't, or won't, do your job. It looks as if I'll have to manage it myself. I want you gone!"

Mr. Bledsoe pursed his lips in clear annoyance, and his eyes flitted about the room, which had gone strangely silent. A quick glance around revealed all eyes were upon us, including those of Mr. and Mrs. Platte. I immediately regretted my fit of temper. Already they believed I had killed their daughter and this display didn't help my case. Heat rose to my face, and suddenly the room felt like a furnace.

To my further chagrin, the sheriff was present, sitting at the bar. It seemed he always found me in a state of turmoil and not at my best—or even close to my best. And what was worse, Mr. Brooks was sitting next to him, a mug of ale in his hand. He gave me a contemptible smile. My insides caved in on me. My, but wasn't I giving him plenty of fodder for his story?

Mr. Bledsoe reached out for my elbow.

"What are you doing?" I demanded.

"Please, shall we sit?"

I shook off his touch and marched toward the booth, keenly aware of the discomfort my tirade had caused among the patrons of the saloon. I glanced at Mr. Brooks, who had taken out his blasted pad of paper and pencil from his breast pocket. I'm sure he would write down every last word I said if his pointy, devil ears could hear me.

I could see the headline of one of his proposed, puerile articles of life in the west now: THE WIDOW ARABELLA PRYCE
LOSES HER MIND.

I had half a mind to rip that pad of paper from his hands and
burn it in the blazing fireplace. Which, by the way, was adding to
my suffering by making the crowded room unbearably hot.
Instead, I scooted into the booth, and Mr. Bledsoe slid in opposite me.

"I'm sorry to see you so distressed, Arabella," he said.

I took in a deep breath, steadying myself to keep from
lashing out again. How dare he speak to me with such familiarity? Once I'd exhaled, I felt more in control of myself. I looked
him directly in the eye.

"This place is going to ruin," I said. "Why have you not seen
to the matters I have laid out? How could you be so careless with
something my late husband entrusted you with? What kind of
man are you?"

His jaw twitched, and his eyes hardened. "Arabella—"

"Mrs. Pryce!" I said with emphasis.

I would have his respect and not have him treat me as
anything other than an equal, not like some simpering woman-
child. Again, I felt all eyes upon us. I took another deep breath.
I really needed to control myself.

"I'm sorry," I said on the exhale, suddenly realizing that I
would get nowhere with this man, or with anyone, with such a
display of temper. "It's been a rather trying time since I've
arrived. And as you can see, I am quite distraught over the
condition of the hotel. Can you please explain to me why it is in
such a state?"

"Mrs. Pryce," he said with emphasis, "the fact of the matter
is, as you know, the hotel is entrusted in your husband's estate.
He has provided a stipend for the care and upkeep of the hotel,
but as you can see, it simply is not enough."

My mouth dropped open. Not enough? This hardly seemed
plausible. William, and now I, had scads of money. Well, I didn't

at the moment. But this hotel was a source of great pride for William. I am sure it was adequately provided for. Perhaps I should have inquired with the lawyer, Mr. Tisdale, about this when I'd learned I was to come and oversee the hotel's operation. I had assumed that even though my allowance was a pittance, there would have been adequate money for the running of the hotel. Where had it gone? A disturbing thought entered my mind.

"Or," I ventured, "the funds were misappropriated."

That statement wiped the condescension clean from his face.

"What exactly are you saying?" A twitching started in the corner of his eye.

I realized in my frustration that I may have spoken impulsively. I decided to divert sightly. "Well, I can assure you, Mr. Bledsoe, I will look into the matter and rectify the situation. No matter what it entails."

He rolled his jaw and then fixed me with the patronizing smile again. "That might prove difficult if you're facing a murder charge."

My mouth dropped open again, this time in utter offense.

"I beg your pardon?" I would not let him get away with this insult. "And that reminds me Mr. Bledsoe. What was *your* relationship with Miss Platte? I understand there was some flirtation between you two—canoodling, in fact, as it was described to me—despite the fact that you are a married man and she was engaged to another."

I held his gaze, remembering the matter of her pregnancy.

"Did you know she was with child, Mr. Bledsoe? Could you have been the father? Perhaps this created a little problem for you? A problem you needed to be rid of?" The words came out before I could stop them.

To my utter amazement, he slapped his hand against the top of the table. I felt the patrons' eyes swivel in our direction once again.

His face reddened and a vein pulsed in his temple. The eye

twitch quickened. "You have overstepped your bounds, Mrs. Pryce. What you have 'heard' about Miss Platte and myself is vicious gossip, and I am insulted at your insinuations. We will continue this conversation at a later time, when you are in a more rational state of mind." He rose from the booth.

I gasped at his imperiousness. "How dare you?"

"Good evening, Mrs. Pryce!" he boomed and then stalked out of the saloon.

I stared after him in disbelief and then felt the hairs rise on the back of my neck at the deafening silence that filled the room. A glance to my left was met with a roomful of stunned faces. I swallowed down my embarrassment and wanted to shrink into the booth. My discomfort was worsened when my gaze met the startling blue eyes of Sheriff Marshall who was still sitting at the bar. Next to him, Mr. Brooks made a point of giving me a hideous, Cheshire cat grin.

To my relief, Sheriff Marshall quickly engaged him in conversation, acting as if nothing at all had happened. The resulting effect was that others lost interest in the spectacle I had created. The rest of the patrons followed suit and continued with their merrymaking.

Completely and thoroughly humbled, I wanted to flee but found myself glued to my seat.

CHAPTER 16

After I had recovered from my complete and absolute astonishment at what had just transpired with Mr. Bledsoe, I set my elbows on the table and placed my head in my hands. Partly because I was distraught at how badly our conversation had gone, but mostly because I was embarrassed at my fit of temper. Such behavior was quite beneath me.

A loud *thunk* on the table shook me out of my despair. I looked up to see Kitty Carlisle standing over me. She'd set a glass of whiskey, a bowl of some kind of stew, and a crust of bread on the table.

She tilted her head toward the glass. "Looks like you could use it."

I picked up the glass, swallowed down the entire contents, and then choked as it burned all the way to my stomach. I eyeballed the mass of brown beans and rice in a thick broth in the bowl in front of me. Its sharp aroma assailed my nose. It actually smelled rather good. I must have been hungrier than I'd thought.

"Another?" she asked. I nodded.

She left, and I tipped the spoon into the bowl and lifted out a small bite. An explosion of flavor hit my tongue, and a slight burning filled my mouth. It was a bit shocking but not at all unpleasant. The sweet, smoky flavor brought my senses alive.

As I ate, I avoided looking about the room as I feared I was still the main object of attention. Again, something I usually reveled in, but this was a different matter entirely. Also, I was afraid I'd see Mr. Brooks scribbling in his notebook of damnation.

The madam returned. She set the glass on the table and then, to my surprise, slid into the booth opposite me. I picked up the glass and sipped at it gingerly. The liquid felt warm this time and quite gratifying.

"Want to talk about it?" She tapped her fingers on the table.

I let out a sigh. "That did not go well."

"It did not," she agreed.

There was something in her dry response I found endearing. This was a woman who didn't mince words, and I found it refreshing.

"I simply wanted to know why the hotel is in such disrepair, and why you—" I took another sip, stalling. I didn't need yet one more person angry at me.

"Why I am allowed to run a brothel out of here?" she finished for me.

"Well . . . yes."

"Look. It's good for business. Mr. Bledsoe thought it would bring in more travelers, and it has. And some of the miners are far away from their families. They get lonely. There are a slew of brothels around here, but mine offers a bit more refinement. My girls are clean, have regular visits to the doctor, and I vet any customer who wants to darken my doorway. I won't tolerate violence against my girls."

"But did my husband agree to this? He never mentioned a word of it to me."

I sipped at the whiskey. The taste was quite growing on me, and I liked the way it warmed my chest and that warmth filtered down to my arms and legs.

"Huh. I wonder why?" she muttered with sarcasm, both answering my question and making a statement of her own all at the same time.

Did I really seem such a buttoned-up snob? I had been accused of snobbery before, which I thought unfounded. I'm an actress after all. An artist with an open mind. Historically, society viewed women in my profession on par with that of harlots. Thank goodness that had changed—for the most part.

But still, I didn't relish the idea of my name being associated with a whorehouse. And, on further thought, I wasn't sure how I felt about the matter in general. Women selling their bodies for money? I supposed there was nothing I could do about that. It would happen whether or not I approved, but under my roof?

My gaze slid over to the bar where Atticus Brooks was otherwise engaged with one of the patrons, pad and pencil in hand. I hoped he'd found some other juicy tidbit to write about besides me. As if he could feel me looking at him, he swiveled his head in my direction and gave an annoying, finger wave, dashing my hopes of such a diversion. The man was relentless. What was he doing? Inserting himself into the investigation of the murder of Narcissa Platte? This would not do. I simply had to find out what had happened and fast.

That reminded me . . . I still wanted to speak with Sally Dean about her confrontation with Miss Platte.

"Miss Carlisle —"

"Kitty," she said. "Call me Kitty."

"Yes. Kitty. What can you tell me about the relationship between Sally Dean and Narcissa Platte? I understand they had an altercation in the street recently."

Kitty frowned. "That's true enough."

"Do you know what it was about?"

She shrugged. "Could have been any number of things. Narcissa Platte treated Sally horribly. Humiliated her at every turn. My guess is that the conceited Miss Platte was jealous.

Everyone loves Sally. Girl has a heart of gold. But Narcissa wanted all the attention. Especially of the male variety."

"I see." That was consistent with what I'd learned to date.

"You can ask her, though." Kitty tilted her head in the direction of Sally, who'd just walked by. "I know with everything in me that Sally would never kill anyone. Girl just doesn't have it in her."

I remembered the sheriff had said as much. "So I've been told."

"Sally!" Kitty called her over.

The young woman, today dressed in an emerald-green bustier and black skirt, approached us with a wooden tray in her hands. There was a hint of wariness in her eyes.

Kitty patted the seat next to her. "Come sit a spell."

I finished the glass of whiskey. My previous distress at my altercation with Mr. Bledsoe had mellowed, and I was considerably calmer.

"But the customers," Sally protested.

I got the sense that I scared her, or intimidated her, or she simply didn't like me, which sent a prick of anxiety straight to my stomach. I admonished myself for my insecurities and reminded myself that not everyone was required to like me.

"They can wait a bit," Kitty assured her.

Sally slid into the booth next to her, then gave me a nod. "Good evening, ma'am."

"Hello, Sally."

"Mrs. Pryce has some questions for you." Kitty patted the younger woman's hand.

"Oh?" A look of terror flitted across her features.

I figured the best way to go about this was to just dive in. "I understand you had a disagreement with Miss Platte in the street not too long ago."

She stiffened. "I did."

"Do you mind telling me what it was about?"

She looked from me to Kitty and then back to me again. "I

really can't say. I'd be betraying a confidence. But I can tell you this: she started it."

"Oh." How to proceed from here, I wondered. Might as well get to the point. "I understand the two of you did not get on."

She swallowed and then lifted her chin. "Narcissa didn't get along with a lot of people. Felt she was far above everybody."

"Kitty said she was particularly cruel to you."

"Yes. That was on account of Mr. Bledsoe."

"Mr. Bledsoe?" I was not expecting this. "What about him?"

"Narcissa thought he fancied me."

From what I'd seen earlier in the saloon—his eyes locked on her—I had thought so, too.

"But he's married." I didn't want to let on that I'd heard about his canoodling with Narcissa.

She gave me a pointed look. "That doesn't stop some men, Mrs. Pryce."

The hurt of the letter pressed in on me again. I was no puritan, but I had always abided by my commitment to William in marriage, and I had thought he'd done the same. But was her statement an indication that he, too, had been tempted by Miss Dean, as well as by Miss Platte? Or was I being too sensitive about the matter?

I suddenly realized my thoughts had digressed. After all, we weren't talking about my husband and me. We were talking about Sally, Mr. Bledsoe, and Narcissa.

"And did he fancy you?" I asked.

She chewed her lower lip. "Lots of men fancy me, Mrs. Pryce," she said, skirting my question.

"But wasn't Narcissa engaged to Andrew Archer?"

Sally gave a nonchalant shrug of her shoulders. "Didn't matter. Narcissa couldn't abide anyone liking me. I think she was sweet on Mr. Bledsoe, but he never paid her much mind. Said she always had her nose stuck up in the air."

I wondered about the sheriff who had come to Sally's defense. Was he one of the men who fancied Miss Dean? Miss

Chatterley had said the sheriff was widowed and was one to keep to himself. But if he'd turned an eye toward Sally, did that bother Narcissa? I wondered at poor Andrew. Did he not know his betrothed was collecting the attentions of men like charms on a charm bracelet? Had he been so blinded by love that he could not see her arrogance?

I would need to speak with him to find out.

"So, Miss Dean—Sally." I smiled at her sweetly, "where were you the night of the murder?"

She hesitated and looked over at Kitty, who patted her hand again. "She was with a customer," Kitty answered for her.

"And who was that?"

Kitty gave me a stern glance. "I'm sorry, but we can't tell you that."

I directed my attention to Sally again. "Where you with this customer all night?"

She hesitated. "No. Right after, he said he had to meet someone and he was late."

"Did he say who he was meeting?"

"It's not my business, ma'am."

"Very well," I said on a sigh. I, too, could not see this young woman killing anyone. Along with others' opinion of her, there was an undeniable feeling in my gut.

Sally rose from the table. "I'd best get back to work."

"Thank you for your time," I said, and she went to the bar.

"Same goes for me. Can't keep the customers waiting too long." Kitty picked up my empty bowl and then nodded at the empty glass on the table. "Another?"

I looked down at the tumbler. I hadn't felt this calm since I'd arrived, and I was enjoying the peace that had settled on me.

"Why not?" I asked.

She gave me a wink and took the bowl away. Before I could blink, another barmaid appeared with a bottle and poured an inch of the liquid into my glass. She was an unfortunate-looking girl with buck teeth and protruding eyes, but she had a warm smile.

I took a mouthful of the liquid and let it rest on my tongue before swallowing. The fiery sensation passed up through my mouth and into my nose. I swallowed it down and then coughed, my eyes watering. Perhaps smaller sips?

Feeling even more relaxed, I leaned against the wooden back of the booth and continued to sip my drink.

I surveyed the saloon, and my gaze rested on the painting of "Bella" hanging over the doorway. Why had William named the garish thing, and the saloon for that matter, after me? The pudgy, reclining nude did not resemble me in the least. Was that how he wished me to look? I had so many questions.

I don't know how long I sat there nursing that glass of whiskey, but soon my mind began to whirl with the information I'd gathered that day, and suddenly I was exhausted. I lifted the watch pendant hanging from the long gold chain around my neck. It was nearing nine o'clock. I had been sitting there for almost two hours. Where had the time gone?

"I must go to bed." I said out loud.

Kitty came back over to the booth and gave me a quick once-over. "You all right?"

"Perfectly. Thank you for the meal, Kitty. And the whiskey." In my dreamy state, I raised the empty glass to her.

She snorted. "It didn't come out of my pocket. It's your saloon." She pointed to the portrait of the chubby nude.

I glanced again at the offending blight. "Oh, yes, I suppose it is."

The reminder of that fact and that this saloon, this hotel, and this mess I was in, all belonged to me weighed heavily on my shoulders.

I turned back to her to find an amused expression on her face.

I narrowed my eyes. "See to it that that thing is removed."

CHAPTER 17

I left the noisiness of the saloon to find the lobby blissfully void of voices. Only the sound of the rain pattering against the front windows and the distant rumbling of thunder filled the emptiness.

No one was there, not even Mr. Pettyjohn, which I found curious if not questionable. Perhaps he had been attending to a guest, I told myself, not wanting to inquire further. I'd done quite enough inquiring for the day.

I walked to the staircase thinking about the events of the day and how they had culminated in that volatile disagreement with Mr. Bledsoe. He'd been so defensive at my questions. Although, in retrospect, I might have been a bit presumptuous in accusing him of murder. Guilty or not, that would make anyone angry. I knew that all too well. And if he was angry at me, I'd be less likely to get the truth from him. I had to try to ingratiate myself to him, as much as I didn't like the idea. And it needed to be tonight. If not, it would fester in my mind and I knew I would not sleep.

On the rare occasions when William and I were together for any length of time, we'd agreed never to go to sleep angry or upset with each other. It was a practice that made things go much more smoothly for us, as things often looked different in the light of day.

I would make amends with Mr. Bledsoe and apologize. I needed him for the operation of the hotel, if nothing else, so I needed him on my side. We had clearly gotten off on the wrong foot, especially in regard to the murder of Miss Platte. It was not a good time for me to make enemies.

I slowly, resolutely, climbed the stairs to the third floor. I did not know exactly which doors led to his rooms. There were four on one side of the stairs and four on the other. I knew which door led to at least one of the Plattes' rooms so I decided to try the doors at the other side. When I approached the one closest to me, I noticed that another of the doors down the hallway was slightly ajar.

I made my way down the hall and peered in. "Hello?"

I knocked a little too hard because the door swung on its hinges and opened farther. I gasped when I saw a person's foot pointing upright and at an angle only a yard away from me. I pushed into the room to find Mr. Bledsoe lying on the ground, blood oozing from his chest. Instantly, everything came acutely into focus, the warming effects of the whiskey suddenly replaced with a surge of hot adrenaline.

"Mr. Bledsoe!"

My heart clanging like the bell on a fire wagon, I rushed over. I knelt down next to him and laid my hand on his cheek. "Mr. Bledsoe?"

His dark eyes, open wide and staring, didn't flicker. The life had gone from them.

He was dead.

I scanned the area around him, looking for what might have caused his injuries. There was an odor in the air—something fragrant, something floral. Perfume?

Then, peeking out from beneath his right shoulder, I spotted something metal glinting in the dim light. I reached for it and pulled out a slender, silver letter opener with a mother-of-pearl handle decorated with ornate silver filigree. Blood smeared the thin blade.

"Mrs. Pryce? What are you doing?"

I spun around to see Atticus Brooks standing in the doorway.

"Good Lord!" His hand flew to his mouth.

"He's dead," was all I could manage to say. His gaze traveled from mine to the letter opener in my hand. Instantly, I dropped it.

"You—" His voice came out in a harsh, accusing whisper.

"No." I shook my head. "No! I found him like this. I didn't do this." My stomach twisted into knots, and my lungs felt as if an anvil had settled on them. I knew how this looked, and on top of the accusation that I had killed Miss Platte and Mr. Brooks's seemingly single-minded desire to disparage me, I knew I was in trouble.

Someone appeared in the doorway behind him. It was Mr. Pettyjohn.

"What's this?" He pushed his way past Mr. Brooks.

"He's dead," I repeated. "I came up after dinner to speak with him, and I found him like this. The letter opener was here." I pointed to his upper body. "Beneath his shoulder."

"This is terrible." Mr. Pettyjohn's face had gone pale. "We need to get the sheriff. And the doctor."

"The sheriff is downstairs in the saloon," I said.

A squeak sounded from behind the men, and I turned to see Maggie's face peering over Mr. Pettyjohn's shoulder.

"Maggie, run and get the sheriff. He's in the saloon," Mr. Pettyjohn said, then turned around, blocking her view. "And then go fetch Dr. Tate."

In a flash, she was gone.

Mr. Pettyjohn closed the door, for which I was grateful. We didn't need to have any of the guests witness this gruesome scene.

Mr. Brooks had taken out his pad of paper and was scribbling something on it with his pencil. I shot up to standing and swiped the pad out of his hands. "Print one word of this and I will have my lawyer sue you for libel. You have no proof of anything."

"Are you threatening me, Mrs. Pryce?" he asked, brows raised.

It took every ounce of self-control I had not to throw the thing in his face. The man was like a pestilence!

"Please," Mr. Pettyjohn stepped in. "Let's not squabble."

Mr. Brooks held out his hand for the notepad, and reluctantly I placed it in his palm with a firm slap, my heart pounding. If he so much as breathed a word of this to my contemporaries in New York, I was finished. Again, I could see another damning headline: BELOVED ACTRESS TURNED NOTORIOUS MURDERESS.

I'd have to send a wire to Mr. Rankin to write a story to counter Mr. Brooks's, should he write one about this incident. Then again, wouldn't that make me seem guilty? Oh dear, I was getting ahead of myself. I needed to remain calm. Since I was owner of this hotel, couldn't I throw him out? Did I have to serve every single badly behaved guest? Certainly that was not the case. Yet, that would give the petulant writer more ammunition in his war against my good reputation.

But I shouldn't be thinking such things now, when a man in my employ was lying dead at my feet.

Duly chastised by Mr. Pettyjohn, we each retreated to our corners and waited for the sheriff and the doctor in silence. Mr. Pettyjohn crossed the room and sat down on the Queen Anne–style sofa, his elbows propped on his knees and his head in his hands.

Thankfully, it wasn't long before the sheriff arrived. Maggie opened the door and let him in. She gaped at the body and began to tremble. Her face paled, and I could see her knees were going to buckle. I started toward her, but the doctor appeared behind her just in time to catch her before she fell.

"What happened?" the sheriff asked.

"I saw her kneeling over the body," Mr. Brooks cut in, pointing at me. "She was holding the letter opener."

I gasped. "You horrible, horrible man!" I moved toward him, to do what, I didn't know, but Sheriff Marshall laid a hand on my shoulder, stopping me.

"Hold on. Everyone just calm down," he said.

By *everyone* I knew he meant me, and it rankled. I was not going to stand by while the venomous theater critic accused me of murder. Again.

"He doesn't know what he's talking about!" I said.

Sheriff Marshall turned to me, hands on hips, his blue eyes regarding me with a flinty stare.

"I repeat, what happened?" he asked.

"I honestly don't know," I said. "I left the saloon and came upstairs. I wanted to speak with Mr. Bledsoe—"

"Would someone get this woman some water, please?" The doctor lifted Maggie her to her feet and took her to the sofa where Mr. Pettyjohn sat in a dazed stupor. The doctor took the crocheted throw that was draped over the back of the couch and placed it over the distraught young woman's shoulders.

"I'll go." I stepped toward the door. I also wanted to fetch Cordelia to tend to the prostrate woman.

"Not you." Sheriff Marshall raised a hand to stop me, as if I would flee the scene. Or the hotel. Or the town. Believe me, the thought had occurred in my mind more than once, but still, I was affronted that he could so readily believe that I would *murder* someone.

"Mr. Pettyjohn, you go," he finished.

"And please get Cordelia," I added. "She will take care of Maggie."

"Mrs. Pryce, please continue," the sheriff said.

I took in a deep breath to settle myself. "As I said, I wanted to speak with Mr. Bledsoe. I didn't know which were his rooms and was prepared to knock on all the doors when I found this door open. I came inside and found him here on the floor."

The doctor left Maggie on the sofa and began to inspect the body.

Mr. Pettyjohn returned with Cordelia, who was holding a glass of water. She looked down at the prostrate body of Mr. Bledsoe. "Oh my goodness." Her eyes met mine. I shook my head in a silent signal that we would discuss this later.

"I'm afraid Maggie fainted." I directed her attention to the sofa. The young woman had come to but looked dazed and was shaking violently. "Please tend to her."

Cordelia complied and sat down beside her. She wrapped an arm around Maggie's shoulders.

"What did you wish to speak with him about?" Sheriff Marshall asked, crossing his arms over his broad chest.

I took in another sharp breath and then let it out. "I wanted to apologize."

"For the argument in the saloon?" His forehead rose in question, causing a fine line to appear in an undulating pattern above his eyes.

A pit grew in my stomach. "Yes."

"What was the argument about?"

"It was about the state of the hotel."

A fierce scratching noise caused us both to turn toward it. Mr. Brooks was busy with his pad and pencil. The sheriff reached out and snatched it out of his hands.

"That's enough, Mr. Brooks." He raised the items in the air, giving a gesture of warning.

"You can't do that!" Mr. Brooks snapped.

"I just did." Sheriff Marshall tucked the pad in his vest pocket. I refrained from smirking with satisfaction at Mr. Brooks, worm of a man that he was.

"I saw her holding the murder weapon!" He pointed to the letter opener lying on the floor.

I thrust a finger out toward Mr. Brooks. "That man is intent on ruining me, Sheriff. In fact, I wouldn't be surprised if he was trying his best to make me look guilty." I turned to Mr. Brooks. "Did you plant that letter in my desk drawer?"

Mr. Brooks let out a laugh. "Absolutely not. I was out that

morning, taking the air. You can ask Archibald. We were together."

I set my hand on my hips and glanced at the sheriff. He gave a nod.

"Mr. Archer vouched for him."

I gritted my teeth. Just because he hadn't planted the letter didn't mean that he wasn't still intent on making my life miserable.

The sheriff bent over, picked the letter opener up by the handle, and turned it in his fingers.

Cordelia approached us. "Maggie seems to be a little better now. I am going to escort her to her room."

"Thank you, Cordelia." I looked over at Maggie. Her face was still white as marble but she looked stronger. Cordelia went to her and helped her to her feet, and the two left the room.

The sheriff held the letter opener up to the light. "Is this what killed him, Doc?"

The doctor looked up from the body. "At first glance, yes. The blade penetrated his heart. It would only be a matter of minutes before he died. But, to be sure, I'll have to do a more thorough examination."

The sheriff turned to me. "What time did you come upstairs?"

"It was around nine o'clock."

"And you went immediately to his room?"

"Yes. I found him on the floor," I repeated.

The doctor stood up and pulled his pocket watch from his vest, taking note of the time. "I need to get him to my infirmary," he said. "Pettyjohn, Mr. Brooks, a hand?"

The two men assisted Dr. Tate in lifting the body.

"Take the back stairs, please," I requested.

"I'll show you the way," Mr. Pettyjohn said to the doctor.

The three men exited the parlor, struggling with the weight of the dead Mr. Bledsoe and leaving the sheriff and me alone.

"I can't believe it." I pressed my palm to my forehead, suddenly feeling quite dizzy.

"Are you all right?" He stepped forward as if ready to catch me if I crumpled in a heap. I was touched at his concern—if it was concern—but I didn't have time for it.

I waved him away. "Yes, yes, I'm fine. Another murder in the hotel. This is just awful."

He rubbed his chin. "And so close on the heels of Narcissa Platte's murder."

"They must be connected," I said. "Have you made any headway into finding who killed Miss Platte?"

He went silent, regarding me with those thoughtful blue eyes. I didn't know what to make of it.

After a long pause, he cleared his throat and then, with a lowered voice, said, "The doctor was able to determine the substance on the fireplace poker."

"And?"

"It was blood."

My heart sank to the pit of my stomach. "So it was the murder weapon?"

He nodded. "Most likely."

My insides swirled with anxiety. "Sheriff Marshall . . . I swear on my career, on my life, I didn't—"

He raised a hand to interrupt me. "I haven't come to any final conclusions yet."

He held my gaze, and I could see the conflict in his eyes. I got the sense that he wanted to believe me, but the evidence was stacking up against me. I wondered that he didn't just march me off to the jail right then and there.

In the stillness, the floral fragrance tickled my nostrils again.

"Do you smell that?" I asked him. The fragrance conjured a notion of familiarity. I had smelled this before, but I couldn't remember where.

"I smell whiskey," he said, giving me a pointed look. "You sure you're all right?"

I firmly set my hands on my hips. "I certainly am."

One of the many things Sheriff Marshall did not know about me was that I could hold my liquor. Or champagne as it were, as it was my vice of choice. I had not had whiskey before, but the effects were similar, creating a warm and tingly feeling and giving way to a slight lightheadedness from time to time. But I was feeling a bit tipsier than I was accustomed to. Even so, I was in complete control of myself.

"You don't smell that? A floral fragrance?" I asked.

He sniffed the air. "Now that you mention it . . ."

"I know that smell," I said, and then it hit me. "It's jasmine. Mrs. Bledsoe was wearing jasmine perfume! She was here in the hotel. Recently. Mr. Bledsoe was called away from our meeting with Mr. Archer to take her home, but what if she came back here and waited for him?"

My nose had helped me solve a mystery before, when my lucky ring had gone missing. The sheriff rubbed a hand over his chin. "You're sure it's her perfume?"

"Yes. Positive. It all makes sense! I've learned from a couple of sources that Mr. Bledsoe fancied other women besides his wife. I witnessed myself how he looked at Sally Dean. She even told me that he— Well, he . . . had made use of her services. What if Mrs. Bledsoe found out about it? Or already knew about it and was fed up?"

Sheriff Marshall visibly stiffened. Did he have feelings for the beguiling barmaid? If so, I pitied the man. Or was it something other than pity I felt? Jealousy, perhaps?

How ridiculous. I set aside my feelings, whatever they were. I couldn't think about that now. I was onto something here.

"And Miss Chatterley and Mrs. Gilroy said they'd seen Mr. Bledsoe and Narcissa together," I continued. "Miss Chatterley even used the word *canoodling!* What if he was the father of Narcissa's child? What if he—or Mrs. Bledsoe—killed Narcissa because of the baby?"

The sheriff frowned. "My, you've been busy."

I opened my mouth in indignation. "Sheriff Marshall, may I remind you that my reputation, and the reputation of this hotel, are at stake. Yes, I have 'been busy' trying to clear my name. Mark my words, sir, I will not rest until I find out who is behind these crimes. And I think we need to find Mrs. Bledsoe. She had motive, means, and opportunity."

He furrowed his brow, but his mouth took on that curve of amusement that always seemed to occur in my presence. "Motive, means, and opportunity? Are you familiar with the workings of the criminal mind, Mrs. Pryce?"

I sighed with impatience at his teasing. It really wasn't appropriate. "Not really," I admitted. "I've read some of Cordelia's books. Sir Arthur Conan Doyle's work, in fact."

"Sherlock Holmes?" He smiled.

"Yes, Sherlock Holmes, if you must know. Now, really, we must go find Mrs. Bledsoe!"

Suddenly, the room swirled, and I faltered. With nothing near to grab on to but the sheriff, I reached for his arm but missed, and in the blink of an eye, his arm had gone around my waist, supporting me. My knees had gone quite wobbly.

"You're not going anywhere." He led me toward the door. "I'll walk you to your room."

As we approached the doorway, Percival appeared in the parlor mirror, holding his pipe aloft, observing the situation—and me in the sheriff's arms. Did I see a look of disapproval on his face?

"What are you doing?" I asked Percival but then closed my mouth, realizing Sheriff Marshall most likely would not have seen the ghost.

"You seemed unsteady on your feet." Sheriff Marshall pulled away from me, releasing me. "Forgive me."

"Tha-that's not what I meant," I stammered. I didn't mean to imply I thought he was being forward, but the presence of Percival in another's company filled me with anxiety. My mother's voice echoed in my head.

What would people think if they knew you saw ghosts? They'd put you away. We'd be ruined. Forever shunned. Keep your mouth shut.

I wobbled, and Sheriff Marshall took hold of my elbow. "Please let me help you."

His voice had such a smooth and calming quality, I couldn't protest. The shock of finding Mr. Bledsoe dead on the floor was wearing away and the effects of the liquor had returned. The mixture of the two turned my bones to jelly.

I gave a brief nod, and he gently slipped his arm around my waist again and led me out of the room.

His nearness and the feel of his arm, solid and sure, holding me steady, guiding me up the stairs, created such an odd feeling within me. This man had seen me at my worst, like a bedraggled cat in the river, accused and suspected of murder, and now with evidence against me. He had witnessed me arguing in public with one of my employees, and he had deduced that I was intoxicated, and yet, he hadn't seemed to have formed an ill opinion of me.

The notion gave me a feeling I hadn't ever experienced before. The tension in my body relaxed, and the turmoil of my mind calmed. I shook my head, not able to reconcile this feeling that was so completely foreign to me. I wasn't sure I understood it completely, but for the first time in my life, I felt that I wasn't being judged. That he accepted me for who I really was—faults, flaws, and all—instead of who I wanted the world to see.

CHAPTER 18

I had slept late, which greatly irritated me. I wasn't typically one to linger in bed. A consistent sense of urgency regularly drove me to rise early and start the day, sometimes even before sunrise. There was always so much I wanted to do, and today was no different. I wanted to follow up on my theory about Mrs. Bledsoe. She seemed the most obvious suspect—the jealous wife —perhaps one out for revenge.

I sat up, ready to jump out of bed when a knifelike pain pierced my head, reminding me of the libations in the saloon the night before.

"Good morning." A voice penetrated the room from somewhere to my right. I turned to see Percival sitting in the armchair next to my bed.

"Oh, it's you," I muttered. Really, this lack of privacy was growing tedious. I placed my fingertips at my temples and circled them in an attempt to relieve the tension.

"You had quite a night last night." He took his pipe from his pocket.

I wrinkled my nose. "Please don't light that. I don't think I could manage the smell right now." I made a mental note to avoid whiskey and stick to champagne in the future.

He sighed, placing the pipe back into his pocket. "Another murder. My, my."

I swiveled my head to face him again. "Did you see who did it?"

"No."

For someone who freely roamed the hotel undetected, who could be anywhere he pleased at any time, why couldn't he be of more help?

"Did you see *anything?* Did you see Mr. Bledsoe enter his rooms?"

"I saw him leave the saloon. Looked angry as a bull."

"Yes. That was on my account."

"Oh? Do tell." He leaned forward in the chair, resting his elbows on the armrests. He crossed his legs at the ankles.

I shook my head, ashamed of my tantrum. "It started with my questioning him about the disgraceful condition of the hotel—"

"Yes," he cut in, his voice hard. "Bledsoe never did appreciate her. His shallowness prevented him from seeing her beauty. He did not have the capacity to comprehend the uniqueness of her design. She was not a priority for him. He was too busy licking Archer's boots."

I lowered my hands. "You mean Archibald Archer?"

"Yes."

"For what reason?"

"He works for him. At the General."

"The General! Mr. Archer owns the General? Our competitor? Why did I not know this? I thought the General was owned by the railway company."

"Well, it is. But Mr. Archer has a vested interest in the railway, and he is the principal partner in the General."

Mr. Blank leaned back in the chair and examined his fingernails.

"Well that doesn't seem right. It's an egregious conflict of interest." I said. A sense of betrayal wormed its way into my heart. "How long has this been going on?"

"He was hired at the General by Mr. Archer shortly after your husband left town."

"How could Mr. Archer do that? How could Mr. Bledsoe have accepted?"

"You forget, my dear Arabella, Mr. Archer owns the vast majority of La Plata Springs. He can do whatever he wants. And Bledsoe is—well, *was*—exceedingly ambitious."

"And obviously lacked integrity!" I added.

Percival nodded. "The whole situation caused quite a bit of upset with Mr. and Mrs. Platte."

"Oh? Why?" I had trouble making a connection.

"The job at the General was supposed to go to young Andrew."

"What?" This wasn't making any sense at all.

"Mr. Platte paved the way for Mr. Archer to get involved with the railroad. In return, Mr. Archer agreed that Andrew would have a job at the General. You see, the Plattes—Narcissa included—could not abide having an artist in the family, snobs that they are. Really, to think they consider themselves above—"

Fearing he was about to launch into something off topic, I cut him off. "But Mrs. Gilroy told me Mr. Archer wanted Andrew to step into his mining company. Hoped he would one day take it over from him." Which, in my estimation, was a bit overbearing. Clearly, the young man had his own ideas for his future. I wondered why he would agree to employment with his uncle. Perhaps the Plattes or Narcissa had worn him down? Or maybe his love for Narcissa overpowered his own desires?

There was only one way to find out.

❦

The burial for Narcissa Platte was to take place that morning. I intended to pay my respects but from a distance. Given what

Mrs. Platte thought of me, it would be best if I did not intrude on the very solemn and personal occasion.

Cordelia, Bijou, and I opted not to take the hotel coach but to walk. I needed the fresh air to think. As we joined several of the townspeople on their pilgrimage to the gravesite, I noticed some of them looking at me askance. Ladies whispered to one another behind gloved hands, and men glanced at me warily. A pang of shame pierced my heart, even though I knew I had nothing to be ashamed of. I had done nothing wrong.

"Is it me, Cordelia, or does it seem that we are getting the cold shoulder?"

She gave me a tight smile. "I noticed the same."

"Are they all so readily willing to believe that I am a murderess?" I couldn't disguise the hurt in my voice, although I tried.

"We are new in town," Cordelia said, trying to comfort me. "I'm sure it's just that. People have trouble with change. And since we've arrived, a lot has happened. Please don't worry yourself over it. They'll come to see that you are a good person."

We stood at the back of the cemetery. Shaded with elm trees, it was a beautiful spot for a resting place. The perimeter of the area was bordered with a rainbow of rose bushes that were in full bloom.

The funeral was a small affair. Of course, Mr. and Mrs. Platte were in attendance, as well as Andrew and Mr. Archer. Mrs. Gilroy and her husband were there, as well as Miss Chatterley, Mr. Pettyjohn, and Dr. Tate. To my surprise, right in the thick of them all stood Atticus Brooks.

Really! He had no stake in the welfare of these people, of this town. How he inserted himself into the fold as if he belonged here was laughable. At least he wasn't scribbling in his notebook, I thought with contempt.

I scanned the horizon, and in the distance, the sheriff watched on horseback.

The priest, wearing black-and-white vestments, read from the Bible. I could not hear what he was saying, but the scene had an air of tranquility, and I hoped the Plattes and the rest of the mourners received some kind of comfort.

The priest made the sign of the cross in the air, and then the group began, in turn, to throw handfuls of dirt in the grave. The last to perform this ritual was Andrew, who also gently tossed in a long-stemmed yellow rose. I wondered at that. Yellow roses symbolized friendship while red roses indicated love. Perhaps he hadn't known the significance of the hues, or maybe the yellow rose was Narcissa's favorite?

He then picked up a satchel and walked away from the scene. He was headed for the river.

"I don't like funerals," Cordelia said. "It's difficult to see people in such pain."

I took in a deep breath and let it go. "Me neither."

The last funeral I had attended was my husband's. I had been so relieved when it was over. I didn't see much benefit in wallowing in grief. The balm for me had been my work.

"I'm going to go talk to Andrew," I told her. "I'll meet up with you later." I held my hand out for Bijou's leash. "I'll take her. The fresh air will do her good."

Andrew walked at a fairly fast clip, and since I was some distance away, Bijou and I had to make haste so as not to lose him.

The river was flanked by a seemingly never-ending forest of majestic trees. As I neared them, I marveled at their rough, knotty trunks and twisting branches. A profusion of leaves clustered on smaller limbs that jutted out at eccentric angles.

I found Andrew sitting on a large boulder at the water's edge at a bend in the river. As I came up behind him, I noticed he was scribbling something in a notebook of some kind. At closer range, I realized he was not writing but drawing. He did not hear me approach due to the roar of the water, so I was able to observe him. The pencil drawing was a portrait of a woman. I assumed it was of his lost beloved—Narcissa—but when I approached, I was surprised to see that it was not.

It was Maggie. The likeness was so accurate it was as if he knew every contour and line of her face—intimately. I remembered their embrace in the hallway of the hotel.

He must have sensed me standing there because he turned around. When he saw me, he flipped the sketchbook shut.

"Hello," I said.

"Good day, Mrs. Pryce."

"I'm so very sorry for your loss. This must be a difficult day for you."

He gave me a weary smile. "Thank you."

"May I?" I pointed to a boulder to the left of the one he was sitting on.

"Sure." He shrugged.

I settled myself on the boulder, and Bijou jumped onto Andrew's, looking for attention. She crawled right into his lap.

"Oh, I am so sorry. Bijou, come here." I tugged on the leash to no avail. She, with her smiling face and wagging tail, would not be moved.

"It's all right." A happier smile broke across the young man's face as he stroked her head. Completely content, she lay herself across his legs and set her head on her paws. "I like dogs."

We sat in silence for a few moments, watching the water rush by—mostly because I didn't really know where to begin. But I was curious about the portrait.

"You have a talent for drawing. That portrait is beautiful."

He looked over at me, his face reddening. "You saw it?"

I nodded. "Maggie?"

He looked away but did not confirm.

"Andrew, I am trying to find out what exactly happened to Narcissa. I hope you don't think that I—"

"I don't." He ran a hand through his mop of hair. "I know you didn't kill her."

"Thank you," I said, truly grateful.

"Do you have any idea who might have done it?"

He shrugged again, still watching the water. "She didn't have many friends. I mean, real friends."

I braced myself for what I was about to say next. "Andrew, did you know she was pregnant?"

He snapped his head toward me in surprise. "What?"

"Did you know she was pregnant?" I repeated, though his reaction indicated he hadn't known.

His gaze shifted away from mine. "No, I didn't," he said, but I sensed he might not be telling me the truth.

"Were you the father?" I pressed.

He closed his eyes and took in a deep breath. Slowly, he let it out. "No," he said.

"You're sure?"

"Yes, I'm sure!" He raised his voice, and Bijou startled. He raised a hand in apology. "I'm sorry, I shouldn't have shouted."

I took his previous, impassioned response to mean that he and Narcissa had not been intimate. "Do you know who might be?"

He scoffed, shaking his head. "Could have been anyone. Narcissa was— Well, she had a lot of male . . . *admirers*."

My heart went out to the young man. Anyone in Andrew's position would suffer a great deal of humiliation and degradation at not being enough for one's partner. It caused insecurity of the worst kind—questioning if they were good enough, or special enough, or worthy of love at all. I was feeling a bit of that myself with the rumor about William and Narcissa floating around.

If that feeling was painful enough, might the person want to snuff out that feeling? Or perhaps the person, or persons, who'd caused it? I remembered how angry Andrew had seemed to be at Mr. Bledsoe the other day. I wondered again if he had just lied to me about knowing of the pregnancy.

"Was Daniel Bledsoe one of her admirers?"

The set of his jaw hardened, the muscles in it flexing. I had definitely hit a nerve.

"She told me about him," he ground out. "He didn't treat her very well."

"I see. Is that why you were so angry with him? Did that bother you?"

"Yes. But not like you'd think. I wasn't jealous. Though it did make me look a fool, didn't it? My fiancé carrying on with other men, and with someone who couldn't care less about her?"

I pulled my upper lip between my teeth, fully empathetic to his plight.

"And you and Maggie?" I ventured.

He grew silent and bowed his head to looked down at Bijou, who in turn, looked up at him adoringly, his previous transgression forgiven.

He stroked her back. "I love Maggie. I always have, ever since we were kids. I was only marrying Narcissa because I had to."

"Why was that?"

"Because my uncle and the Plattes made an arrangement." His mouth twisted into a sneer. "They made it plain that both Narcissa and I would lose everything if we didn't marry each other. She didn't want to marry me any more than I wanted to marry her.

"I don't much care about myself. I'd find a way to make a living—maybe with my art—eventually. But Maggie's mother is ill. Maggie is all she has left, and she doesn't make enough money to—"

I raised my eyebrows in question, encouraging him to continue.

"That is . . . Mr. Bledsoe didn't pay her enough to take care of herself and her ma. I needed to help support her." He snickered. "So I guess you know my secret now. That I love Maggie. For a long time, the only person who knew was Sally."

Right, I thought. Sally had mentioned not betraying a confidence. Had it been Maggie's?

"I won't say anything," I assured him. "Well, I must get back to the hotel."

I stood, and something to the right of us caught my eye. I sucked in a breath when I saw Percival Blank sitting on a boulder near the water's edge, smoking his pipe. He'd mentioned he liked to come down by the river from time to time. How long had he been sitting there?

"Pardon?" Andrew said.

"Oh, it's nothing." A wave of heat rose to my face at my reaction to Percival. I glanced back at him. He was pointing to Andrew's satchel that had been placed on a boulder to Andrew's right. I shook my head, not understanding. His pointing became more exaggerated. He wanted me to see something in the satchel. But how could I do so with Andrew sitting right there? Then an idea struck.

"Oh my!" I said, wobbling on my feet. I went to the boulder and sat down between Andrew and the satchel.

"Mrs. Pryce? Are you all right?" Andrew asked.

I held up a hand. "Yes, yes, I'm fine. Just a little light-headed. I'm still getting used to the altitude, I suppose."

"Shall I walk you back to the hotel?"

"No, that won't be necessary. It's already passed." I laid my hand on the satchel to push myself to my feet and shoved it off the rock.

"Oh dear, I'm so sorry." I bent down to pick it up and was surprised to see something had tumbled out of it. From the leather whipstitching and tan-colored fringe, it could be none other than a buckskin jacket.

The guests who'd found Narcissa dead on the landing had mentioned a man in a buckskin jacket walking down the hallway on the night of her murder. My breath froze in my lungs, and I looked over at Percival, who returned the glance with raised eyebrows.

"Don't worry about it." Andrew lifted Bijou from his lap and set her down on the ground. He stood and picked up the satchel, shoving the coat back into it.

Bijou raised herself on her hind legs, dancing at Andrew's feet, wanting more attention from him. Chuckling, he bent down and tousled the hair on her round little head.

Still in shock at the discovery, I couldn't help but think that with Narcissa dead, the arrangement between her and Andrew would no longer be in effect. He'd be free to continue with Maggie.

Yet, Bijou's behavior toward him was puzzling. She had a sense about people and she was showing me that Andrew was a good, loving, and caring person. Someone who most likely would not commit murder. But then again, if he was such an attentive and obliging person, he might do anything for those he loved.

Anything.

CHAPTER 19

I had just opened my mouth to question Andrew about his whereabouts at the hotel on the night of Narcissa's murder, but Percival stepped between us and shook his head.

Perhaps he was right. I was alone out here with Andrew. If he had killed Narcissa, my further questioning of him might land me another swim in the river. A permanent one.

Bijou and I left Andrew to his thoughts. The young man certainly seemed to have a lot on his mind. And I couldn't help but think that a guilty conscience might add to that preoccupation.

I walked along the river, my mind reeling, the image of the buckskin jacket etched in my thoughts. Indeed, Andrew had motive to want to be rid of Narcissa. Yet, it stood to reason that buckskin coats would be a staple here in this western town. It could have been anyone. Still, I would have to mention this to Sheriff Marshall.

The pathway along the river ran parallel to the back entrance of the hotel, and Bijou and I made our way there. Sally Dean and Maggie stood near the door, talking. As I got closer, it became apparent that they were passing something back and forth between them, and then Maggie doubled over, coughing.

They were sharing a cigarette, and it was apparent that Maggie was not in the habit of smoking.

I shook my head. This would not do. Women smoking in public was greatly frowned upon in New York City, and I imagined it was no different here. Granted, a few of the actresses I had employed at the theater partook of the habit, but I had insisted they do it in the privacy of their homes, not in my place of business. I ran a respectable theater, and I would run a respectable hotel.

"Put that out please," I said as I approached.

Maggie gasped when she saw me, which only contributed to the irritation in her lungs, and she sputtered another round of coughing.

Sally Dean coolly exhaled a steady stream of smoke in my direction, her gaze fixed on mine in what was clearly a challenge.

"Please," I said again.

With a roll of her eyes, she dropped it to the ground and snuffed it out with the point of her delicately heeled boot.

"If you are to remain employees of the hotel, I would ask that you please not smoke in or around the vicinity. What you do elsewhere is no concern of mine, but when you are at work, there will be no smoking."

Sally Dean suppressed a laugh at my request, and I realized the irony of what I was asking, as she was in the most disreputable profession of all.

I sighed. That would have to be taken care of, too, but not now. I had other things to contend with, and now that my hotel manager was dead, it all fell to me.

Maggie, on the other hand, crumpled into tears. "I'm so sorry, Mrs. Pryce. I was just trying it. Sally said it might calm my nerves."

Sensing the young woman's distress, Bijou raised herself on her hind legs and pawed at Maggie's skirt.

I felt for the girl and could commiserate. Two murders in the span of one week. It was enough to set anyone on edge.

Sally put an arm around Maggie, and I pulled a handkerchief from my reticule.

"Here." I handed it to her and gently pulled Bijou away.

"Thank you," she said. She wiped her eyes but to no avail as another wave of tears dampened her cheeks.

"What is it, Maggie?" I implored.

She shook her head and then blew her nose. "It's nothing, ma'am. I'm sorry."

"I hardly think it's nothing. This has been a very trying time. You've been crying for the past couple of days. I have half a mind to send you home until you can get ahold of yourself."

"No, please don't send me home, ma'am. I'll stop." She let go a sob, clearly not able to tamp down her emotions.

"But you are so distressed." I insisted.

"She needs to work, ma'am," Sally cut in. Then I remembered what Andrew had told me. She needed the money to take care of her mother.

"It's just too awful," she wailed. Bijou gave a yip and jumped up to comfort her once again.

"What's too awful?" I said, pulling at the leash.

She gulped in air. "Mr. Bledsoe!"

I frowned in sympathy. "Yes, it's terrible what happened to him. Do you know something about it?"

The question brought on even more tears. I took her by the hand and gave it a little squeeze. "Maggie, please tell me."

She looked up at me with sad, if not bloodshot, eyes. "I shouldn't have told him."

"Told Mr. Bledsoe what?"

She shook her head. "Not him. Andrew. I shouldn't have told him. He got so angry."

"Angry about what?"

She blew her nose again, and then finally, the tears stopped. She took a moment to collect herself. "Please don't fire me, ma'am. Sally's right. I need the work."

"I'm not going to fire you, Maggie." I released her hand.

She sniffed. "You see, Mr. Bledsoe——" She took in a deep breath and then continued. "Mr. Bledsoe . . . made advances."

"With you?"

She nodded, and her eyes welled up, the tears threatening to return.

"I see." I bristled at the notion. Having endured similar treatment in the past I had absolutely no tolerance for men like Mr. Bledsoe. "And that made Andrew angry because you and he . . . ?"

"Yes." She squeezed her eyes shut, I assumed to staunch another flood of tears. Bijou pulled away from me, and again, I bent down to pick her up.

Maggie opened her eyes and blinked the tears away. "Mrs. Pryce, I'm afraid that Andrew may have——"

"Killed Mr. Bledsoe?" I finished for her, my heartbeat picking up a tick.

She pressed her lips together.

"And what about Narcissa?" I asked, recounting my previous theory. "She stood in the way of you and Andrew being together, didn't she?"

A look of horror washed over her face. "Yes, but . . . he wouldn't! He was also angry at Mr. Bledsoe on her behalf."

I blinked. "What do you mean, on her behalf?"

"He— Oh dear!" Her eyes opened wide with terror. "I've said too much. I just— It's just— Oh, it's just too much to bear!" She succumbed to another bout of crying. Sally gently rubbed her back, trying to comfort her.

And then it dawned on me. "You mean, the pregnancy. Andrew knew Narcissa was pregnant. Did he suspect Mr. Bledsoe was the father?"

She nodded. "Narcissa wouldn't say it was him. But that's what Andrew thought. Oh, if he——" Her knees crumpled, and she sank to the ground. Bijou let go with desperate barking. I set her down, and she crawled into Maggie's lap. The young woman instinctively wrapped her arms around the little dog.

She'd just confirmed what I had suspected: Andrew had lied

to me. But from what I'd gathered about his gentle nature, I found it hard to believe that he would kill an unborn child. But then again, Narcissa did pose a big problem for him and Maggie, and her being pregnant would only complicate matters.

"Maggie, was Andrew at the hotel the night of Narcissa's murder?" I asked.

"He— Well I was working late . . . on account of being so far behind. I was supposed to meet him at my mother's house for dinner, but when I didn't show . . . he was worried and came to . . . to check on me."

"Is that all?" I pressed.

She gave a short, vigorous nod and then buried her face in Bijou's silky fur. It seemed she was holding back something, but she was so distraught I wasn't going to press her. Perhaps I would try again after she'd calmed down.

I glanced at Sally, whose eyes were wide with surprise. Her face had lost all its color, and she pressed her hand to her mouth.

"Sally? Are you all right?" I asked her.

"He couldn't have," she muttered.

"Who?"

She looked up at me with round eyes and then swallowed.

"Please, Sally, what is it? If you know something, it's important you tell me."

"Mr. Bledsoe . . . the night of Narcissa's murder." She swallowed. "I hope Kitty doesn't get mad at me for telling you this, but since he's dead and all . . . That night, he was with me. He was angry about something . . . and rougher than usual. I asked him what was wrong, and he said, 'That girl is ruining my life.' At first, I thought he was talking about his wife, but she's no girl. Then I remembered he'd asked one of the other saloon girls to deliver a message to Narcissa earlier that evening."

"What was the message?" I asked, my pulse racing.

"To meet him later that night at the General. I thought it strange because he said he was sick of her mooning around him all the time."

"How long was he with you?" I asked.

"He was with me from around nine o'clock 'til around eleven forty-five."

My heart sank. Then he couldn't have killed Narcissa. Discouraged, I blew a deep exhale through my lips. I was no closer to the truth than I'd been in the beginning.

"The doctor said the time of death was approximately ten o'clock but most likely a little earlier," I said. "So if Mr. Bledsoe did not kill Narcissa, who did? And who killed him?"

Maggie looked up at me with pleading in her eyes. "I don't know for sure that Andrew did it, Mrs. Pryce. It's not like him. He's really very sweet natured. I am just scared, that's all. Please don't say anything, Mrs. Pryce. Please, I beg you. I shouldn't have—"

She pressed the handkerchief to her mouth with a shaking hand. The poor girl was completely beside herself with worry. It was understandable. The odds were definitely stacked against Andrew as far as motive for both murders was concerned. But I wasn't entirely convinced. As much as I wanted to exonerate myself for these murders, I didn't want to make false accusations.

"It's all right, Maggie. I won't say anything for the time being."

Andrew, after all, wasn't the only person with motive.

❦

I stopped at the front desk before I went upstairs. Mr. Pettyjohn was there going through some papers. I scanned the lobby for Clarence. In all the recent commotion, I'd forgotten that Percival had seen the bellhop leave my rooms.

"Have you seen Clarence?" I asked Mr. Pettyjohn.

He looked up at me over the rim of his spectacles. "He's been ill. I received a letter from his mother."

"Oh dear. Is it serious?"

"I don't know, madam."

I flinched at his utterance of *that word* but didn't say anything about it.

"Why didn't you tell me about this before now?" I asked with some irritation. After all, I was in charge of the hotel and all of its goings on now.

"I didn't wish to bother you, madam. You've had rather a lot to contend with." He said the last two words with a lilt in his voice. Whether it was an accusatory lilt or a sympathetic lilt, I couldn't be sure. My insecurities ran to the former.

I pressed down the anxiety rising in my chest. "So who has been fulfilling his duties in his absence?"

Mr. Pettyjohn sighed. "Me, of course. We are rather short of staff here," he said pointedly, accusation clear in his voice now.

I wanted to respond by saying that it wasn't my fault Mr. Bledsoe had been well on his way to sending the hotel into ruin, but given the man had been dead less than twenty-four hours, I refrained. "I understand, Mr. Pettyjohn. I will rectify the situation as soon as possible. Hopefully, young Clarence will return to work shortly."

Bijou and I made our way upstairs to my rooms. When we arrived, Cordelia was seated at the love seat, completely immersed in a book. Bijou went straight to her water dish and then to her bed under the window.

"I'm going to change out of this dreary dress," I said, looking down at my black satin and lace frock that I kept close at hand for funerals and other somber occasions.

"Would you like me to help you?" Cordelia offered.

"That's all right, I can manage."

I went to the bedroom, my mind still occupied with Maggie's fears that Andrew had done in Mr. Bledsoe.

I sat down on the bed, ruminating on the conversation.

"Penny for them." A quiet male voice broke the silence.

I turned to the mirror. Percival was seated in the chair's reflection next to the bed.

"Oh, it's you," I said absently.

He frowned. "Glad to see you, too."

"I'm sorry."

"It doesn't seem like you to be so pensive. From what I've seen, you are a woman of action. Always bustling about."

I sighed. "I'm afraid Andrew may have been the one who killed Mr. Bledsoe. And maybe Narcissa."

"Afraid? Isn't that what you wanted? To find the guilty party in order to clear yourself?"

"Yes. But . . . as much as I want to find the killer, or killers, and put this behind me, I hate to think it was Andrew. It just doesn't feel right."

"But you saw the buckskin coat in his satchel," Percival said. "And you said a man wearing a buckskin coat was seen in the vicinity of the crime."

"Yes, but that's not proof that he killed her." My thoughts trailed to Andrew's predicament. "Although, he must have been so angry at the position he'd been put in."

"Yes. From what I'd overheard at the river about the arrangement for his marriage to Narcissa—a woman he didn't love and who, by the way, was having her way with other men, Mr. Bledsoe included—it's not hard to believe that Andrew is a frustrated and angry young man."

"He believes he had no choice in the matters of his own life," I added. "And I know how that feels."

He puffed on his pipe. "Oh?"

"I know what it is like to live under the oppression of someone else's ambition. I did so for most of my life. Up until I married William at the age of twenty."

"Tell me more," he said, settling further in the chair, his gaze and his attention completely focused on me.

My first instinct was to button up. I did not like wallowing in my past, and I had said too much of a personal nature already. I made it a practice to never share my feelings with anyone. I had been trained to suppress them, to bottle them up, save them, and draw on them for a convincing performance. But the way in which he asked made me want to divulge more. It was as if he was allowing me permission. Besides, I knew he would keep my confidence. Who else would he tell?

I gazed down at my intertwined fingers in my lap. "I had become a theater phenom by the time I was twelve. Not because I had a burning passion for the stage but because my mother wanted it." I looked over at him again. "She dictated everything in my life. I've never told anyone this, other than her—in fact, I haven't even thought about it for a long time, but as a young girl I fancied the idea of becoming a novelist. But she said there wasn't enough money in that, and I needed to support us—in grand style, I might add. She wanted me to become rich and famous. I think that drive stemmed from her own frustrations over my father's leaving us."

"So she lives vicariously through you," Percival finished for me, regarding me through a haze of smoke.

"Yes," I said, sadness piercing my heart. "Sometimes I think I am just a means to an end for her."

"I'm sure it's not as bad as that." He tapped the back of his pipe with his fingers, ridding it of the ash, which disintegrated into thin air. "Your fame gives her life meaning. Her sense of worth is wrapped up in you. Sounds familiar."

I looked over at him. "You mean Narcissa and her mother?"
He nodded.

I thought about how hard my mother had driven me to succeed. Every penny we had was spent on acting classes and voice lessons, even at the expense of putting food on the table sometimes.

"My mother was thrilled when William approached us one night after a performance," I said, thinking out loud. "She had read about him, and his wealth, in the papers. She practically threw me at him. He, too, was a means for her end, but it did not go according to her plan. When I married him, she lost all control of me and my career."

"Did that make her angry?"

I nodded. "Very. We haven't spoken or exchanged letters in quite some time. I send her an allowance, of course, but that's it."

He settled deeper into the chair. "That must have been hard for you. To be denied your novelist dreams."

"It was."

"It's not too late, you know. And now you have all the money you need."

"Not exactly," I said with a huff. "Not until I finish my year-long incarceration."

Percival cocked his head in confusion. "Incarceration?"

I gave him a truncated version of the conditions of my being in La Plata Springs. Just the main points. Then I waved a hand in the air, dismissing the subject. I didn't feel like having a long discussion about it.

"I won't further bore you," I said. "But back to Andrew and the Plattes. I completely understand the boy's anger. Believe me, the thought of being rid of my mother had crossed my mind many times. But, fortunately, instead of murder, I turned to marriage."

CHAPTER 20

The following day, my conversations with Andrew and Maggie weighed heavily on my mind. As much as I did not want to be suspected of Narcissa's and Mr. Bledsoe's murders, I didn't want Andrew to be a suspect, either, despite the more than convincing reasons he might want to kill them. I knew I should speak with Sheriff Marshall about Andrew's buckskin coat and my conversation with Maggie, but I wanted to explore the options a bit further first.

There were two other people whom I had questions about: Mrs. Gilroy, who was heartbroken over her son leaving on account of Narcissa, and Prunella Bledsoe, who had been woefully wronged by her husband and Narcissa's flirtations. As to Narcissa's unborn child, it was pretty clear that Andrew was not the father, so that left Seth Gilroy and Daniel Bledsoe as the most likely candidates. Unless it had been William, I shuddered, who had left La Plata Springs right around the time she conceived. I certainly couldn't ask him about it, though.

I decided to start with Prunella Bledsoe. The night her husband had been killed, the unmistakable aroma of her perfume had hung in the air. She might have been the last person to see him alive.

Once downstairs, I stopped at the reception desk. "Good morning, Mr. Pettyjohn."

He gave me a nod. "Madam."

I gritted my teeth. "Please, Mr. Pettyjohn, *Mrs. Pryce* or even *Arabella* will do."

He nodded again.

"Has Clarence returned to work?" I asked.

"No, mada—Mrs. Pryce."

I pressed my lips together. If he did not return tomorrow, I resolved to pay him a visit. As his employer, it would be a nice gesture. And as a suspect falsely accused of murder, it was a necessary part of my investigation.

I had Mr. Pettyjohn summon the hotel's stagecoach driver.

A bear of a man, with a considerable paunch and a grizzled beard drove the coach up to the front of the hotel. "'Lo, Mrs. Pryce. Mine name's Paul Ellis." He greeted me as he helped me into the coach. "Pleasure to meet you. I am grieved to hear about your husband, ma'am. Please accept my condolences."

His mannerisms belied his looks. At first glance, he reminded me of a hardened and tough cowboy, but his gentle way and cultured speech said something different.

"Thank you, did you know William well?"

He gave a small nod. "Fairly. He used the coach quite a bit. We also went out on horseback. He wanted to learn every inch of this area, and he asked me to be his guide."

"Ah. I see."

"Where would you like to go today?"

"I'd like to see Prunella Bledsoe. Do you know where she lives?"

"Indeed I do." He closed the coach door. "It's a couple miles downriver. Pity about her husband, too. What a terrible mess."

"Yes. I'm going out to check on her and pay my respects."

"That's kind of you." He tipped his hat and then climbed up to the driver's seat.

A little niggle of guilt stabbed my gut at the white lie. But it didn't seem right to say I was actually going to her home to interrogate her about her husband's murder.

We made our way out of town from the opposite direction I had come days earlier with the sheriff. The road led onto a grassy plain. The sun shone brilliantly, warming the land, and a cool breeze filtered in through the window of the coach, bringing with it the calming aroma of pine. I took in the view of the majestic mountains surrounding us. The air was so clear, it was as if the trees on the mountainside were in miniature, and so close I could reach out and touch them. Billowing white clouds made their slow progression across the crystal blue sky.

I tilted my head out the window to take in more of the clean air. There was someone on horseback coming toward us. As the rider neared, I could see it was a man with long, flowing dark hair adorned with a single eagle feather. He wore a colorful, striped blanket wrapped around his shoulders. His face was round, and flat, and proud.

Mr. Ellis stopped the coach. He and the man exchanged a few words that I could not understand, and then we were off again.

I leaned out the window. "Who was that?"

"A man of the native tribe. They live along the river just over there." He pointed farther in the distance where several light-colored, conical structures were clustered. I had heard of the teepee but had never seen one.

"Fascinating," I said under my breath. "Are they friendly?" I had heard about the embittered wars fought between the white man and the Indians out here in the West.

"For the most part. If we show them respect. They were here long before us, you know. We invited ourselves into their home. The least we can do is to be gracious guests."

"Quite," I agreed.

We continued on and finally came upon a homestead surrounded by a rustic split rail fence that snaked around the property in a zigzag fashion. Mr. Ellis got down to open a gate to drive the coach through. After he'd done so and closed the gate again, we made our way to the house. It was a large, three-storied, salmon-colored structure with white gingerbread detailing, built in the Queen Anne–style with a steep roof, intersecting gables, dormers, and a wraparound porch.

"I won't be long," I said as Mr. Ellis helped me down from the coach.

He gave my hand a gentle squeeze. "Take your time."

A young woman in a black dress with a white pinafore and white cap on her head answered the door.

"I'm Arabella Pryce," I introduced myself. "Is Mrs. Bledsoe in?"

The girl showed me into the house. The interior of the home was as grand as the exterior. Mrs. Bledsoe had excellent taste.

She led me to a brightly lit room at the back of the house, built almost exclusively of glass. A sunroom. Greenery and floral blooms contrasted with the ruggedness of the mountain views through the windows. There were several pieces of white wicker furniture about, with fluffy, floral cushions, including a quaint little writing desk accompanied by a broad-backed chair that were placed against the floor-to-ceiling windows. What a lovely spot to pen correspondence, I thought.

I had to admit, I was envious of the sheer comfort and cheeriness of the dwelling. My rooms at the hotel seemed dreary in comparison.

Mrs. Bledsoe stood over one of the plants, which was elevated on a bronze-and-marble plant stand. She was picking off the dead blooms and placing them in a basket that hung from the crook of her elbow. She turned when she heard us enter.

"Mrs. Pryce to see you, ma'am," the girl said, and then she was gone.

Mrs. Bledsoe set down her basket and came over to me, her hands clasped at her waist. The familiar, saccharine scent of her jasmine perfume enveloped me. I wrinkled my nose.

"Hello, Mrs. Pryce." At closer inspection, her complexion

was sallow and dark moons hung below her eyes. She indeed looked like a grieving widow.

"I am so very sorry for your loss," I offered.

Her jaw tightened. "I'm told you found him," she said. I detected the hint of a southern accent.

"Yes, I—"

"Or rather, you were found hovering over his body with the letter opener in your hand."

I gulped and then raised my chin. I reminded myself I had nothing to be ashamed of. I had done nothing wrong.

"Yes. But please understand. I didn't kill your husband."

She considered me for an uncomfortable number of seconds that actually felt like minutes. "What can I do for you?" she finally asked.

"I am trying to find out exactly what happened. May I ask you some questions?"

Before she could answer, the girl entered the room again. Behind her was Sheriff Marshall.

"The sheriff, ma'am," the girl said and turned to leave.

"Claudia, wait." Mrs. Bledsoe raised her hand. "Bring some refreshments."

"Yes, ma'am." The girl gave a slight curtsy.

"Mrs. Bledsoe." Sheriff Marshall nodded. He then looked over at me. "Mrs. Pryce. What are you doing here?"

I detected a hint of suspicion in his voice.

"Simply paying a visit," I said, hoping I sounded sincere.

"She said she had questions about Daniel's death," Mrs. Bledsoe stated.

I winced at her bluntness, my feelings of guilt at my motives for being there raising their ugly heads.

The sheriff regarded me with a cynical lifting of his brows.

"I'm only trying to help. Why are you here?" I asked him.

He pressed his lips together in a tight smile, which seemed to indicate he did not feel the need to answer my question.

He turned to Mrs. Bledsoe. "Please accept my condolences."

"Thank you." She swallowed, blinking her eyes as if to keep back tears.

"I know this is a difficult time, but I, too, have some questions." He darted a look at me.

"Well," she said with a note of exasperation, "then we might as well sit down."

She led us over to a white wicker table surrounded by four chairs. The sheriff pulled one out for her.

As we settled ourselves in, the girl returned carrying a tray with three glasses, a ceramic pitcher, and a plate of biscuits.

"Here's your iced tea, ma'am." Claudia set the platter on the table and then poured for us. I hadn't realized how parched I had been until I saw the tea. I took a large sip and nearly choked. The tea was so sweet it made my back teeth ache.

The sheriff cleared his throat. "Mrs. Bledsoe, when did you last see your husband?"

"It was at the hotel."

"I know you occupy both households, Mrs. Bledsoe," he continued. "Were you staying there with him at hotel at the time?"

Her lips twitched, and she looked down at her hands in her lap. "No. I was there to gather some of my things to bring back here to the house."

"What time was that?" I asked.

The sheriff darted another look of annoyance at me.

She pressed her lips together. "It was around seven o'clock."

My heartbeat sped up. That had been just about two hours before I'd found him and right around the time he'd left me in the saloon.

"Was everything . . . all right between you two?" I asked gently.

Her forehead pinched, deepening the crease between her eyebrows. "I don't see how that is any of your business."

"Mrs. Pryce," the sheriff broke in, holding up a hand to silence me. "Please."

Irritated, I blinked at him, the back of my neck prickling.

He turned his attention back to Mrs. Bledsoe. "How was Daniel that evening?"

"He was upset." Her eyes shifted to me. "Angry."

"Angry about what?" the sheriff asked.

"Her." She nodded in my direction, and I squirmed in my seat.

"Do you know why?" the sheriff continued.

He knew why and I knew why, I thought with a twinge of regret at my argument with Mr. Bledsoe.

"He said that she was intolerable." She glared at me, and there was an edge of bitterness to her voice.

Intolerable? Really? I think not.

"Did you see anyone else on the third floor around the time you were with your husband?" the sheriff continued.

"No."

"What about when you left? Was there anyone nearby?"

"No."

I let out an exasperated sigh. This was getting nowhere. "Mrs. Bledsoe, do you know of anyone who might wish to do your husband harm?" I interjected.

From the corner of my eye, I could see Sheriff Marshall's jaw tense.

Mrs. Bledsoe turned her gaze to me. "He and the young Mr. Archer, Andrew, had words."

"When was this?" the sheriff asked.

"About a week ago. The young man came here. Pounded on the door like he would break it down. Daniel went outside with him. I could hear shouting but couldn't entirely make out what they were arguing about. I heard the young man mention that—" Her mouth turned downward in distaste. "That girl. His fiancée. Narcissa Platte."

"Why would they be arguing about her?" I asked.

Her mouth twitched again. "I have no idea. But Andrew threatened my husband. They nearly came to blows. Thank goodness our farmhand stopped him. Threw that ruffian off the property."

"Mrs. Bledsoe, how well did your husband know Miss Platte?" I asked.

Her face went stony, except for her small, dark eyes, which blinked rapidly. "She was a resident at the hotel. He knew her as well as any of the residents, I suppose," she said flatly.

"Are you sure?" I pressed.

The sheriff slowly turned his head toward me. I didn't look at him but could feel his blue-eyed gaze scorching through me. He really shouldn't have been so vexed with me. I was only trying to help him stop painstakingly beating about the bush.

"What are you implying?" Mrs. Platte ground out.

"You said Mr. Bledsoe and Andrew were arguing about her. I'm just trying to find out why."

Her eyes narrowed. "I've told you, I don't know."

"Do you take stock in the rumors that your husband had a relationship with Miss Platte? Do you think that is what your husband and Andrew were arguing about?" I asked.

Her mouth dropped, and she gasped. "I beg your pardon?"

"Mrs. Pryce—" the sheriff broke in, but I pressed on.

"If the rumors are true, don't you think that would make Andrew angry? And if you knew about it—"

Her face contorted in rage. "How dare you!"

"Mrs. Pryce!" The sheriff reached out and laid his hand on my forearm.

"Get out of my house." Mrs. Bledsoe pointed her finger toward a glass door that led to the backyard.

"I apologize, Mrs. Bledsoe. I—" Sheriff Marshall said in an attempt to calm her.

"You too! Get out!" She stood up from her chair, reached for a hand bell on the table, and rang it furiously. In seconds, the maid appeared.

"Show them out," Mrs. Bledsoe demanded. Still holding the

THE PRYCE OF CONCEIT 185

bell in her hand, she pointed it toward the door. The girl, her eyes wide, went to it and opened it.

I glanced up at Sheriff Marshall, whose face was like a thundercloud. Swallowing, I ducked my head and headed for the door. As I passed by the wicker desk, I spotted a writing set on the corner of it and stopped in my tracks. The set was made of mother-of-pearl and silver filigree, and consisted of an inkwell, ink blotter, wax tool, seal, ink pen, and fountain pen. It was the exact pattern of the instrument that had killed Daniel Bledsoe. And this set was missing something. The letter opener.

"Ma'am?" The maid held her arm aloft toward the open door.

Stunned at my discovery, I looked at her blankly and then turned to Mrs. Bledsoe. "This is beautiful," I said, nodding toward the writing set.

Mrs. Bledsoe folded her hands at her waist. "It was a gift from my husband."

"But the——" I was about to mention the missing letter opener when the sheriff took me by the elbow.

"Let's go," Sheriff Marshall said sharply.

Once outside, I whirled around to face him. "Didn't you see that?"

"See what?"

"The writing set?"

"What are you talking about?"

I pointed back toward the sunroom. Mrs. Bledsoe and the girl were still standing there, Mrs. Bledsoe glowering at us.

With my elbow in his grip, the sheriff marched me around the corner of the house so that we were out of view. "Now what are you going on about?" he asked.

"The letter opener was missing. That writing set was exactly the same style as the letter opener that killed Mr. Bledsoe. We need to ask her about it."

"I don't think now is the time," he said.

"Why not? It's the perfect time!"

"The woman threw us out of her house. We need to let her

cool down a bit. I don't think she'll be compelled to answer any more questions at the moment."

"Because she is probably guilty," I whispered loudly.

"You insulted the woman." He let go of my arm and placed his hands on his hips.

I took in a deep breath, trying to steady my racing pulse. "She clearly knew something about her husband and Narcissa," I said as calmly as I could. "And she admitted she'd been in her husband's rooms at the hotel near the time he died. And the letter opener of her *matching* writing set is missing."

"That doesn't mean she killed him."

"But don't you think it's suspicious? It seems pretty clear she was the last person to see her husband alive."

"Not necessarily."

I blinked up at him. "What do you mean?"

"Andrew was seen coming down the stairs around the time of Bledsoe's death."

"What? By whom?" My heart sank at the news.

"I can't say."

"That's not proof," I insisted. "Although . . ."

I hesitated, deciding if I should mention Andrew's buckskin coat and Maggie's confession that he had also been in the hotel at the time of Narcissa's murder. I didn't want to say anything. Despite the fact that my neck was on the line, I found myself moved by Maggie and Andrew's story. But if he was the murderer, could I live with myself if I withheld information from the sheriff?

"Although what?"

I took in a deep breath. "Remember when the couple who found Narcissa mentioned a man wearing a buckskin coat leaving the second floor?"

He nodded. "I do."

I told him what I knew.

"Why didn't you tell me before?" the sheriff asked.

"I'm telling you now."

We stood staring at each other in some kind of standoff, his indigo gaze rooting me to the spot.

"But I still think Mrs. Bledsoe is suspect," I said finally. "I'm going to go back and ask her about the letter opener."

I turned to go, and he grabbed my arm again and yanked me back—a bit too hard. I slammed into his chest, knocking him off-balance. To save himself from falling backward, his arms went around me, clenching me in an embrace so tight my forehead grazed the stubble on his chin. I looked up into his face, and our gazes locked. He smelled of leather and spice, and his arms felt solid and true.

Time stood still. His eyes traveled to my mouth, and I could've sworn he was about to kiss me. Then suddenly he released me, and I had the sensation of being adrift, lost and unanchored in myself.

"I, um, I'm sorry," he said, backing away from me. He was clearly as flustered as I had been that first day when the dog had knocked us to the ground in front of the hotel. I found his boyish embarrassment endearing.

"Seems you can't get enough of me." I smiled.

Queenie whinnied in the distance and came hurriedly trotting toward us as if she wanted to break us apart. She halted at his shoulder.

"Well, I guess I'd best get back to town," he said, taking up the reins hanging loosely around the horse's neck.

"Toodle-oo." I waved my fingers at him, thinking that as soon as he left, I'd go back to ask Mrs. Bledsoe about the letter opener.

"But not until I see you to your coach," he added, holding his arm toward it. "After you."

I wrinkled my nose at him and marched toward the coach. I'd just have to find another opportunity to question Daniel Bledsoe's widow.

CHAPTER 21

The following morning as I sat at the desk in the parlor drinking my tea and skimming over Miss Chatterley's tabloid, I thought about the conversations I'd had with Andrew and Maggie, the visit to Mrs. Bledsoe, and my intimate encounter with the sheriff. I smiled at the remembrance. But I was being silly. The man and I had absolutely nothing in common. And my life was in New York.

"It's unseemly. That cowboy sheriff is beneath you." My mother's voice popped into my head, confirming my previous thought that Sheriff Marshall and I had nothing in common. Or was it that I felt that way because of how my mother had preconditioned me with her overbearing opinions?

I hadn't spoken to her since William died, and only then because she had insisted on coming to the funeral. Instead of mourning my husband, though, she had taken the opportunity to try to weasel her way back into my career. She had not been successful. After that, I had refused to see her.

I dismissed the voice. I had more important things to think about than my mother or my romantic life.

Romantic life? I nearly laughed out loud at myself. I didn't have the time or the inclination for such things.

"You seem amused about something."

I looked up into the mirror to see Percival sitting on the love seat behind me, one leg crossed over the other.

"It's nothing," I said, waving my hand in the air.

"Making progress on your investigations?" He took out his pipe, and the familiar spicy aroma instantly filled the room.

"I think so." A pang of worry shot through my stomach at telling the sheriff about Andrew's presence in the hotel on the night of Narcissa's murder. It still didn't feel right that he'd committed the crimes.

"Really? What kind of progress?"

I told him about Mrs. Bledsoe and the writing set.

"So you and the sheriff went out to the Bledsoe place together?"

I blinked at the question. Why did that matter?

"No," I said. "We met there. It was quite by accident."

"I see." He seemed satisfied with that answer and puffed on his pipe. "I am inclined to agree with you about Mrs. Bledsoe. Having observed her and her husband, it seemed they were always quarreling about something. I don't know how the man could stand it."

I pulled back my chin, affronted. "How *he* could stand it? I know that Prunella Bledsoe is not an agreeable sort, but by all accounts, her husband was not faithful. Perhaps that was what they argued about. Hell hath no fury and all."

"So you think she killed her husband?" He opened his mouth, and several smoke rings floated out.

"I believe she may have."

He finished his exhale. "And Sheriff Marshall doesn't agree?"

"I think he just needs something a bit more concrete than conjecture."

"Ah . . . Where is the letter opener now?"

"I don't know. The last time I saw it was when I found Mr. Bledsoe dead in his rooms. I suppose either the sheriff or the doctor has it."

"Did you ask the sheriff?"

"No. I . . . I didn't get the chance."

After our little moment, the sheriff couldn't seem to get away from me fast enough. He nearly pushed me into the coach and gave implicit instructions to Mr. Ellis to take me back to the hotel immediately.

"But what if I don't want to go back to the hotel?" I had said to him through the coach window, affronted that he had the nerve to dictate where I went and when. I had wanted to go back to speak with Mrs. Bledsoe again.

"Then I will have to deputize Mr. Ellis and treat you as a prisoner. You are still a suspect."

The words had been like a dagger to my stomach. He still wasn't entirely convinced I was innocent. I withered at the notion.

Percival cleared his throat quite loudly.

Realizing I had been staring into space, I blinked and then stood up from the chair to physically distance myself from the girlish musings over a man I had no business being interested in.

"Where are you going?" Percival asked.

"Mrs. Bledsoe is still at the top of my list of murder suspects, but there is someone else I need to speak with. Mrs. Gilroy. She said that her son had been courting Narcissa before he left town."

"Ah. And don't forget about the pregnancy," Percival added.

"Yes. You don't suppose that Seth and Narcissa had . . . well, you know?" I circled my hand in the air, not wanting to be unladylike and give voice to the subject of Narcissa's intimate love life in mixed company.

Percival frowned. "I suppose it's possible. She obviously slept with someone."

I balked at his frankness but realized he only spoke what I myself had intimated.

"Yes," I agreed. "Had things perhaps gone too far with Seth before their breakup?"

"How far along was she? Do you know?" he asked.

"About four months. Mrs. Gilroy said that her son left town sometime after that."

I recalled Narcissa's body lying at the foot of the stairs. "At the time of her death, I never would have suspected that she was pregnant," I said. "But her voluptuousness, as well as tight corseting, might have made it easier to hide. Still, it would stand to reason she couldn't have been more than twelve to sixteen weeks along at the most."

"So, if you are correct, Seth could have been the father. Perhaps that is why he left? He wasn't ready for the responsibility," Percival mused.

"I don't know. At any rate, Mrs. Gilroy had been pretty upset about his leaving."

"Maybe she wanted to make Narcissa pay for driving her son away?"

"Could be. That's why I want to speak with her again." I grabbed my hat, which had been sitting on the desk, and arranged it carefully on my head.

"Oh, before I go, you mentioned that you saw the bellhop, Clarence, in my rooms. Have you seen him recently?"

He shook his head. "No. But I have discovered something of interest."

"Really? Pertaining to the murders?"

"Perhaps."

"Well?" I wished he would get on with it. "What have you found?"

"Rats. More dead rats."

A prick of irritation arose. "What does that have to do with the murders? Have you been up to your tricks again, Percival?"

"No. When I was returning from a sojourn down by the river, I saw some dead rats in the rubbish bin outside at the back of the hotel."

"Ugh!" I didn't want to be reminded. "The infestation. Obviously, Maggie had poisoned them and disposed of them. What of it?"

"These rats did not look like they'd been poisoned. They were bloody and had deep wounds, as if they'd been skewered."

I wrinkled my nose in disgust. "Again, Percival, what does this have to do with the murders?"

"Have you forgotten about the fireplace poker?" he asked. "Didn't the sheriff say that in addition to the sticky substance, he'd seen short, light-colored hairs on it?"

"Yes . . . And? Oh!" I finally caught on. "You think someone used the fireplace poker to kill the rats? Not Narcissa?"

He shrugged a shoulder. "Could be. If Mrs. Bledsoe *is* guilty, perhaps she used the letter opener to kill both victims."

I supposed it could be possible. "Thank you, Percival."

While this line of logic was, indeed, food for thought, I wasn't sure how it would help me in the moment. We still knew nothing for sure.

"And there is one more thing, dear." He turned over the bowl of his pipe, and the ash shimmered out into the air. "There are still two possible suspects you have not queried at all."

"Oh? Who?"

"Mr. and Mrs. Platte."

My chin dropped in surprise. "The Plattes? You think one of them is responsible for the murders? That they would kill their own daughter?"

He shrugged again.

I shook my head. "No. They had too much riding on Narcissa and her future. Why go to all the trouble of arranging a marriage for her?" I secured the hat to my coiffure with a hat pin.

"But what about Bledsoe?" he asked. "If he killed Narcissa, and they knew about it . . ."

"But he couldn't have. He was with Sally Dean at the time of Narcissa's murder."

THE PRYCE OF CONCEIT   193

"He could have been a threat to Narcissa and Andrew's impeding nuptials."

"That would mean they killed him after Narcissa was already dead. That doesn't make sense. Besides, I think the sheriff spoke to them at length. And I doubt they'd want to speak with me, seeing as Mrs. Platte thinks I had some vendetta against her daughter."

He turned both palms up. "The sheriff might have missed something. Could be worth your while."

"Very well. I'll think about it."

"And what about young Andrew?" he asked. I got the distinct impression he was trying to stall my departure. He'd never been so chatty before, but I was anxious to go.

I sighed. "The buckskin coat and what Andrew and Maggie revealed to me definitely make Andrew look guilty of one, if not both, of the murders. But I have no real evidence, only motive for any one of my suspects. But I hate to think that Andrew would have killed either one of them. I like him."

"You need to trust your instincts." He folded his hands at his waist.

I don't know why, but I was taken aback by his comment. Not in a bad way. His words made me feel assured. I supposed it was because no one had ever said them to me before. I had never been encouraged to take my own counsel, although I always did anyway. It was then I realized that I had always been told what to think, by my mother primarily, but also, to some degree, by William.

My thoughts were interrupted by a knock at the door that sent Bijou into a rousing chorus of barking. Percival vanished from the mirror.

"Hush, girl!" I scolded. Though it was nearly nine a.m., it was still early by some accounts and I didn't want her disturbing the guests.

I answered the door to find Sheriff Marshall standing there.

Upon seeing me, he swiped his hat off his head. He did not look me in the eye.

Heat rose up my neck and into my face. "Good morning," I greeted him, trying to ignore the flutter in my stomach. Really, this was ridiculous.

"Mrs. Pryce." He finally regarded me with his bright gaze. "I hope I'm not disturbing you."

"Not at all. Do come in." I said in my most business-like voice. I opened the door wider to let him through.

"I'd like speak with you about Daniel Bledsoe." His gaze shifted to his hat in his hands.

"Again? I was just going out," I said.

"It will only take a moment," he assured me.

I nodded, then gestured toward the love seat. "Please, sit down. Would you like some tea?" I really didn't want to take the time to pour any. Besides, it was probably cold at this point, but I thought it rude not to ask.

"Um, no. Thank you. Don't care much for tea." He lowered himself to the love seat. He was so tall and so long, he practically dwarfed it, looking a bit like Alice in the house she'd grown too large for in *Alice's Adventures in Wonderland.* I suppressed an amused smile and took the chair perpendicular to him. "Very well."

"I'll just get to the point, Mrs. Pryce. There have been several accounts from people in the saloon on the night of Mr. Bledsoe's murder—the night the two of you argued—that you threatened him."

I scoffed, that dagger again piercing my stomach. Or was it my heart? It didn't matter. It still hurt.

It must have shown on my face because before I could respond, he raised a placating hand. "I'm just trying to find out what happened."

I sucked air in through my nose, trying to steady myself. "This is insulting, Sheriff Marshall. Why on earth would I want to kill Daniel Bledsoe? There are plenty of others who knew him much better than I. Plenty of others who had motive. Why aren't you talking to them? Am I such an easy target? The new woman in town that everyone despises?"

He pulled back his chin in surprise. I hadn't meant to sound so defensive. I quickly gathered my wits about me again.

"What about Mrs. Bledsoe and the letter opener?" I arched an eyebrow.

"I went back last evening and asked her about it. She said her husband had misplaced his and asked if he could take hers to the hotel. So that's how it got there."

"Well, she would say that, wouldn't she, if she were the guilty party?"

He didn't answer but simply looked at me, his expression dubious.

I raised my chin to cover the anxiety rising in my chest. "Who said I threatened Daniel Bledsoe?"

"According to these accounts, you said, and I quote, 'I want you gone.'"

I slapped my hands against my thighs. "Well, yes, I did say that, but not that I wanted him 'gone' as in dead. I was angry. I meant, I wanted him 'gone' as in fired."

"So you fired him?"

I thought back to our argument. "No. Not really. Not officially. Like I told you before, I was angry at the neglected condition of the hotel. I spoke out when I shouldn't have. It was a conversation that should have happened in private."

I neglected to tell him that I had basically accused Daniel Bledsoe of being the father of Narcissa's baby—and her killer, which was the real reason he'd been so angry at me.

"In truth, I didn't really want to fire him. I needed him to help me get the hotel back to its former glory. Like my husband and Mr. Blank had intended for it to be. Again, I ask you, why would I kill him?"

"It runs deeper than that." He set his mouth in a hard line.

"It does? In what way?"

"Because of Bledsoe, you stood to lose the hotel."

"Excuse me?" That made no sense to me at all. "How would that be possible?"

We sat, our gazes locked for some time. It was as if he was trying to decide if I truly didn't know what he was talking about, which of course, I didn't. I could think of no reason why Daniel Bledsoe would be a factor in whether I maintained ownership of the hotel or not.

"There is a lien against the hotel," he said eventually.

"What? What are you talking about?"

"Bledsoe had some repairs made several months ago. Quite extensive. He hired a construction company to do the work. He neglected to pay the bills so they filed a lien against the hotel. If the bills aren't paid, the hotel goes to said construction company."

"But how would my killing Mr. Bledsoe help?"

"He has sole financial authority over the hotel's accounts at Archer's Savings & Loan. You do not. With him out of the way, as the hotel's owner, you would be able to claim the accounts."

"What?!" This was like some kind of unending nightmare. "Why Archer's bank? My husband set up the hotel's accounts in New York and then sent funds to Mr. Bledsoe for the running of the hotel. Unless—" My stomach caved in on itself.

Unless he'd appropriated the funds to start new accounts.

He'd been stealing from the hotel. My voice froze in my throat, and I couldn't speak.

"I don't like to say this, Mrs. Pryce, but that seems like a strong motive for murder to me."

I shot up from the chair, my pulse throbbing in my ears. "Are you serious?

He looked up at me with, dare I say, a crestfallen expression. "I'm afraid so."

Nearly unable to breathe, I paced the floor in front of the coffee table and attempted to draw air into my lungs.

This wasn't happening. Bledsoe had as much as admitted the

hotel "couldn't afford" to pay the bills. And what repairs? I had seen no evidence of any. Yes, he had taken the money and set up accounts in the hotel's name. And yes, it was definitely a motive for murder.

I stopped and looked over at the sheriff, who was watching me intently. I went over to the love seat and sat next to him, our knees touching.

"You have absolutely no evidence against me. Only conjecture." I stated flatly.

"I know. But, I need to take this information into consideration."

"I knew nothing of this lien," I said. "Or these accounts. You have to believe me."

His deep blue gaze searched mine.

"Well, say something!" I pleaded. "You don't really think I could do something so conniving, do you?"

How could he look like he wants to kiss me one day and then think me capable of murder the next? He still hadn't said anything. Was I getting through to him?

He sat there, mute, which spoke volumes. I couldn't ignore the wave of pain coursing through me.

"I don't even want to be here!" I shouted. "I could care less about this hotel, this town, and everyone in it! I wish I had never set foot in La Plata Springs!"

The injustice of it all seized me in its grip. What had I done to William for him to punish me so? To make me pay for simply being myself? Yes, I enjoyed the finer things in life and yes, I enjoyed the adoration of others. It might even be possible that I can be a bit full of myself, but did I really deserve this?

CHAPTER 22

"Either arrest me or leave." I narrowed my eyes at the sheriff.

"I'm not going to arrest you . . . for now," he said, rising from the love seat. "But I'll say it again: don't leave town, Mrs. Pryce."

I screwed up my mouth and blinked, fighting back angry tears. I was ready to go on a tirade but held my tongue and, instead, showed him to the door. Little did Sheriff Marshall know, I was already serving an unjust sentence. I had half a mind to leave my inheritance behind and take the next train out of La Plata Springs. I had a viable career. I could support myself.

You don't have a head for business, Arabella. Never have. Stick to what you do best.

My mother's voice penetrated my thoughts. Even though I had taken a much larger role in the business concerns of my career, I had never wholly managed my own financial affairs. My mother and William had always taken care of that. And, now I had Mr. Tisdale and Mr. Blackstone back in New York managing things for me. If I walked away from the hotel and my inheritance, I could very well be completely lost.

I sighed, realizing it would be easier just to bide my time, carry out my sentence, and then hire a new manager for the hotel, sell the damned place and go back to New York.

The fact remained: I was stuck here.

"I believe you." A voice broke the silence. Percival had appeared again. "And I believe you will get to the bottom of this, Arabella." His eyes were soft, and a warm smile lit up his features. I had not yet seen such tenderness in him, and it moved me.

"Thank you," I managed, making my mind up to refuse to let this beat me down. "I will carry on."

"You will," he assured me.

The front door opened, and he popped out with a snap of his fingers like the flip of a switch.

It was Cordelia and Bijou returning from Bijou's morning constitutional. Maggie was behind them with a bucket and broom to clean out the ash from the fireplace.

Cordelia removed her hat. "What a lovely day it is."

Her eyes were lit up like the sunrise. She seemed to be taking to life in these wilds. I didn't understand it. She never much liked to be outdoors. It would take all I had to get her to ride a bicycle with me through Central Park.

"You really should take the air, Arabella," she said. "You look a little pale. Are you feeling all right?"

"I'm fine." I straightened my blouse. "I'm going to visit Mrs. Gilroy. Care to join me?"

"I'd better take care of some of your correspondence. I'm afraid I've gotten behind. But I'll fetch your coat for you."

"Thank you. By the way, has Clarence returned?"

"No."

"I hope he's recovering. Perhaps I will pay him a visit as well." I turned to Maggie, who had knelt down next to the fireplace. "Do you know where his mother lives?"

She faced me. "His mother?"

"Yes. His mother sent Mr. Pettyjohn a note saying the boy was ill."

"Clarence doesn't have a mother," she said. "She died two years ago. His dad up and left after that. He lives alone."

"Really? Well then who wrote the note?"

"Don't know, ma'am. Maybe Mr. Pettyjohn was confused. He goes a little batty sometimes."

"Does he?" That didn't instill much confidence. He'd seemed fine before. Was I going to have to find yet another employee to run the front desk, as well as additional maids and now a hotel manager? Hopefully one who wouldn't swindle me. I swallowed the feeling of overwhelm rising from my gut.

"Not all the time, ma'am," she said with an assuring smile.

"Oh dear," I said on a sigh.

Downstairs at the reception desk, I found Mr. Pettyjohn sorting through some papers. He was so focused on his task, he didn't hear me approach.

"Good morning, Mr. Pettyjohn."

Taken by surprise, he jumped. "Oh, good morning, madam."

I gave him a prim smile, in no uncertain terms showing him my displeasure at his greeting.

"Oh, I mean, Mrs. Pryce," he said.

I nodded in acceptance of his correction. "Mr. Pettyjohn, the other day you mentioned that Clarence's mother wrote you a note claiming the boy was ill."

"Yes, she did."

"Maggie made mention that the boy has no mother. She died two years ago."

His brows pinched down over his nose in confusion. "Did she?"

"Do you still have the note, Mr. Pettyjohn?"

"I believe I do." He opened the drawer to his right and pulled out a piece of paper. "Here you go."

I took the note from him and gasped. It was written in the same leftward sloping hand as the letter that had been found in my desk drawer! Narcissa's handwriting. But that wasn't possible

. . . She had already been dead when the sheriff took the note out of the drawer. How could she have written this note days later?

"Oh my goodness!" I pressed my fingers to my mouth. "This is proof that Narcissa did not write the note to William," I said under my breath.

"I beg your pardon, ma—Mrs. Pryce?" Mr. Pettyjohn blinked up at me.

"I have to go see the sheriff," I said. "And then I need to find Clarence. Do you know where he lives?"

"I've heard him mention Masterson Grove, downriver, a time or two. But I'm not certain that is where he resides."

"How far is it?"

"A few miles to the south of us, Mrs. Pryce."

"Thank you, Mr. Pettyjohn."

The street was already busy that morning with people out on their errands. As usual, they nodded to me in greeting but still looked a bit stiff in my presence. It would definitely take some time for me to ingratiate myself to the townsfolk, if I could at all.

Perhaps, I would throw a party at the hotel once the matter of the two murders was resolved. Everyone loves a party. I would *make* them like me—after, of course, I proved my innocence. And got the accounts sorted out at the bank because once this was all over, I would be sending a wire to my solicitor to claim those accounts at Archer's bank. To do so now would only make me look guilty.

As I was walking past the hotel, I spotted Mr. Archer and Mr. Brooks standing in front of said bank, Archer's Savings & Loan. A knife of fear cut through my chest. If Atticus Brooks learned what I just had about the hotel's accounts, and that I did not have access to them, he might come to the same conclusion the sheriff had: I had even more motive to kill Bledsoe. The thought made my stomach ache.

The man lived to see me squirm. Perhaps he had written the

letter found in my desk, put Clarence up to planting it, and then had done something to Clarence to keep him quiet and sent the note to give to Mr. Pettyjohn. Could he be that devious? For once I wished I could see that incriminatory notepad. I certainly couldn't ask to see it. He'd never willingly comply to a request from me. But the sheriff could certainly ask.

I crossed the street in an attempt to avoid the pair, but I was not successful.

"Mrs. Pryce!" Mr. Archer called out.

I stopped and slowly turned around, fixing a well-rehearsed smile on my face. He beckoned me over. Reluctantly, I crossed the street again and stepped up onto the boardwalk.

"You're looking fine this morning," he said, his eyes bright.

"Thank you," I said. "Good morning."

Bijou, excited at the opportunity for making new friendships, stood on her hind legs and pawed at Mr. Archer's shins.

"Hello," he said with a chuckle and bent down to ruffle her ears. She yipped with pleasure. "How is your investigation going?" he asked, straightening.

My eyes shifted to Mr. Brooks who regarded me with a wry grin, as if he could see right through me. The man made my skin crawl. I tried my best to keep my paranoid thoughts at bay.

"Well," I answered, "I was just going to the sheriff with an important development."

"Really? What is this development?" Mr. Brooks asked in an infuriatingly condescending tone, pulling his pad of paper from his coat pocket. My heart lurched. If only I could see it!

His face had broken into an oily smile that I couldn't quite make sense of. My emotions were too raw and I felt like a crystal vase that had developed a crack that would cause me to shatter. But I couldn't allow him the satisfaction of witnessing my fragility.

I stiffened my spine. "I'm not yet ready to discuss it."

I certainly didn't want to divulge anything to Mr. Brooks for his infernal story. Had he done any investigating at all, or was he merely listening to gossip on the street or in Bella's Saloon?

"But rest assured," I continued, "I am making progress."

"And what about Daniel Bledsoe?" he asked, scribbling something on his pad. "What about his murder? You were seen holding the murder weapon when—"

My stomach twisted into a knot.

Turning her attentions to Mr. Brooks, Bijou growled and then barked, making him flinch. She took hold of his pant leg with her teeth and tugged. I did nothing to stop her.

"Go away," he said, kicking at her. She did not relent, and he bent down to push her off him, giving me a view of the notepad. The handwriting on it was a nearly illegible scrawl, and it looked nothing like the script on the letter or Clarence's note.

The revelation left me with mixed feelings. So Atticus Brooks wasn't trying to frame me for murder. He was just delighting in the fact that someone else was.

"Come now, Atticus!" Mr. Archer stepped in. "You can't be serious, man. Why in the world would Mrs. Pryce want to kill Bledsoe? Put that pad of paper away. I insist!"

Bijou barked furiously, and not wanting her more upset, I shushed her.

It seemed that the lien on the hotel, and Mr. Bledsoe's fraudulent accounts, were unknown to Mr. Archer. I recalled that Mr. Bledsoe also had worked for him at the General. Had he defrauded Mr. Archer, too? And using his own bank? If so, the deviousness was astounding. I wanted to ask Mr. Archer about it but not with Mr. Brooks there. And not until I had proof of my innocence.

I refused to look at Mr. Brooks with that disturbing smile on his face and his damning questions. But since I had Mr. Archer there, I thought I would ask him about Andrew.

"Mr. Archer, how is your nephew holding up?"

The muscles in his jaw twitched. "He's— Well—" He gave

Atticus Brooks a sideways glance. "The sheriff came and got him this morning. He's in jail."

My heart fell to the pit of my stomach. "But why?" I asked, even though I knew. The sheriff must have arrested him for one or both of the murders.

"Bet that tickles *you* pink." Mr. Brooks smirked at me. Oh, yes, he was determined to see me guilty.

I glared at him. "It doesn't." In fact, it made me feel rather sick.

I turned to Mr. Archer, choosing to ignore the embittered writer. "I don't believe Andrew killed Mr. Bledsoe. I believe that whoever killed him may have also killed Narcissa, but as I've said, I'm not convinced it's Andrew. Are you aware that Narcissa and Mr. Bledsoe had a romantic relationship?"

Mr. Archer's face reddened, and a vein at his temple pulsed. "If you'll excuse me, Mrs. Pryce. I must go. Good day." He tipped his hat to me and walked away, leaving me in the sour company of Mr. Brooks, who, after a moment of staring me down, also took his leave.

I watched Mr. Archer walk down the street, his head bowed, his steps quick.

It seemed I had hit a nerve.

⚜

The Sheriff's Office and jail stood at the at the end of the main street, set apart from the other buildings. Outside, tied to the hitching rail, Queenie was taking a snooze.

I entered to find the sheriff seated at his desk, which was strewn with papers. Across the room stood two cells, one occupied by Andrew Archer who sat on the cot, his elbows perched on his knees and his head in his hands, the other, empty.

The sheriff looked up from his work when I entered. "Mrs. Pryce," he said, rising from his chair. "What can I do for you?"

"I've discovered something that I believe is integral to the case."

The sheriff glanced over at Andrew and then took me by the elbow and led me back outside so that we might speak in private.

I took the note from my reticule once again and handed it to him. "Look at the handwriting."

Immediately, recognition flashed on his face. "Hold on a minute," he said. He went back into his office and then returned with another piece of paper. It was the letter that had been left in my drawer. "It's identical."

"Yes. This is a note that Mr. Pettyjohn received when Clarence didn't turn up for work. It's signed Beatrice Hays, but she's been dead for two years."

"So Narcissa couldn't have written the letter to your husband."

"Exactly! Whoever wrote these notes, wrote them *after* Narcissa was killed. Someone is playing a game here. Furthermore, we haven't seen Clarence at the hotel for a couple of days."

"He might know something about one or both of the murders."

"That's what I think, too. I hope nothing has happened to him." Then I added, "Why is Andrew in a cell? Did you find more evidence against him?"

"Not exactly. He's here because he and his uncle had an altercation over at the General. The boy lost his mind and attacked Archer. The display of violence doesn't help his case."

"No, it doesn't. And it doesn't help mine, either, does it?" I quipped, still insulted and a little hurt at the sheriff's doubts about my innocence.

He bit his lip and looked away from me. Immediately, I regretted my sarcasm. I needed his help. It wouldn't do to give him more reason to doubt or dislike me. Although, I was surprised that he would listen to me or discuss the case with me at all given the circumstances. It gave me a sliver of hope that he might not think me completely evil and capable of murder.

"Do you know what they were fighting about?" I asked.

"Neither of them would say. One of the witnesses said it had something to do with Archer's plans for Andrew. Another said they heard something regarding the murders, but they couldn't remember what."

"I see. Did you ask him why he was at the hotel on the nights of both murders?"

The sheriff nodded. "He said he went to check on Maggie—she was late for dinner—but he didn't know anything about either murder until after the fact."

"Do you believe him?"

"At this point, I'm not sure what I believe, Mrs. Pryce."

No wonder Mr. Archer hadn't answered my question as to why Andrew was in jail. I felt for the young man. He was trapped beneath the overpowering thumb of his uncle. I wasn't surprised at the outburst. A person can only take so much.

"I wonder if he wrote these letters," the sheriff said under his breath.

"Why on earth would Andrew want to frame me for Narcissa's murder? That makes no sense."

"Well there is one way to find out." The sheriff went back into the office, and I followed closely behind. He took a piece of paper and a pen from his desk and a book from the shelf and held them out to Andrew through the bars. "Write something for me. Just a sentence or two."

A look of confusion crossed Andrew's face. "What for?"

"Just do it please."

Andrew got up from the cot and took the items. Setting the paper on top of the book, he scrawled some words and then handed it all back to the sheriff. I peered over Sheriff Marshall's shoulder.

He had written, *Let me out of here please.*

I stifled a grin. The handwriting was slanted to the right, with small, tight letters. Almost the exact opposite of the other notes.

The sheriff and I exchanged a glance.

"Thank you, Andrew," he said.

"There is one more thing, Sheriff," I said. "I'm not sure it pertains to the case, but—" "Go on."

I told him about the dead rats and their condition in the trash bin at the back of the hotel. "Do you think it's possible the blood on the fireplace poker is rat's blood?" I asked.

He rubbed his chin in thought. "I suppose so. We could talk to the doc about it."

"That won't be necessary," Andrew, still standing at the front of the cell, piped in.

"What do you mean?" I asked.

He bit his lip, hesitating.

"Speak up, son," Sheriff Marshall said.

"It was rat's blood."

"How do you know?" I asked.

He took in a deep breath. "Because I killed those rats. Like I told the sheriff before, the night Narcissa was killed, I'd gone to check on Maggie. One of the hotel guests, who had been staying in a room on the second floor had complained of rats in their room. They checked out and went over to the General. Anyway, poor Maggie was crying—said she couldn't keep up with the workload as it was, much less take care of the rats. I told her I'd take care of it, at least the rats in that particular room."

"So you used the fireplace poker from my room to kill them?"

He nodded.

"But Cordelia and I were in our rooms. How did you even get the fireplace poker?"

"Maggie was going up there to put one last log on the fire— to keep the place warm. You must have been asleep."

It was true, both Cordelia and I had been exhausted.

"Why didn't you mention this before?" the sheriff asked.

"Well, I told you I was there, Sheriff, to visit Maggie. I just didn't mention the rats because—"

"Because?" I prodded.

"Maggie was already in trouble with Mr. Pettyjohn. I don't work in the hotel so I shouldn't have been in that room. Please, Mrs. Pryce, she's working ever so hard. I hope I didn't just get her into more trouble."

"How did the fireplace poker end up in the annex?" the sheriff asked.

"When she saw what a mess it was, she told me to leave it back there and she'd clean it, but I guess she forgot about it. Then when you noticed it missing from Mrs. Pryce's room and thought it could be the murder weapon, she hid it." He looked over at me. "She didn't want to get you in trouble, ma'am. Nor did she want anyone to know I'd been in that room to kill the rats. She panicked. She's terrified of losing her job."

I gave him a brief smile. While touched at Maggie's concern for me, I wished she had just come out and told the truth about Andrew killing the rats. It would have at least solved one mystery.

"Well that answers the question about the fireplace poker, but why were you at the hotel the night of Mr. Bledsoe's murder?" I asked.

"Same reason. To help Maggie." He darted a look at the sheriff. "But I didn't kill him. I swear."

The sheriff gave a brief nod and then walked over to the chair at his desk, removed his gun belt from the arm of it, and placed it around his hips. "I'll be back in a while."

"So when are you going to let me out of here?" Andrew asked him.

"When I feel that you've cooled down."

"Where are you going?" I asked the sheriff.

"I'm going to find Clarence."

"I want to go with you," I said.

He gave me a dubious look. "I don't think that's a good idea."

"Please. I've brought you evidence," I reminded him of the note. "The least you could do is allow me to see it through."

He hesitated for a moment, his eyes searching mine. My heart lurched, and I cursed it.

"You can ride?" he asked. "I mean, on your own?"

A spike of anxiety stabbed me in the chest. I hadn't thought of that. I had only ridden a horse twice in my life. Once when I was a girl and my mother, who was being courted by an avid horseman, took me out with them for a ride through the park. The sidesaddle he'd perched me upon was far too large for me, as was the horse. When the animal had spooked at a bird darting out from a tree, he'd jumped violently to one side, toppling me off him. I had broken my wrist. The other time I'd ridden was in tandem with the sheriff.

"I'll take the coach," I said.

He shook his head. "It'll be faster on horseback. But if you can't ride—"

"I can ride," I cut him off. "Of course, I can ride," I lied.

Really, how hard could it be? And I was no longer a child. Surely, I could control a horse now.

"All right," he said. "Let's go to the livery and find you a horse."

❧

At Archer's Livery and Blacksmith, we met Bob Parkhurst, a very large, young, and strapping colored blacksmith and farrier who ran the place. He picked for me a small, dappled gray mare with a sweet face and kind eyes, and tied her to the hitching post. I was immediately put at ease by her countenance.

"Bessie here will take good care of you, ma'am," he said, revealing perfectly straight, white teeth. Then he headed back inside the livery while I moved slowly toward Bessie. When I touched her soft nose, she knickered at me.

Mr. Parkhurst returned with a saddle in hand and placed it on her back.

"I'm to ride astride?" I asked.

"'Fraid so," he said.

I wondered how I would manage the volume of my skirts. When Mr. Parkhurst finished saddling and bridling her, he gave Bessie a few stout pats on the neck and pulled some sugar cubes from his pocket. He set them under the mare's lips, and nuzzling his palm, she took them in her mouth and crunched them with relish.

"She's ready to go," he said with that dazzling smile. "Let me give you a leg up."

"Oh yes. Thank you." My mouth had gone dry, and I could barely get the words out. I glanced at Sheriff Marshall, who was sitting atop his horse watching the proceedings.

I approached the saddle and laid one hand on the front of it and the other on the back.

"Give me your foot." Mr. Parkhurst bent down next to me and formed a little cradle for my foot with his hands. I placed the toe of my right boot in them.

"Other foot," he said, looking up at me with a grin.

Heat rose to my cheeks and my gaze slid over to the sheriff, who regarded me with amusement. I chose to ignore him and offered Mr. Parkhurst my left foot. He hoisted me in the air with such force, I almost toppled over the saddle, but I managed to right myself by grabbing onto the mare's mane. I swung my leg over her and landed in the saddle with a thud. Poor Bessie grunted with the impact. To my horror, I saw that my skirts were riding high above my knees.

Mr. Parkhurst gently pulled down the fabric to cover my left leg, but my right was exposed for Sheriff Marshall's pleasure. I jerked my skirt down over my knee. The sheriff's chuckle made the heat in my face intensify.

I shook off my embarrassment and took hold of the reins from beneath, clucking to Bessie. "Get up," I said.

Mr. Parkhurst reached up and placed my hands over the top of the reins, then rotated my wrists to face each other with my thumbs resting on the leather. "You're riding her, not driving her," he said with that mesmerizing smile.

A glance at the sheriff revealed that his amusement had turned to something else. Perhaps annoyance?

"Shall we go?" I asked, not wanting to detain him further.

He let loose a sigh. "Yep. It's going to be a long afternoon."

CHAPTER 23

We plodded along in silence, which shouldn't have surprised me. Aside from the fact that Sheriff Marshall was a man of few words, conversation was made even more challenging because we had to walk single file down the narrow trail that led us through a thick coppice of trees. Also, Bessie did not seem the least bit interested in keeping up with Queenie.

Try as I might to speed the mare up, she was unmoved by the enthusiastic tapping of my heels against her side. Periodically, the sheriff would turn around to check to see if I was still there, but the silence continued between us, growing wider and darker like a yawning cavern.

Finally, we came upon an area where the waters were quieter and less tumultuous. The trail broadened slightly, giving us a reprieve from the dense thicket of forest. I took advantage of the opportunity to ask the sheriff some questions about his own investigations.

"Have you spoken with Mrs. Gilroy?" I shouted ahead.

"About what?" he asked over his shoulder.

"About Narcissa's murder."

"Yep."

I wanted him to continue, but he didn't offer anything more.

"I understand that Narcissa broke her son's heart," I added. Still nothing.

So I proceeded. "She said her son left town because of Narcissa. She seemed pretty angry about it. Do you think it's possible Mrs. Gilroy could have killed Narcissa for revenge? For causing her son to leave town? Doesn't that seem like a plausible motive?"

He shook his head. "It's a stretch at best."

"How so?"

"Seth Gilroy didn't leave town because of Narcissa. He left town to get away from his mother."

"What do you mean?"

"In Betty Gilroy's eyes, no one was ever good enough for her boy. Not even Narcissa. If anyone broke Seth's heart, it was his mother. Narcissa and Seth both got tired of her interfering so they agreed to go their separate ways."

"How do you know this?" I asked, surprised at this bit of information.

"I've spent some time with the boy. We used to go fishing together."

"Well, was he heartbroken over the breakup?"

"Not really. I don't think the relationship was that serious. Narcissa was a handful. Truth be told, I think he was a bit relieved."

"But Mrs. Gilroy wouldn't think *she* was the reason her son left town. She blames Narcissa. So we are back to motive."

"Mrs. Gilroy didn't kill Narcissa Platte," he said flatly.

"How can you be so sure?"

He pulled Queenie to a halt and turned around in his saddle to better speak with me. "She and her husband were returning from Addison that night. They were on the road and didn't arrive until early the next morning to open the bakery."

I stared at him, incredulous that he would let me go on. "Well why didn't you say that before?"

His eyes lit up with amusement. "It was interesting to see

how your mind works. You're very inquisitive. You ask a lot of questions."

Exasperated, I sucked in a breath. Apparently, I was a great source of entertainment for the sheriff—and not the kind of entertainment by which I made my living. I forced myself to set aside my annoyance.

"But what about Daniel Bledsoe?" I asked. "If Mrs. Gilroy knew about his alleged liaison with Narcissa, perhaps that angered her in defense of her son?"

"You're reaching, Mrs. Pryce," he commented over his shoulder.

I rolled my eyes. He was right, of course.

"But do you think Seth may have been the father of Narcissa's unborn child?"

"I doubt it."

"Why do you doubt it?"

"Narcissa didn't seem that interested in Seth."

"But they *were* courting."

"Like I said before, Mrs. Pryce, it was short-lived."

The trail narrowed again, and we were soon flanked on either side by towering pine trees and thick undergrowth. The bushes tugged at my skirt, and where my lower legs were exposed, sharp, thin branches scraped at my stockings. I feared they would be torn to shreds.

Sheriff Marshall and Queenie successfully skirted a menacing low-hanging branch. Steeling myself for our approach, I tried to steer the mare away from it. It was at that moment Bessie decided it was finally time to catch up to them. She lurched forward, and the branch scraped her flank. She reared up, nearly unseating me, and when she came down again, she sprang forward, squeezing between the sheriff's horse and the wall of trees. She took me careening down the pathway at breakneck speed.

My heart in my throat, I tried desperately to pull back on the reins, but the mare lifted her head high in the air, giving me no leverage with the bit. I heard Sheriff Marshall shouting some-thing behind me, but it was all I could do to keep my seat. I gripped the saddle horn, screaming like I'd never screamed before as we zigzagged through the maze of trees.

Suddenly, the forest opened up and we entered a lush meadow, but it did nothing to stop the mare. We were headed straight for a lean-to at the edge of the river.

My heart hammering against my ribs and the air having vanished from my lungs, I tried again to pull back on the reins with one hand while keeping a death grip on the saddle horn with the other, but Bessie kept her head high. The sound of Queenie's thundering hooves came up behind us. Soon, the horses were neck and neck. Sheriff Marshall reached over and took hold of one of my reins, and we finally came to a stop.

The sound of my pulse roared in my ears and my body hummed with adrenaline. "Get me off this horse!" I shouted.

Bessie pranced, threatening to pull herself out of his grasp. Terrified she would take off again, I leaped from the saddle but got my foot caught in the stirrup and fell to the ground on my back with a *phoof!* Pain shot through my ankle, which was still trapped in the stirrup, as Bessie danced around, jerking me about.

"Come here!" the sheriff growled at the horse, taking a firm hold of the bridle. She finally quieted, but she trembled all over and her sides heaved. White foam coated her neck.

"Can you get your foot out?" he asked.

"I can't... It hurts!" I yelped.

"Steady, girl," he murmured to Bessie. "You just stand."

Still holding on to the bridle, he got down from his horse.

Whereas I had previously been embarrassed at the exposure of my legs while mounting the horse, having dismounted in such a ridiculous way with my leg high in the sky, my skirts were now aptly wrapped around my waist, exposing all my undergarments to God and everyone—everyone being the sheriff. Now I wanted to die. There was no graceful way to cover myself.

Seemingly nonplussed, Sheriff Marshall carefully removed my foot from the stirrup and gently placed it on the ground. I winced as the blood rushed back into it, making it feel like it was on fire.

"Please get me up," I demanded. "And don't look at me!"

"What?"

"Don't look at me," I repeated.

He turned his head, and placing his hands under my arms, he hoisted me to my feet. Another stab of pain radiated up from my ankle.

"Ouch!" I cried, hopping on my good foot.

"You really should let me take a look at that ankle," he said, still holding on to me. A quick glance at his face made a flush of heat rise to mine. He was smiling! And dare I say, doing everything in his power not to chortle.

"I'm glad you are so amused at my expense. I could have died, and you are laughing."

He straightened his face, but the merriment did not wane from those damnable blue eyes. "I'm not laughing. It's just—"

"Just what?" I snapped.

"It's just, I thought you said you could ride."

I sucked in a breath, infuriated at his cheek. I wouldn't dignify his remark with a response. I decided to keep on task. "How far are we from Masterson Grove?" I asked.

"It's just around the bend here." He pointed to a curve in the river.

I released myself from his grasp and attempted to set out without his help, but pain shot through my ankle, forcing the air from my lungs. I nearly toppled to the ground again.

"Come on," he said.

"Come on, what?"

His hands went around my waist, and before I could protest, he had lifted me up onto Queenie's back.

"What are you doing? I don't wish to be up here."

"You can't walk on that ankle. You need to ride." He then placed his foot in the stirrup and clambered up behind me.

"I'd rather not," I stated vehemently. I didn't wish to ride ever again in my life.

"Well, I'd rather. I shouldn't have let you come along in the first place. You're a suspect in a murder case. It's not protocol."

My hackles rose. "Well then, I suppose you'd wished you'd put me in the cell next to Andrew's?" I quipped.

"You'd certainly have been safer," he said.

I didn't turn around but could tell he was smiling.

৩৯৩

Masterson Grove was a cluster of approximately twenty-four shanties next to the river. There weren't many residents about, not that we could see anyway, but we spotted a woman doing her wash upstream. We approached her, and the sheriff asked if she knew where Clarence lived. She pointed to one of the larger buildings.

He steered the horse toward it, and after helping me down, Sheriff Marshall led me over to the porch steps. In a swift movement, he swept me up into his arms and mounted the stairs.

"Stop doing that!" I said in protest. "I'm perfectly fine to walk on my own."

He didn't say anything in response, just gently set me down.

"Clarence?" He knocked on the door. "Clarence, it's Sheriff Marshall."

We heard some noises from within, and finally, the door opened just wide enough for Clarence's face to fit through. I was relieved to see that he was there, and seemingly all right.

He looked up at the sheriff, and then when he met my gaze, he slammed the door shut.

"Clarence, open the door," the sheriff said. "Don't make me come in there after you."

"We just want to talk with you, Clarence," I said. "To make sure you're all right. We understand you've been ill."

After a few seconds, his face appeared in the doorway again.

"Can we come in?" the sheriff asked. "I need to ask you some questions."

Clarence shook his head.

"Who wrote the note that was given to Mr. Pettyjohn?" Sheriff Marshall asked.

"What note?" the boy finally said.

"The note saying that you were ill," I added. "The note from your mother?"

He shut the door again.

"Come on, Clarence," the sheriff said. "Last chance before I come in there."

There was no response. The sheriff and I exchanged a glance.

At last, the door opened and Clarence stepped out. His hair was turned up on end, and his clothing was mussed. "I'm not sick." He folded his arms protectively over his chest.

"Why haven't you been at work?" I asked, and his eyes grew wide with fear. "You're not in trouble," I assured him. "I just want to know. We need you at the hotel."

"I'm sorry, ma'am. I . . . I can't go back there." His bottom lip quivered.

"Why not?"

"I just can't."

The boy seemed frightened. It was understandable with the two recent murders.

Sheriff Marshall, probably sensing the same thing, relaxed into a more casual stance, probably trying to put the boy at ease. I was glad because I feared he might be intimidating the boy.

"Clarence, we need your help with our investigation into the deaths of Miss Platte and Mr. Bledsoe," he said. "We think the note given to Mr. Pettyjohn saying you were sick may be a clue. Did you write it?"

His eyes widened again, and he shook his head. "No, sir. No, I didn't."

"Then who did?" the sheriff asked.

The boy's gaze fell to the floor. "I dunno."

"I think you do." The sheriff raised himself up again and puffed up his chest, instantly reminding me of a giant lion. I guess he thought intimidation was the tactic needed.

"Maybe I should bring you in," he said.

The boy's face paled. "N-no. Please, I don't want to go to jail. I—I don't know who wrote that note!"

The sheriff pushed past him and went into the shack. Wincing, I hobbled in after him. My ankle throbbed.

The place was dark, with only dim light coming through a small window at the back. It smelled of something stale. I wrinkled my nose. The furnishings consisted of a pallet on the floor and a wooden table with two chairs. Another chair sat in the corner. Its cushion was tattered and frayed.

A basket lined with a linen kerchief and containing some bread, cheese, and two apples sat on the table. It didn't look like something the boy would put together.

"This is lovely," I said. "Did someone give this to you?"

He nodded.

"Who?" the sheriff asked.

Clarence pressed his lips together and blinked up at Sheriff Marshall with big eyes.

"All right." The sheriff took him by the arm. "Let's go." He started to pull him toward the door.

The boy's face froze in terror, and he let out a whimper. "Mrs. . . . Mrs. Gilroy," he stammered. "She—she gave me the basket."

"Mrs. Gilroy?" I said. "That was kind of her."

"Yes, ma'am," Clarence said. "She said she hadn't seen me walking to and from work and was worried about me."

"If you're not going to work at the hotel, you must be

running out of money." The sheriff pointedly glanced around the room.

"I get by."

"I'd like it if you came back to the hotel, Clarence." I said. "You do a good job. I could increase your wages."

His mouth turned down, and his chin trembled slightly. "I'll be fine."

"Well, the offer stands." I smiled. "The job is there for you whenever you want it."

His gaze slid from mine, but I could see that moisture had pooled in his big hazel eyes. A range of emotions flitted over his features and finally settled on a hardness that was startling.

"There's something I have to tell you, Sheriff," he said, his gaze drifting to the floor.

I let out a breath. Finally, we were getting somewhere!

"What is it, son?" Sheriff Marshall asked.

Clarence screwed up his face again. "I—I saw her. I saw her do it."

"Who?" I blurted. "Saw what?"

He raised his eyes to the sheriff's. "It was her." He pointed at me. "I saw her stab Mr. Bledsoe."

His words knocked the breath from my lungs and the room spun.

"Come again?" the sheriff asked with caution.

"You heard what I said." The boy looked down to the floor again.

"It's not true!" I said. "It's not true, I swear it." I looked up into Sheriff Marshall's face. "The boy wasn't even there!"

"I—I was," Clarence said. "I had just come up the stairs after you to take some firewood to one of the guest rooms."

My mouth dropped open. "Why? Why are you lying!?"

Tears swelled in his eyes again, but he wouldn't look me in the face. He just stood with his arms crossed and clenched to his chest.

"Clarence?" Sheriff Marshall prodded.

The boy pushed past us and fled out the door, leaving me and Sheriff Marshall gaping at each other.

"He's lying," I said. "Why would he lie? And he's lying about the note, too. He knows who wrote it. Don't you see? The boy is under some kind of duress. Someone is making him do this!"

The sheriff stood mute, his eyes searching mine. In them I could see so many things. Confusion. Question. Disbelief. And pain.

He gently took me by the arm to lead me out of the shack.

I pulled it away. "Say something!" I said.

He just shook his head and took hold of my arm again. "Let's go back to the hotel," he said quietly.

His refusal to either accuse me or support me was devastating. Why was this happening to me? Who hated me so much that they would do this? And why? What had I done? The injustice of it all tore through me like a tornado.

Preoccupied with the torrent of confusion, anger, sorrow, and abject terror, I hadn't paid mind to my injury and put my full weight on my foot, searing it with agony. I let out a yelp and was about to topple over, but the sheriff's arm went around me to support me as we left the shack.

Once outside, I spotted a fallen tree trunk just past where the horses were tied. Feeling the need to wrest myself away from him, and longing to sit, I wriggled out of his grasp and hobbled over to the tree trunk and sat down with an audible exhale through pursed lips. I set my elbows on my thighs and my head in my hands. Tears burned at the back of my eyes. How had I ended up in this hell?

"How's the ankle?" Sheriff Marshall asked, looming over me.

I raised my head. "It's terrible. Terrible! This is all just terrible!" I couldn't keep back the tears.

"Let me have a look," he said quietly. He knelt down and gingerly picked up my foot. He slowly and carefully untied the laces of my boot.

As I watched him, that familiar—yet again, completely inappropriate—flutter in my stomach returned. How could that be when I was so angry? Angry at him. Angry at William. Angry at this intolerable predicament I found myself in. But the fluttering continued, making me somewhat short of breath.

When he removed my boot, a stab of pain delivered me from my silly, girlish feelings. My ankle had swelled to twice its normal size. He examined it with tender fingers, and the warmth of his hands against my stockinged skin sent a tingle up my leg.

He slowly rotated the ankle, and I sucked air in through my teeth at the discomfort.

"Doesn't seem broken," he said. "But you've got a pretty bad sprain. You really shouldn't put any weight on it. Let's get you back to the hotel." He stood up and held out his hand, his gaze settling on mine. I didn't want to take his hand, still wanting to hold on to my anger, but when I looked up into his face, into those heart-melting eyes, I found myself helpless to do so.

"Please believe me," I whimpered. "I am not a murderer."

He didn't respond but encouraged me with a nod to take his hands. I put my hands in his, and he brought me to my feet. Cautiously, he wrapped his arm around my waist and supported me as I limped toward the horses.

"I think I can ride Bessie again," I said quietly.

He shook his head. "No. Can't risk you getting hurt any worse than you are already. Not on my watch."

I knew there was no sense in arguing with him, and quite frankly, the pain in my ankle and the outrageous injustice that had just been done to me was taking up every last bit of energy I had.

"May I?" he inquired, nodding toward the saddle.

I hesitated, looking up into his face. There was no more amusement in his eyes, only concern and . . . something else. Was it pity or tenderness?

Our gazes locked, and the pupils of his stormy, sea-blue eyes had widened. My breath caught, and a magnetic force drew me closer to him. He inclined his head toward my face, and my heart beat furiously against my ribs. I could scarcely breathe. Was he going to kiss me? I tilted my head back, breathlessly waiting for his lips to touch mine, but then he blinked and pulled back. My heart stuttered, and I wanted to fling my arms around him, but I refrained.

My throat closed up, and I swallowed. Unable to speak, I gave a quick nod and placed my hands on his shoulders.

He gently lifted me up and set me onto the saddle.

CHAPTER 24

Back at the hotel, the sheriff helped me into the lobby and led me to the staircase, the spell of our encounter broken.

Luckily, there were no guests present. I didn't feel like facing anyone at the moment. Only Mr. Pettyjohn at the reception desk, and Mr. Johns, the miner who had helped Maggie the other day, occupied the room. Mr. Johns was cleaned up and looking smart. He stood sentinel at the doorway to Bella's Saloon.

"Goodness," Mr. Pettyjohn said as I hopped past with the sheriff guiding me. "What's happened?"

My emotions running rampant and afraid I would burst into tears, I remained silent.

"She twisted her ankle," Sheriff Marshall said. "I'll help her upstairs."

"Shall I have Mr. Johns fetch Dr. Tate?" Mr. Pettyjohn asked, nodding toward the man. He then directed his attention to me. "Mr. Johns has a bad back and can no longer work in the mines. I took the liberty of hiring him to help around here. I hope you don't mind?"

I shook my head in answer to both questions. A day ago I might have taken umbrage with Mr. Pettyjohn overstepping his bounds, but today, what did it matter? Clarence had just sentenced me to the gallows.

"You can send the doctor up later," the sheriff said. "I think she needs to rest right now."

Once he got me upstairs, we entered the parlor to find Cordelia writing at the desk. Probably working on the glowing reports of my inspiring life in La Plata Springs for the *New York City Times*. Glowing, indeed.

"Arabella!" She jumped up when she saw my condition. "Good Lord, what's happened?"

At seeing my only true friend, I could no longer hold back my tears. I pulled myself from Sheriff Marshall's hold and went to her, tears streaming down my face. She wrapped her arms around me.

"What is going on?" she asked the sheriff.

He let out a sigh. "We found Clarence."

"And?"

"He claims he saw Mrs. Pryce . . . He saw her . . ." He couldn't seem to get out the words. Was that a sign that he believed me? Or perhaps that he wanted to believe me?

"Saw her what?"

I pulled away from her. "He claims he saw me stab Mr. Bledsoe."

Her eyes and mouth opened wide. "What? You can't be serious? That's just not true."

"Were you with Mrs. Pryce in the saloon that night?" he asked. "Did you see her come upstairs after Mr. Bledsoe?"

"Well, no, I was up in my room. But—but this is ludicrous!"

I closed my eyes, shaking my head, still not able to comprehend why this was happening.

"I'm not going to take you in," the sheriff said. "But I'm afraid you'll have to keep to your rooms."

I whipped around to face him. "Keep to my rooms? Are you serious?"

"I'm afraid so."

"You're locking me up? For a crime I did not commit?"

"We now have a witness to the crime." His gaze shifted from mine. "I'm sorry."

"But Clarence is lying!" I shouted.

"Please." He raised his hands to placate me. "Let me get this sorted out. Just stay put."

My anger flared. "I will not! This is absolutely absurd."

"Then I'll have to put a guard at the door."

I stared at him, dumbfounded. Not only did I find myself in this backward, backwater hole but now I was here under lock and key, making my imprisonment complete.

"Please leave," I said to him, the tears threatening to return.

With a sheepish look, he ducked his head and left the room. My heart squeezed and my chest ached. I bit my lower lip to distract me from the feelings.

"Why did Clarence say that about you?" Cordelia asked.

My ankle burning, I reached for the desk chair and sat down. I leaned my elbow against the desk and placed my head in my palm. "I don't know."

It was then I noticed the newspaper sitting on the corner of the desk. And it wasn't Miss Chatterley's one-page chit.

"Is that the *Times?*" I asked.

Cordelia quickly swiped it off the desk and folded it in half. "Yes. I picked it up today, but you need to rest that ankle. Let's get you to bed."

"Did Mr. Rankin's story come out? Did he use the information you've been sending him?"

She swallowed, and her face reddened. "Not yet. I was just . . . I was just writing to him. He probably needs more details of your life here."

She was keeping something from me. I could tell by the red splotches blooming on her neck.

"Well, let me see it." I held my hand out for the newspaper.

She tucked it under her arm. "You've had an awful day. Let

me help you get undressed, and then I'll go fetch you some tea and pastries. Does that sound nice?"

I narrowed my eyes at her strange behavior. "Don't patronize me. Give me the paper."

She clutched it harder to her side.

"Cordelia!" I lunged at her and ripped it away.

Her hands flew to her mouth. "Don't read it," she said behind her fingers.

I started to flip through it and then my eyes settled on the headline: ARABELLA PRYCE, THE TOAST OF NEW YORK, ACCUSED OF MURDER.

The byline read *Atticus Brooks.*

All the air was sucked out of the room, and my insides caved in on themselves. Mr. Rankin had betrayed me. We'd had an arrangement, and yet, he'd published that snake's article over my story. I was ruined. My reputation was completely ruined. Not only here but in my beloved New York. I had been worried about being forgotten, worried about my name being out of print, worried that I'd lose the love and admiration of my public, so damn worried about my celebrity and how I looked in the eyes of others . . . and now?

Terror rose up from my stomach to my chest, and I vomited it out in an anguished sob. I would have nothing. I'd lose every-thing that mattered to me. I'd be reviled, loathed, degraded. I'd be exposed. Everyone would see the real, unworthy me. Someone who was undeserving of all the things I craved.

"Oh, Arabella!" Cordelia cried. "Come now." She took hold of my hand.

With the life drained from me, I sat rooted to the chair. I couldn't move, couldn't breathe.

She took a firm hold of my arm and pulled me to my feet. Like a lifeless robotic automaton, I let her take me to the bedroom. I was vaguely aware of the discomfort in my lower leg, but the pain in my ankle was nothing compared to the crushing ache of my heart.

She guided me to the bed, turned down the covers, and then undressed me down to my shift. After she took the pins from my hair, she got me into bed. I leaned back onto the pillows, taking no comfort in their soft support. She placed another pillow under my foot and then took a blanket from the wardrobe drawer and tenderly draped it over me.

I closed my eyes, begging God to let me sleep. To let me sleep and never wake up again.

CHAPTER 25

My sleep had been fitful all night, filled with horrible dreams, anxieties, and dread. The betrayal of Mr. Rankin had sliced through me like a sword newly taken from the fire, hot and burning. Brooks's article was damning, but his erroneous conclusions were backed with no real evidence. It was just a libelous piece of salacious gossip. How could Mr. Rankin have printed it?

When morning came and I awoke, Bijou was perched next to me, panting in my face. She wanted to go out, but I couldn't make myself rise. My ankle ached, and I didn't want to face the day, to face the responsibilities of the hotel, to face my utter humiliation at being locked up. I couldn't even open my eyes to face the world, knowing everyone would think me a murderess.

The image of Sheriff Marshall's handsome face appeared behind the curtain of my eyelids, and my heart wrenched. I thought he had believed me. I thought we'd had a connection. But he had imprisoned me in my room. Had he succumbed to the lie that I was the culprit in not only one, but both murders? The reality of that possibility darkened my world, which was even more distressing and outright confusing. I did not have feelings for this man. The two of us never would have worked.

Our worlds were too different. But then why would the thought of his poor opinion of me, if he did think me guilty, hurt so much?

Bijou let out one of her impatient yips. I pulled her close to me and buried my face in her silky fur. Anxious to be let out, she squirmed out of my grasp and let go another bark. I should get up and open the door for her, but my limbs felt like lead.

"Arabella? Are you awake?" Cordelia had stepped into the room.

Unable to face even her, I remained with my eyes closed, feigning sleep. Bijou scampered to the end of the bed and yipped.

"Okay, girl," Cordelia whispered. "Let's go for a walk."

She left with the dog, and I burrowed myself farther under the covers, longing to go to sleep again, but the thoughts whirling through my mind made it impossible. It didn't matter. I would not get up.

In the darkness of my little cocoon, I shut out all the demons poking and prodding at my thoughts. I wanted oblivion, and soon, my mind wandered. My thoughts became fractured, incomplete. I was sinking into an abyss of swirling waters, going down, down, down when suddenly, a pool of coolness penetrated the blanket. I ignored it, wanting to drown in my own darkness, but the frigid sensation grew deeper. I flung off the covers to see Percival Blank sitting on the bed next to me.

With a groan, I yanked the blanket over my head again.

"Giving up so easily?" His buttery voice infiltrated the barrier.

Easily? My life had been ruined. There was nothing easy about it. I didn't want to talk to him.

"Go away," I demanded, my voice muffled by the fortress of blankets.

"I will not."

I remained still, hoping he would get tired of waiting and go off on some ghostly errand to leave me alone in my misery.

"I saw the newspaper," he said. "That has to hurt."

Really? Was he here only to add to my degradation?

"I have asked you to leave," I said.

"And I've told you I will not."

I ripped off the covers, and they whooshed right through him. "Then you are not a gentleman!"

He gave a shrug, apparently unconcerned with my comment. "Why are you so unkind to yourself?" he asked.

I gave a snort. "I beg your pardon?"

How could he say such a thing? I had not been "unkind" to myself. I had been trying to defend myself against the injustice done to me.

"You aren't deserving of this."

I sat bolt upright.

"Yes, I *know* that! I am not deserving of someone hating me so much that they would do this to me, including my own husband! If he had truly loved me, he would have let me stay in New York, comforted, taken care of, surrounded by people who actually care about me! Not sending me to this horrible town to be set up for humiliation and ridicule."

He raised an eyebrow. "Is that what you think? That your public *truly* cares about you?"

"Yes! They do. They clamor to be around me. I receive flowers, gifts, invitations to the finest houses. People crave my company."

He let go a sigh. "Who is your best friend?" he asked.

"What an absurd question! I have many."

"I'll ask another way. Who is someone, a person, with whom you feel a deep kinship, with whom you can let yourself rest? Who, among your *many* 'friends,' do you feel you do not have to perform for?"

I blinked, so dumbfounded at his last question that my mind went completely blank.

He continued. "Don't you think that perhaps your husband wanted you to experience people who want nothing from you?

People with whom you can just be yourself. Arabella the person, not Arabella the actress?"

"But there are people here who want to see me hanged!"

He smiled. "Did you ever consider that this murder case isn't about you?"

I blinked and shook my head, trying to make sense of what he'd just said. "What? Are you serious? Not about me? This is all about me! It's a conspiracy to get rid of me, to deny me of my livelihood, to rip my inheritance away from me."

"You only think that because you believe it's what you deserve."

His words sucked the air from my lungs, and a burning tingle started at the back of my eyes and deep into my nose.

"Don't give up, Arabella," he said softly. "This isn't about you as a person. This is about someone else. Someone who needs a scapegoat. You just happen to be convenient. New in town."

"Yes, but who is it?" I asked, my voice quavering. "Do you know? If you know, why aren't you telling me?"

"I'm not keeping anything from you, Arabella. I don't know. I only know what you've told me and have developed a theory. It seems that the killer is someone who carries a great deal of shame, so much so that they are in denial of their actions. It is too abhorrent for them. That is why they are using you. They don't have anything against you personally."

"You sound sympathetic to this person," I said, affronted. "Of course they should feel shame. They've killed someone— perhaps two people."

"Not everyone feels shame, my dear. Some people are simply diabolical."

"Well, framing me makes this person diabolical. They are using me because they don't want to face the gallows!"

The doorknob clicked, and Percival vanished.

"Oh, you're up." Cordelia entered the room. Bijou raced toward the bed and took a flying leap onto it. She scampered over to me, jumping up to lick my face. I stroked her head, thinking over Percival's words.

"How are you feeling today?" she asked, her voice cheery.

"How do you think?" I snapped.

Her forehead wrinkled, and she looked at me with apologetic eyes. Percival's question rang in my head. *With whom can you be yourself?*

The answer suddenly came to me. It was Cordelia. She was the only person who did not seem to want anything from me. When I'd offered her a raise last year, she'd refused it. Said she had everything she needed.

She always believed in me unconditionally. She did anything I asked of her. She was understanding and loyal. She eased my worries. She put up with my demands, my fits of temper, my conceit. She was a true friend.

"I'm sorry," I said. "I shouldn't have snapped at you."

"It's of no matter. I know you are still upset—and rightfully so." She went to the wardrobe. "Shall I lay out your clothes, or would you like for me to bring you breakfast in bed?"

"Seeing as I can't leave my room, what is the point of getting dressed?" I asked.

"You will feel better, I promise."

She was right. I never could abide wallowing about in bed.

"I'll get up," I acquiesced.

"Good for you, dear." She examined the contents of the wardrobe and picked a lavender skirt and a white shirtwaist embellished with lace. She laid out my shift, my corset, and my stockings.

"I can't make out Clarence's part in this whole affair," I said, mostly to myself. "Who has him so terrified that he would tell such a damaging lie?"

"Did he give any kind of hint of who this person could be?" she asked, sitting down to polish my boots.

"No. Nothing. Only that he was afraid."

"The poor boy. Living on his own," she mused. "The sheriff

told me about your visit with him yesterday—after you went to bed."

"I see. What exactly did the sheriff tell you?" The fluttery feeling that had consumed me when I looked into his eyes now seemed like complete folly. Was I so desperate for attention that I had conjured up a feeling of connection between us? I silently chastised myself for my senselessness.

"Not much. Just that the boy wouldn't say more. It's so sad that he has no parents. He has a roof over his head, though," Cordelia continued. "Which is a good thing. And before he stopped coming to work, I'm sure he ate at the saloon. Mr. Pettyjohn said that Mr. Bledsoe at least saw to the employees getting one meal a day. But how is he getting his meals now?" Her voice took on a tone of concern. "If he's left his employment—"

"Mrs. Gilroy brought him a basket," I said absently.

"Oh, well, that was nice of her. I wonder if she's been taking care of him since he left the hotel?"

"Yes. I wonder, too. Perhaps she knows why he hasn't returned to work or what has him so frightened. I'd like to speak with her."

Cordelia stopped polishing and looked up at me with dubious eyes. "I'm afraid that's not possible. Sheriff Marshall has deputized Mr. Johns, and he is sitting guard at the door. Sheriff Marshall told him that you are not to leave, and no one is to come see you except him."

The sting of Sheriff Marshall's need to keep me jailed and locked up returned. "Did he now?" I asked. "Well, that is a problem."

"I could try talking with her," Cordelia offered. "I'd like to go to the bakery anyway."

"Hmm. Yes. Why don't you."

"I'll go directly after I get you dressed."

"I can manage. You go on."

"But your ankle."

"It feels much better this morning," I said, not sure if that was the case. I hadn't yet put any weight on it.

Cordelia's eyes lit up. I knew she was eager to help in any way she could, and I was grateful.

She left me to get dressed.

I flung the covers off my legs to take a look at my foot. The swelling had gone down considerably, but it was still a little bloated. I rolled my ankle and winced. It was still sore, but better.

Dressing was a bit of a challenge, but I could do some of it while seated on the bed.

My boots were another matter entirely. The button-ups definitely would not do, but I managed to squeeze my foot into my white leather and canvas lace-ups. I found that pulling the laces taut around my ankle gave me ample support and the compression helped to ease the pain.

Once completely attired and with my waterfall of hair loosely coiled at the back of my head, I was ready for the day.

A sinking feeling pervaded my stomach. I was ready for the day to sit in my rooms, locked away from the world. It was so unfair.

I went into the parlor and opened the front door. Sure enough, Mr. Johns was sitting in a hard-backed wooden chair next to the door. He quickly stood up at my presence.

"So you are my jailer?" I asked him. "And also the new bell-man. My, you have quite a lot to do."

He looked at me sheepishly. "Sorry, ma'am. I'm just following orders. Mr. Pettyjohn said—"

"I know." I held up my hand and then went back inside.

Jailed in my own hotel, by my own employees. It rankled.

How was I to continue with my investigation? The sheriff was obviously more than capable, and he seemed determined to find Narcissa's killer, but I doubted he would put much more effort into finding the killer of Daniel Bledsoe. He had his prime suspect under arrest: me. I had not yet been charged, of course, but if he could not find evidence to prove my innocence, it would only be a matter of time. And, he had nothing so far as to the murder of Narcissa Platte, so it would stand to reason that he would focus his attentions there.

Either way, it did not look good for me.

CHAPTER 26

I went to the love seat near the bay window to think. I
recalled what Percival had said, that the murderer of at least
one or possibly both victims was someone filled with shame at
what they'd done, and that I was the most convenient scapegoat.

From the manner in which both crimes were committed—a
head wound and fall down the stairs, and death by letter opener
—it seemed both murders had been crimes of passion, done in a
moment of anger or despair. Shame and regret would naturally
follow.

I thought about all the people who had been hurt by
Narcissa or Mr. Bledsoe.

Mrs. Bledsoe seemed the most obvious culprit. Hurt and
humiliated by her husband's philandering, she perhaps had
reached her breaking point with his relationship with Narcissa.
And if she had heard rumors about my William and Narcissa,
and Mrs. Platte's accusations against me, it would have been easy
for her to set me up as the killer.

Then there was Andrew. He'd admitted to using the fireplace
poker to kill the rats, but were they the only living beings he'd
killed? He could have been lying about exterminating the
vermin. While he didn't seem like a person who'd intentionally

murder another, he struck me as someone who would show intense remorse at having committed such a violent act against another human being.

Next was Maggie. There might have been a likelihood of her wanting to do away with Narcissa. She stood in the way of Maggie's potential happiness with Andrew. But she was such a meek yet sweet girl. I couldn't imagine her actually doing anything about it.

And why Mr. Bledsoe, then? It's true Maggie had confided that he'd made advances, and surely that would anger both Maggie and Andrew, but murder seemed excessive. The two murders had to be related, didn't they? Having occurred so closely together? It would seem too much of a coincidence.

Sally Dean also had suffered under Narcissa's cruelty. And she'd had a relationship, if you could call it that, with Mr. Bledsoe. Had her feelings for him run deeper than she'd said? Was he more than just a customer? Jealousy and revenge were indeed strong motives, but according to everyone who knew her, vindictiveness did not seem consistent with Miss Dean's nature.

With revenge in mind, I again thought of Mrs. Gilroy. But Sheriff Marshall had said that Mrs. Gilroy had been out of town on the night Narcissa was murdered. However, if she'd suspected Narcissa having an affair with Daniel Bledsoe, and was angered at the betrayal against her son, she might have killed both Narcissa and the hotel manager, but the sheriff had said that was a stretch. Begrudgingly, I had to agree.

In my mind, Prunella Bledsoe still was the top suspect for several reasons. It seemed everyone knew about her husband's relationship with Narcissa, but no one was quite sure the extent of it. Had it been a flirtation or something more serious? Either way, it would have been humiliating for a displaced wife.

The timing of her visiting Mr. Bledsoe's rooms also fit with the time of his death, and there had been the scent of her perfume lingering in the air. But the most damning reason of all was the missing letter opener from her writing set. She hadn't denied that the letter opener found under Mr. Bledsoe's body was hers, nor why it had been there.

Was Sheriff Marshall pursuing the same line of reasoning? It hadn't seemed so, but it was hard for me to tell. He was such a difficult man to read.

Something Percival had said suddenly popped into my mind. He'd mentioned that I had not spoken with everyone involved in the case, and he was right. I had not yet spoken with the Plattes.

The sheriff had, I'm sure. Probably more than once. He would be keeping them abreast of his investigation if nothing else. The killer, whoever it was, had destroyed their lives. Unfortunately, they thought that person was me. I frowned. Perhaps what Mrs. Platte had said was true, that William had been pursuing Narcissa. It would stand to reason that she would think the jealous wife would be out for revenge. After all, isn't that what I thought about Mrs. Bledsoe?

Percival also had hinted that one of the Plattes could have killed their daughter. I still could not believe this was likely, given how they had put so much stock into Narcissa's future. Yet, if they knew about the pregnancy, and knew that the father was not Andrew, wouldn't that have angered them? Disgraced them and their standing in the community? Perhaps my ghostly friend had a point.

I wondered if the Plattes were currently in their rooms. Mrs. Platte might be, but Mr. Platte most likely was not. He was probably at the railroad office. It might be worth a try to talk with Mrs. Platte, though—if she would allow it.

I'd have to take my chances. But how to get past Mr. Johns at the door?

But of course!

"Percival?" I called out to the empty room. "Percival, I need your assistance."

I waited. I had tried to summon him before to no avail. He seemed to appear only when he wished to.

"Please, Percival. It's important."

To my relief, his transparent figure materialized. "You're out of bed. I'm glad to see it. And you have that attractive spark in your eyes once again."

"I wouldn't go that far, but I am feeling better." I stood from the love seat and went to the desk.

"How's the ankle?"

"Sore, but better."

"You have a look of determination about you," he mused.

"I'd like to speak with Mr. or Mrs. Platte, or both, but I cannot get out of here with Mr. Johns standing guard."

"Yes, that does pose a problem. What would you like me to do?" He placed his hands behind his back.

"I'd like for you to create a distraction. Some kind of disturbance that would draw Mr. Johns away. Perhaps in Mr. Bledsoe's rooms? Then I can sneak downstairs and call on the Plattes."

"I think that is a grand idea," he said with that devilish smile.

"Are you sure you don't know who committed these crimes?" I asked again, just for good measure.

"I assure you, my dear, I do not. I have only been a casual observer of this investigation, and I want to make sure you leave no stone unturned."

"Right," I said, a little dubiously.

I opened the desk drawer to retrieve the key ring Mr. Pettyjohn had given me and stuffed them into my skirt pocket. It wouldn't do to lock myself out while Mr. Johns was preoccupied with the commotion Percival was going to cause.

"Ready?" he asked.

I nodded, and then he popped out of sight.

I perched myself on the desk chair, waiting, straining to hear. All that sounded was the clock on the mantel piece over the fireplace, and the low, rapid thud of my pulse in my ears.

Then a loud crash came from downstairs. It sounded like glass shattering. I went to the door and opened it.

"Oh my goodness!" I said. "Did you hear that?"

Mr. Johns had stood up from the chair.

"Yes, ma'am. Sounded like something breaking."

"Do you know where it came from?"

"Sounds like maybe on the third floor."

Another loud crack penetrated the hallway. Something else had broken. Percival was having a right jolly time in Mr. Bledsoe's rooms.

"Someone is tearing the place apart!" I cried. "Do something Mr. Johns!"

"But the sheriff said—"

"Oh, don't be silly! I promise I won't leave the hotel." It wasn't a lie. I didn't intend to leave the hotel.

"I've been instructed that you are not to leave your room," he added.

Another smash of glass.

"If you'd like to keep your job here, Mr. Johns, I demand that you go find out what is going on and put an end to it. Do you understand?"

He regarded me with skepticism for a few moments but then fled down the stairs. I heard him knock loudly on Mr. Bledsoe's door. "Who's in there?" he shouted.

I limped out into the hallway and down the stairs to see him try the doorknob.

My heart stuttered. The door was locked! He tried again, and miraculously, the door opened and he went in. And then I remembered the doorknob was in the reflection of the mirror in Mr. Bledsoe's parlor.

Taking my chance, I tiptoed down the stairs. The Plattes' rooms were on the opposite end of the hallway from Mr. Bledsoe's rooms, so I had to hurry past. My ankle flared with pain, but I refused to let it slow me down. Luckily, Mr. Johns was preoccupied with whatever he'd found in Mr. Bledsoe's rooms.

Quietly, I knocked on the Plattes' door, and to my surprise, it creaked open. Someone must be in.

"Hello?" I whispered. "Mr. Platte? Mrs. Platte?"

There was no answer. Instead of inquiring again, which might alert Mr. Johns down the hall, I stepped inside and closed the door.

"Hello? It's Arabella Pryce. Mrs. Platte?"

Only silence greeted me. I entered the parlor and then looked in each one of the two bedrooms. One was masculine in décor and contained a double bed, which led me to believe it was Mr. and Mrs. Platte's. The other bedroom had softer features with lace curtains and a single, canopied bed with a floral bedspread. A mirrored vanity with various perfume bottles, a flower vase, and two hat stands with exquisite hats placed upon them sat under the window.

I wondered if Mr. Johns was still in Mr. Bledsoe's rooms. Surely not. By this time, he'd probably gone to get Mr. Pettyjohn to come assess the damage. How soon before Mr. Johns realizes I'm gone? I wondered. Then I realized he may not notice at all. He may think I was still confined in my parlor.

I started to turn to leave when something caught my eye. One of the vanity drawers was opened a fraction. Instinctively, I went to close it, but it jammed. I slid the drawer open to try again, but the edge of a book caught it. I pulled it out.

It was a diary.

Curious, I opened it. Delicate handwriting filled the pages. The script was nothing like the letter that had been found in William's desk drawer. The letters here slanted to the right and had long, curling lines with wisps at the end of each word. It was beautiful.

I scanned through to the middle and stopped when my gaze fell on the name *Daniel*. I lifted the book closer to my face and gasped.

Daniel took me out in his carriage today. We went to Holiday Meadow and had a picnic, and he confessed his love for me with a pair of beautiful emerald earrings! I knew it. I just knew he loved me!

. . .

The letter found in the drawer had mentioned that William had given her emerald earrings. What were the odds that both men did so? It was highly unlikely. I read on.

I told him it wouldn't be proper if we did what he wanted us to do, but when he confessed his love for me, all propriety went out the door! It was glorious. I tingled from head to toe for hours!

He said he would leave his wife, and I told him I would break it off with Andrew. I never wanted to marry him anyway. He and that mouse Maggie have made no secret their feelings for each other, which, by the way, is quite humiliating . . . as is an arranged marriage. But it doesn't matter. Daniel has lots of money. I don't need mother and father's . . .

I skipped to a later entry.

He has not spoken to Prunella about a divorce. It has been weeks. And when we are together he is distant, distracted. I wonder if he does not love me anymore. So I have not spoken with Andrew. Why would I, when Daniel has not kept his promise?

Poor Narcissa. She had been duped into giving herself to Daniel Bledsoe on the promise that he would leave his wife. Obviously, he'd had no intention to. My suspicions were confirmed as I read on.

He has lied to me. Tonight, he told me he could not leave his wife or he would lose everything. Her family is filthy rich. They were the ones who got him in with Mr. Pryce to manage the Arabella. I argued that he would still have his position with Mr. Archer at the General, but he said it wasn't enough.

How dare he not choose me over his pruney wife or the money? Oh, what am I to do?

When I told him I was with child, he was angry. At me! Like it was my doing alone! I don't know what to do. Since Andrew and I are still engaged, I tried to seduce him. It made sense. Everyone would think the child was his. We got close to doing the deed—I know I am irresistible to most men—but then he pushed me away and said he couldn't. He claimed it was to preserve my honor, but I know it was on account of that dog-faced Maggie.

And then I read something that completely surprised me.

I'm leaving La Plata Springs. I can no longer bear to be here. I don't want a life with Andrew, and I can't stomach the thought of seeing Daniel every single day. He says that things won't change between us, that we can carry on the same once I am married. But how do I explain the child to Andrew? I'll be disgraced.

I flipped through more pages.

Mr. Pryce has come to my rescue!

My stomach clenched, and I wondered if I should read on. Could I bear to read the truth? I wasn't sure, but I couldn't tear my eyes from the page.

He saw me crying one afternoon, and I don't know what possessed me but I told him everything, even that I didn't want to marry Andrew.

I also told him I'd had a terrible fight with Mother. Somehow, she'd suspected my condition. She, of course, assumed it was Andrew's. Father was about to go over to the Archers and give him what for, but I stopped him. I told him it wasn't Andrew's, but I would not reveal the father's identity. Both Mother and Father were spitting mad.

I left the hotel and went out onto the street to calm myself. It was there that I ran into Mr. Pryce and told him everything.

William did have a way of putting people at ease.

He didn't do anything about it at first but comfort me. But several days later, he told me that, if I wanted, he would arrange for me to go to Denver. He has a friend there, a wealthy widow. I could spend my confinement with her, and then she would help me place the child with a loving family. He agreed to accompany me to speak with Mother and Father about the plan. He also offered me his rooms upon his departure, should Mother and Father be disagreeable, which they were. I stayed there one night, but Mother insisted I come back to their rooms. She said it was unseemly . . .

I remembered the blond hairs in the hairbrush and smiled. William and Narcissa had not been lovers. I felt bad for even considering it. I should have known that William would not have betrayed me. The hardness in my heart at his demands that I come to La Plata Springs began to melt a little. I read on.

We would tell Andrew that I was ill and needed more time to recover before we married. Once the child was born, I would return . . .

I skipped a few more pages.

· · ·

I can barely contain my excitement! Daniel has sent me a note. He said he has some good news and would like me to meet him at the General at midnight. He apologized for his harsh treatment and said he loves me!

He must have changed his mind. He must not be able to live without me. Oh! What shall I wear? Perhaps the cranberry velvet gown. He said it brought out the color of eyes. I will render him helpless . . .

I looked at the date. It was the night I had arrived. The night of her murder. Had Daniel wanted to lure her into a tryst to do away with her? Was he waiting in the stairwell? But the time of Narcissa's death was not consistent with that theory, I recalled. And Mr. Bledsoe had been with Sally Dean at that time.

A door slamming upstairs jolted me from my thoughts. Had Mr. Johns discovered I was gone? Or had Cordelia returned? She would be worried to find me not there. I'd been away too long. For all I knew Mr. Johns would have gone to fetch the sheriff by now. I had to get back to my rooms.

I tucked the diary under my arm, and as I crossed the parlor to leave, something glinted in the sunlight on the desk at the window. It was a substantially sized, miniature crystal obelisk. A paperweight. Sunlight streamed through it, splashing a rainbow of color onto the desk. The top of the thing was oddly misshapen. My curiosity got the best of me again, and I went to the desk and picked it up.

A section of it had been broken off. I sucked in a breath. The missing piece was roughly the same size as the shard of thick glass I'd found on the landing on the night of Narcissa's murder. I had completely forgotten about it after I tucked it away in the pocket of my skirt!

I turned the paperweight in my hand. Could Mr. or Mrs. Platte *really* have killed Narcissa and all their hopes and dreams with her?

I perused the collection of glass and crystal knickknacks in all shapes and sizes that lay on the desk. Some had dried flowers embedded in them, some had cloisonne designs. My gaze slid over to an envelope tucked under another paperweight. The return addressee on the envelope was magnified beneath the glass. It read, *Mrs. Pretencia Platte,* which was not at all surprising, but the individual letters of the name were. They were decidedly slanted to the left. I bent down and peered closer. The handwriting . . .

Mrs. Platte had written the letter the sheriff had found in William's desk drawer! And the note for Clarence.

With shaking hands, I put the envelope in the diary and tightened my grip on the obelisk. All three were pretty damning evidence, at least of Narcissa's murder. Sheriff Marshall would have to see this.

I was just about to turn the knob of the door when someone pushed through it.

It was Mrs. Platte.

CHAPTER 27

I clutched the diary and paperweight to my chest. When my gaze met Mrs. Platte's, her eyes burned right through me.

"What are you doing in here?" she snapped.

I swallowed my trepidation and raised my chin in defiance. No, make that outrage. She had wanted to pin her daughter's murder on me.

"I know what you've done," I said.

She looked down at the diary and paperweight in my hands. "Give those to me," she snarled.

"No. They are evidence. As is the envelope I found on your desk. With the same handwriting as the letter you forged in Narcissa's name and the note you wrote for Clarence."

She slammed the door shut and stood between me, it, and any chance of escape.

"Get out of my way," I said, my voice lowered.

She reached for a wooden box on the desk opened it. It was a writing set. She pulled out a long blade. A letter opener.

"You're not going anywhere." She rushed toward me, pointing the blade at my face.

"Who did it?" I stepped away from her. "Who killed your daughter? Was it you or your husband?"

She inched closer toward me. "How dare you?"

"You won't use that on me." I tried to sound confident. "I'm in your rooms. How would you explain that?"

"I'd tell them you were hiding in here. That you threatened me with this." She held up the letter opener. I wasn't certain, but I thought what I could see of the handle had same detail as the one that was used to kill Daniel Bledsoe. But how could she have gotten it? Sheriff Marshall had taken it from the scene so it could be studied further.

"Where did you get that?" I asked, nodding toward the letter opener.

She smirked. "Some beau gave the set to Narcissa. She was always getting gifts from men."

"It looks like the letter opener used to kill Daniel Bledsoe."

I wondered if Daniel Bledsoe had bought two identical writing sets—one for his wife and one for Narcissa.

She huffed. "Does it? Well, it will sure come in handy. Because I had to defend myself with it. From the beautiful, jealous, vengeful Mrs. Pryce, who is already suspected of killing twice."

She was so calculating, it sent a chill through me.

"They won't believe you," I said but wasn't certain of it.

"They'd believe me over you, the self-absorbed, envious, conceited out-of-towner, who couldn't face the fact that she stood to lose the hotel and that she had already lost her husband . . . to my daughter "

"William and Narcissa didn't have an affair and you know it." I held up the diary. "She was having an affair with Daniel Bledsoe."

Her eyes narrowed. "I should have gotten rid of that."

"Why did you do it, Mrs. Platte?" I continued to slowly back away from her, my ankle on fire. I startled when the heel of my good foot bumped into one of the parlor chairs, stopping me. Unable to see a means of escape, my anxiety reached a fever pitch. I had to stay calm.

"Why would you kill your own daughter and the child she was carrying?"

Mrs. Platte flinched as if I'd hit her. Finally, there was a chink in the iceberg.

A look of sadness flashed over her face. "She ruined everything," she said, her lower lip quivering. "All our plans for her. It would have been perfect. But then she had to go and sully herself with that cad, that two-timing scoundrel. If it weren't for him, she would have married Andrew."

"But she refused," I said.

"Yes. What did it matter that he loved another? He would have grown to love Narcissa. He will someday have ownership of the entire town. My girl would have had the best of everything. She would have—" her voice faltered "—*been* the best."

"But she would not be deterred from Daniel Bledsoe, would she? On the night she died, he said he had good news for her."

Her face hardened again. "He was never going to leave his wife! Narcissa was acting the fool running after him. He was using her. I had to stop her."

I pictured the scene in my mind. Narcissa and her mother in a terrible fight. Harsh words exchanged. Shouting.

"You tried to strangle her," I said flatly.

"I only wanted to make her shut up about that reprobate Bledsoe!"

"But she struggled out of your grasp. She left your rooms and fled down the stairs." I held up the obelisk, turning it in my hand. It caught the sunlight streaming through the window. "I wonder, did you throw it at her?"

She blinked rapidly, and her mouth turned downward, her chin quaking. She came closer, holding the letter opener up to my face, the point aimed right between my eyes. I tried to take a deep breath but couldn't manage it. My heartbeat thrummed through my head and roared in my ears.

"I didn't mean to—" Her voice cracked with emotion.

"And Daniel Bledsoe?"

The color drained from her face, and the area around her mouth had turned white. "He'd made her a fool. A simpering, lovesick fool. If she hadn't gotten pregnant with his child, we never would have argued, and I never would have—" she shuddered. "He had to pay for what he'd done. And your husband . . ." Her eyes flared again. "Your husband was going to take her away from me."

"He was only trying to help her," I said.

She held the letter opener so close, my eyes were crossing. I had to do something, and do it quickly, but with her close proximity, I couldn't move. I had to come up with something that would distract her. She'd seemed to falter when I'd mentioned the unborn child before.

"How did it feel to know you killed an innocent baby?"

She flinched again, and her eyes flared with anger. "I told you, I didn't mean—"

As I had hoped, the question threw her off guard. Taking advantage of the moment, I raised my good foot and kicked her away from me. Standing on my injured ankle sent knives up into my leg, and I almost fell but caught myself.

The impact of my foot forced her backward. She stumbled and must have stepped on the hem of her skirt. She dropped to the floor on her backside.

I shambled to the door and flung it open. "Help! Mr. Pettyjohn! Mr. Johns! Someone, I need help!"

I stepped through the doorway and let the items in my arms fall to the floor. Hastily, I pulled it shut behind me and reached in my pocket for the key ring. It would only be a matter of seconds before she stood up and came after me. I fumbled with the keys, trying to find the one that fit the lock to their rooms, but my hands were shaking so much I could hardly make them work. I tried one, then another, my heart in my throat. Finally, the third one slipped into the keyhole. I turned the key and heard a satisfying *click*. I had successfully locked her in.

She pounded on the door. "Let me out!" she shrieked.

"Pretencia!" Mr. Platte came bounding up the stairs. When he saw me, he stopped. His face paled. "What's wrong with Pretencia?"

The pounding on the door continued.

"I know everything, Mr. Platte," I said, holding up a hand to prevent him from coming closer. I threaded my fingers through the keys to use as a weapon if necessary. "I know your wife killed Narcissa and Mr. Bledsoe."

"Get me out of here!" The door rattled with her continued pummeling.

Mr. Platte's gaze fell to the diary, the obelisk, and the envelope at my feet.

His face crumpled with emotion, and he covered it with his hands.

"She was so angry," he said, shaking his head. "I heard the shouting and came out to see what they were arguing about, but I was too late. By the time I reached them, Narcissa had fallen—"

A loud thumping sound moved toward us. Mr. Pettyjohn, Mr. Johns, and Sheriff Marshall had raced up the stairs. Behind them trailed Atticus Brooks.

"There she is," Mr. Johns said, pointing at me.

Sheriff Marshall eyed me with a mixture of impatience and anger. "What are you doing, Arabella?"

The sound of my name on his tongue sent a thrill through me. It was a completely inappropriate feeling to have, given the situation, but I couldn't help it. But for some odd, if not infuriating reason, it filled me with warmth. Flustered, I shoved the sentiment aside.

"What I'm doing is solving your case," I said haughtily. "I have evidence and a confession from Mrs. Platte that she killed both Narcissa and Daniel Bledsoe."

"I didn't mean it!" A muffled wail came from behind the door. "It was an accident. My girl! My beautiful girl . . ."

"Dear God," Mr. Johns said under his breath.

Mr. Pettyjohn shook his head, and his eyes were filled with pity.

The sheriff held his hand out for the keys. Silently, I gave them over.

Horace Platte had sunk to the floor, and with his head in his hands, he sobbed.

Sheriff Marshall opened the door. Mrs. Platte had crumpled to the ground. On her hands and knees, she rocked back and forth, wailing. Gently, the sheriff brought her to her feet and led her out of the room.

He made eye contact with me as they went, and I thought I detected the warmth of a smile in them, and dare I say, a hint of relief. My heart skipped a beat.

"Mr. Pettyjohn," he said, still holding my gaze, "take the evidence and bring it to the jail, would you?"

"Yes, sir." Mr. Pettyjohn gathered the items at my feet.

"I'll call on you later," the sheriff said to me.

I gave him a curt nod.

Sheriff Marshall helped Mrs. Platte down the stairs, and Mr. Platte, Mr. Pettyjohn and Mr. Johns followed them. That left me with alone with Mr. Brooks.

His previous injustice toward me made my temper rise. He slowly looked away from the retreating foursome and met my gaze. I regarded him with a pointed glare. "Well, Mr. Brooks." I crossed my arms over my chest. "Where are your silly notepad and pencil. now? I daresay you have another story to write."

CHAPTER 28

T EN DAYS LATER . . .

Sipping my tea and savoring my second, buttery strawberry biscuit, I re-read the article printed in today's *New York City Times* for the seventh time, a smile plastered on my face. STAGE STAR ARABELLA PRYCE EXONERATED, SOLVES DOUBLE MURDER CASE IN LA PLATA SPRINGS, COLORADO, the headline read.

Oh, how it must have galled Mr. Brooks to have to retract his previous story and print this one, which was, after all, the truth.

"You haven't set that paper down since I brought it to you." Cordelia put on her light, summer coat and gathered Bijou's leash from the desktop. Bijou sprang up from her bed and stood on her hind legs to assist Cordelia in attaching the leash.

"I'd like to save it. Please cut it out and put it in my scrapbook."

"Of course. I'll do so after I take Bijou for a walk. Would you like to come along?"

Bijou rose up on her hind legs and rested her little paws on my skirt. I scratched the top of her head. "I don't think so. I'd like to finish my tea."

"Very well. See you later."

They left, Bijou doing a little dance at Cordelia's heels. I settled deeper into the love seat and gazed out the window. The trees at the banks of the river were lush in their plumage, and the green of their leaves was in stark contrast to the deep-cerulean sky. I had never seen a sky so brilliantly blue or clouds so gleaming white and round, like blossoming cotton bolls. I never had imagined Colorado would be so beautiful. I had envisioned it dry and empty, a desert wasteland, but in its own way, it was a little Eden. If I had to complete a year-long sentence at the far ends of the world, at least I would do it where the landscape was a vision to behold.

The sound of someone clearing their throat pulled my gaze from the window. Percival, in his transparent state, had appeared next to me, leaning casually on the other arm of the love seat, his legs crossed at the knees and his pipe held aloft. A coolness wafted over me, and the smell of tobacco filled the room.

"Where have you been?" I asked. I hadn't seen him since that day the sheriff had marched Mrs. Platte to the jail.

"I've been around. I spent some time down at the river, walked through the town. And I've been at the hotel."

"But you haven't been to see me." I tried but couldn't disguise the disappointment in my voice.

"Oh, I've seen you," he said with that devilish smile. "You've been quite busy with things here at the hotel. You've hired some new staff. You're having the place painted. Making some much-needed repairs."

I sighed. "Yes. It's been an effort. And with very little funds to spend. The hotel's account at Archer's Savings & Loan has been nearly drained. And I can't account for where it went."

With the death of Mr. Bledsoe, and with the help of my lawyer in New York, I was able to claim the account. It shouldn't have been that difficult, but to my surprise, Archibald Archer had been uncooperative at first. In the end, he acquiesced.

"Perhaps Mr. Bledsoe misappropriated the funds," Percival suggested.

"I think that's obvious. But what did he do with the money?" I wondered out loud. "I still cannot access my personal accounts in New York until the year is over. I have a monthly allowance, but it's not enough to cover all that needs to be done here."

"And what about the lien against the hotel?"

"It was filed by a company called Billings Building and Co. Mr. Tisdale is looking into the matter. We don't know if the will stipulated a clause for a situation like this. I certainly hope it did. If the hotel is out of my grasp, I will lose my inheritance. I *mustn't* lose the hotel."

"You will find a way, I'm sure," he said and puffed on his pipe.

I sighed. "My mother is right. I know nothing about business. My talents are limited to the stage, throwing glamorous parties, dressing well, and living a civilized life."

"Not necessarily. It seems you can now add solving crimes to your list of talents." He held the smoke in his mouth, seeming to savor it.

"Not really," I mused. "I was just trying to save my own skin."

"You certainly helped Sheriff Marshall in the process—and Andrew, and Sally Dean, and most of all, Mrs. Bledsoe. Mrs. Platte could have easily tried to pin the murders on them, as well. I'm sure they are all grateful to you."

I scoffed. "Not hardly. I'm not very well-liked here." Saying the words were like stabbing myself with a dagger.

Percival reached out and laid his transparent hand on my arm, causing a coolness to penetrate to my very bones. "I doubt that is true."

"But it is. I've been here for almost three weeks and have not gotten so much as one invitation to lunch, or dinner, or even tea down at Gilroy's Bakery."

He let go a chuckle. "Oh, dearest Arabella. This is not New

York City. You are not among high society. They do things differ-
ently here."

"Clearly," I said with a hint of sarcasm. "I just thought they
would have warmed to me a little more after I had proven myself
innocent of the murders and solved the crime—with your help
of course."

He shook his head with a smile. "It was all you, my dear. You
just needed to see things from a different perspective."

"Well, thank you for helping me to see that different perspective." I raised my teacup to him. "And to your concern about the
people of the town warming to you, you must remember it's not
been that long since you've arrived in our fair little city. And
since then, there have been two deaths and now two funerals.
There hasn't been much time for socializing."

He did have a point there.

"I'm sure, in time, they will see the beautiful person you are,
inside and out," he said.

Our eyes met, and I was moved by the tenderness in his gaze.

"How do *you* know whether or not I'm beautiful on the
inside?" He, too, had only known me for not quite three weeks.

"It's something you gain in death. A knowing. A different
kind of wisdom that people don't have in their earthly lives."

I looked down at my teacup, uncomfortable with his confidence in what he thought he knew of my nature. I had trouble
believing it myself.

"Well—" I raised my chin "—it doesn't matter anyway. In a
year, I'll be gone. Back to my life in New York. Back to my
public, if they haven't forgotten me by then, and back to my
beloved theater and my craft."

My craft, where I could put on a mask and sink into the
mind, motivations, love, and pain of someone else. Performing.
Where it was comfortable.

There was a knock at the door, and when I looked up,
Percival had vanished. I set my teacup down and answered it.

"Sheriff Marshall," I said in surprise. "I hadn't seen him in quite a few days, either. I was still a little hurt—well, all right, angry—that he had not believed in my innocence and felt the need to sequester me to my rooms. "What brings you here?"

He swiped his hat off his head. "I'd like to speak with you, if I may." He ran a hand over his hair to straighten it.

I opened the door wider and gestured for him to come in. "Tea?" I asked. At his soured expression, I remembered he didn't care for it. "Never mind. What do you want to speak with me about?" I folded my hands at my waist.

"Can we sit?" he asked.

I went over to the love seat, and he took the chair that sat perpendicular to it. He fiddled with his hat in his hands. I had to admit I was taking a little enjoyment in his discomfort.

"I believe I owe you an apology," he said, his indigo eyes meeting mine. I tried to ignore the flutter in my chest. "And a debt of gratitude."

"Oh? Really?" I didn't want to give him an out. I wanted to hear this apology.

"I'm sorry if I caused you any distress."

"Over what? Sending me to my room like a child? Jailing me like a criminal?"

"Well, I'm not sorry about that."

"Is that so?" I asked, galled at his bluntness and now wondering where this supposed apology was going. I was about to ask him that very question, but he spoke first.

"Yes, it is. You seem kind of accident prone. I did it for your own safety."

I stared at him, open-mouthed. His gaze never shifted from me, and the seriousness of his expression suddenly struck me as funny. Despite my efforts to stay mad at him, I laughed out loud.

At first, he seemed surprised at my response, but then his face broke into a smile—a beautiful, breathtaking smile—and he laughed along with me.

"Is that really why you put a guard at my door?" I asked, still giggling.

"Well, if I'm being honest, not entirely." His smile faded ever so slightly, and the jovial mood dissipated.

"You thought I might be guilty," I finished for him.

He looked down at his hat in his hands. "I had a hunch you didn't commit either one of those crimes, but I had to be sure. It's my responsibility to see that the residents of La Plata Springs are safe and that justice is served." He raised his eyes to meet mine again. "I hope you understand."

His obvious sense of duty and justice made it hard to be mad at him forever. In fact, I quite admired his loyalty to the town and its inhabitants. No matter how I felt about Clayton Marshall, he was a decent man.

"Yes," I said softly. "You were just doing your job."

An awkward silence filled the space for a few moments. He then caught my gaze again, and an electric heat crackled in the room.

"How is Clarence?" he asked, changing the subject. "Has he returned to work?"

"Yes. It's good to have him back. But he won't talk about what happened."

"I suppose it's because he feels bad about lying, saying he saw you kill Bledsoe when it was Mrs. Platte he saw. And planting the letter before that."

"But why would Clarence do something so underhanded?" I wondered aloud.

"He said Mrs. Platte had seen him take some food from the saloon. She told him that if he spoke out to anyone about what he'd seen her do to Daniel Bledsoe, she'd make sure he was put in jail for theft. She told him to say it was you who killed Mr. Bledsoe, should anyone ask. Said if he came back to the hotel, she'd see him locked up. He feels terrible about what he did to you. It was good of you to let him come back to work."

"I've been wondering, how did he get the keys to my rooms?" I asked.

The sheriff gave me a sympathetic look. "That was on

account of Mr. Pettyjohn. The morning after Narcissa's death, he'd gone up to Mr. and Mrs. Platte's rooms to check on them. They offered him tea, and he set his keys on the side table. He accidentally left them there."

"Oh dear," I sighed. Maggie had mentioned that Mr. Pettyjohn could be a bit absentminded, or had she said something else? *Batty* perhaps?

The sheriff continued. "Mrs. Platte gave Clarence the keys and told him to plant the letter in your rooms. When he was done, he took the keys back to reception and put them in Mr. Pettyjohn's drawer."

I nodded. "I only wish the boy had come forward with what he knew right away."

"I know. But it's hard to say what goes on in the mind of a child. Especially one who has had so much loss."

"The poor thing. He must have been so frightened."

Another silence filled the room. After a moment or so, he stood up. "Well, I best be going."

I set my teacup down and rose from the love seat. "Thank you for stopping by."

He cocked his head, and a gentle smile crossed his face. "I wondered if you'd do something for me."

I blinked in surprise. "What is it?"

"Would you join me in the saloon for lunch?"

"Right now?"

"Yes," he said with a chuckle. "Right now."

I looked over at the empty biscuit plate. I didn't think I could eat another thing. But finally, someone had invited me to something. Even though it was only a dodgy bowl of rice and beans in the saloon. I found I couldn't refuse.

"I suppose I could," I said.

He held out his arm for me to take. "Let's go, then."

I smiled and wrapped my fingers around his pleasingly firm upper arm.

When we entered the saloon, I was surprised to see that the

entire town was there. Every single table, chair, and booth were occupied, and many people were seated at or stood near the bar.

All heads turned toward us and then people began to stand up and applaud. Among them were Mrs. and Mrs. Gilroy, Constance Chatterley, Dr. Tate, Mr. Pettyjohn, Mr. Johns, Kitty Carlisle, Sally Dean, Maggie, Andrew, Mr. Archer, and Clarence. Many of the others I had not yet met.

Not understanding, I gaped at them, their faces full with joy as they clapped with abandon. In the corner of the saloon, seated by herself and wearing black widow's weeds, Mrs. Bledsoe raised a wineglass in my direction and gave me a nod.

I was so taken by surprise, I could barely breathe. What was this all about? My eyes traveled across the room to the front door. A banner, hanging above it, had been placed over the offending portrait of the woman who was not me, and read, WELCOME, MRS. PRYCE.

Kitty strolled up to us, hands on hips. "Good afternoon, Mrs. Pryce," she said with a smile. "Can I get you something?"

Sally came up behind her. "We had planned this party before you got here. We had hoped to have it the day after you arrived, but, you know, with Narcissa and all . . . and then Mr. Bledsoe, and—"

"She gets it, Sally," the sheriff said.

I pressed my hand to my chest, completely overwhelmed. Cordelia appeared at my side and wrapped her arm around my shoulders. Bijou yipped happily and ran over to Clarence who picked her up. She thanked him with several wet kisses all over his face.

"What can I get ya?" Kitty repeated.

I shrugged my shoulders. "Champagne?" I asked with hope in my voice.

"You got it," she said and went to the bar.

Mr. Pettyjohn approached me. "Finally, a proper welcome for you, madam."

I was still so taken aback by it all, I didn't even mind his use of that dastardly word.

"Thank you," I said, but then a horrible thought struck me. I leaned closer to him and whispered, "Are we paying for this?"

His gaze went to one of the booths in the back where Mr. Archer was seated.

"He took care of it," Mr. Pettyjohn said.

Mr. Archer raised his glass to me, and I gave him a grateful smile.

I looked up into Sheriff Marshall's face. "You knew about this? The whole time you were up in my room, you knew this was going on?"

He smiled and nodded.

I pulled back from him and looked up into those smiling blue eyes. "What made you think I would agree to come to lunch with you?"

He let loose a chuckle. "Like I said before, you can't seem to get enough of me."

❧❦❧

Continue with Arabella's Adventures!

Scan the QR code on the next page to sign up for Kari's newsletter and to claim your FREE copy of *The Pryce of Delusion*, the prequel novella to The Pryce of Murder series! You will also be the first to know when Book 2, *The Pryce of Deceit*, will be available for preorder, in addition to learning about exciting give-aways and other news!

Did you enjoy *The Pryce of Conceit?* If so, you might want to share the love with other readers. The best way to do that is to leave a review. You don't have to write much, just a few sentences about your reading experience.

You can leave your review and/or star rating on Amazon, Bookbub, Goodreads or all three!

To leave your review on Amazon, use the QR Code below!

ABOUT THE AUTHOR

Empowered women in history, horses, unconventional characters, and real-life historical events fill the pages of award-winning author Kari Bovée's articles and historical mystery musings and manuscripts.

She and her husband, Kevin, spend their time between their horse property in the beautiful Land of Enchantment, New Mexico, and their condo on the sunny shores of Kailua-Kona, Hawaii.

ALSO BY KARI BOVÉE

The Grace Michelle Mysteries

The Annie Oakley Mystery Series

A Ruby Delgado Mystery
A Southwestern Stand Alone
Bones of the Redeemed

Made in the USA
Coppell, TX
08 July 2023